FERAL

N.L. MCLAUGHLIN

TWISTED SKY

*Always and forever for my best friend
and partner in crime,
Robert*

"We're in the middle of a storm, ain't we, honey?"

BONNIE PARKER - BONNIE & CLYDE

ONE

FIFTEEN YEARS AGO, KOSOMA, OKLAHOMA

THE SOFT THUD of her boots on the damp earth vibrated through her legs. A horrifying, guttural scream, the final breath of her brother, echoed in her head, clawing at her sanity. The air around her was thick with the scent of fear and blood.

Keep going! Don't look back! She commanded herself.

Maggie sprinted through the woods, holding the toddler tightly against her chest. The child's small body trembled in her embrace; his sobs muffled against her shoulder. "Mama!" he cried.

"Shhh, shh, shh," she whispered as she scanned the shadowy forest. She couldn't continue running aimlessly. Panic swelled within her as she realized she didn't have a clue where she was or where to go for help.

From the dark, dense pines surrounding her, a coyote's sharp bark cut through the stillness, the eerie sound reverberating through the woods. All around her, the forest was alive with movement.

The coyote's bark was answered, and then another joined in, until a symphony of wild yips and howls filled the darkness that surrounded her. The pack was closing in.

Nightmare visions of the red barn swam forward in her mind.

She must keep moving. If they caught her, she would suffer the same fate as all the other poor souls who stumbled into that hellish compound.

She ran.

Her heart pounded in her chest; each beat a deafening pulse in her ears. She could almost feel the monsters breathing down her neck.

In the distance, a glimmer of light flickered through the trees.

Headlights! There must be a road up ahead!

Keep going! Don't stop!

The toddler squirmed, twisting and turning against her grip, a muffled whimper escaping his lips. "Zee-zee."

She clutched him tightly. Shh, shh, we're almost safe. We're almost there.

Above her head, the sky was a gentle blend of blue-gray, subtly infused with the pink of dawn. The beginning of a new day. She had never been so relieved to witness the sun come up.

Exhausted and in shock, she pushed herself to continue forward.

The asphalt road appeared like a dark ribbon in the distance, visible amidst the trees. Hope exploded in her heart. The road! A jolt of energy, like an electrical current, shot through her, revitalising her weary legs and urging her forward. The ground seemed to spring beneath her feet.

Coyotes barked and chattered in the dense forest all around her.

She stumbled out of the trees and onto the road, the rough pavement scraping her skin. The child wailed; he was terrified.

The sharp, insistent blare of a vehicle's horn pierced through the night, making her whip her head up just in time to see a pair of headlights rushing toward her. The service truck screeched to a halt, missing her by inches, its brakes seizing and releasing a plume of black smoke and the smell of burning rubber.

She glanced behind her. An enormous beast hovered in the shadows, its eyes glowing ominously. It sprang forward, a spectacle of brown fur and bared teeth, its revolting smell washing over her as it missed her by inches.

Seizing the opportunity, she scrambled to her feet and ran to the passenger door of the truck, screaming, "Help me! Please!"

Out of the woods, a band of coyotes appeared, snarling with teeth bared, poised to attack. They surrounded the vehicle, their hot breath steaming in the cool morning air.

She flung the door open and found herself staring into the face of a confused middle-aged man. "Please," she begged as she climbed into the seat and quickly pulled the door closed. "Go!"

A piercing, chilling howl, sharp as shattered glass, sliced through the air, followed by a heavy, unnerving silence.

"What the fuck?" muttered the man, staring out at the pack of coyotes that gathered around them. "Nah," he said. "Fuck this." He threw the vehicle into gear and then roared the engine.

The beasts refused to move.

He blasted his horn.

Nothing.

"Please, just go!" she shouted. The toddler's cries filled the cabin. "Mama!"

With a grunt, the man stomped on the gas pedal; the vehicle jolted forward with a sudden surge of speed.

A single beast launched upwards, landing with a jarring thud on the truck's hood. The impact sent vibrations through the cab. The creature thrust its body at the windshield, over and over. A snarling, frothing mess of gnashing teeth and deadly claws scrabbled at the glass in a violent frenzy.

The vehicle plowed into the coyotes, sending them scattering in a panicked flurry of high-pitched yelps. With the creatures behind them, the driver stomped his foot on the brake pedal. As the truck stopped abruptly, the creature on the hood collided against the windshield, then soared upwards, crashing to the ground several feet away.

Without hesitation, he slammed the accelerator once more.

As they sped away, leaving the nightmare behind, Maggie

breathed a sigh of relief. A shiver of exhaustion coursed through her ·
frame. The toddler's body trembled in her arms. Tears streamed
down his face as he cried out for his mother.

The poor child had no idea his mama was dead. Another body
dangling in the barn on meat hooks alongside Maggie's brother James,
his girlfriend Deanna, and her best friend, Kayleigh.

Her thoughts shifted to her brother. His sacrifice had bought her
escape. But at what price?

She gazed down upon the child sitting on her lap, his breath
hitching in his chest as he clutched a tattered stuffed animal. What
was the reason for keeping him in that old house? They killed his
family. So, why did they leave him alive? How long had he been a
prisoner of those wretched beasts?

He struggled against her grasp, calling out to his mother.

As she looked out at the blur of trees scrolling past her window,
she rested her cheek atop his head and whispered, "We're safe now."

TWO
PRESENT DAY

A SUDDEN, frantic pounding on his bedroom window jolted Luca awake just before midnight. The sound was like four desperate hammer blows. He pushed aside the dusty plaid curtain and found his cousin Jax staring back at him.

His eyes, wide with amphetamine-fueled anxiety, met Luca's across the cracked glass. "Come on out boy!" He took a long drag from his cigarette and stepped away from the trailer, glancing around nervously at the darkness.

Curious about what had Jax so agitated, Luca paused, studying his cousin intently. He had an uneasy feeling about something, but couldn't quite place it. This wouldn't be the first time Jax dragged him from a warm bed and into trouble. In fact, the odds were very high that this was gonna be one of those instances.

With a shrug, Luca ran his fingers through his messy blond hair, quickly threw on some clothes, and left his room.

He tiptoed down the hallway, the gloominess of the stained wood-paneling seemed to press in on him as he passed the many framed photographs that hung on the walls. From infancy to his teens, the carefully preserved display represented the last vestige of his mother's presence in his life.

Moving silently, he entered the cramped kitchen, carefully stepping around the sink piled high with dirty dishes, some of which were a week old. Grease and spicy sauce covered every surface. No one bothered to clean it up anymore.

His father lay snoring loudly on the living room sofa; the sound was enough to raise the dead. The old man rarely slept in his bedroom anymore, preferring to drink himself unconscious on the musty sofa. Empty beer cans were scattered all over the filthy shag carpet near him. The heavy, noxious smell of stale cigarettes, rancid alcohol and sweat permeated the air.

Luca didn't have to worry about disturbing anyone else; it had been just him and the old man for quite some time now. It was hard to believe that two years had passed since he last saw his mom, Emmeline.

He never found out why she left. Did she meet someone else? Or had she finally just reached her limit and snapped? Whatever the reason, one day, while he was at school and the old man was out hunting or work—on any given day, it could be either—she silently packed her suitcase and disappeared without a trace. Luca was never invited along, and, as far as he knew, she made no attempt to contact him. There wasn't even a goodbye. It was as if she had dropped off the face of the earth, leaving everyone wondering where she had gone. One day she was there, the next she wasn't. As if that wasn't bad enough, all of this went down just two weeks before his birthday. So much for sweet sixteen.

At first devastated, and then angry, Luca made a conscious effort to push thoughts of her, and particularly her departure, from his mind. It simply hurt too much.

The only good thing that came out of that entire period was the old motorcycle his uncle gave him as a birthday gift. Though rusty and needing repairs, the bike gave Luca a chance to escape. He just had to repair it first. It took four months of hard labor and steady focus before he heard the first rumbles of life. That first ride was pure bliss. While it didn't eliminate the pain of having been abandoned, it definitely dulled the sharpest edges.

As he opened the front door, its rusty hinges groaned loudly in complaint. Luca paused and glanced back over his shoulder. He wasn't worried that his father would care that he was going out at such a late hour. For the most part, they were more like weird room-mates than father and son. It was more that just waking the old man was enough to trigger an angry tirade that would result in a fistfight. Luckily, as it so happened on this night, his father never even stirred.

Outside, the warm, humid air was filled with the sound of crickets and frogs calling out to find their mates. Luca shut the door firmly behind him and waved his arms around his head in a futile attempt to shoo away the cloud of mosquitoes, fireflies and moths hovering near the dim yellow light of the front porch. He vaulted the railing and hurried around behind the trailer to where a visibly nervous and fidgety Jax waited.

"It's about time, couillion," he said. "What took you so long?"

"Had to get past the old man," said Luca. "What are you doin' here?"

Jax wiped his hands off on his dirty jeans. "I found a bunch of money in the bayou." He pulled a wad of cash from his pocket and held it out.

"Woah!" Luca reached out for the money, only to have his cousin pull it back. "Where did you get all that?"

"You hard of hearin' boy? I just told you," said Jax, thumping the side of Luca's head with each word. "I found it out in the bayou." He stuffed the money in his jeans. "I was fishing out by old man Guidry's cabin."

"Ain't he dead?" asked Luca, suddenly aware of what compelled his cousin to go all the way out there at such a late hour.

With a mischievous glint in his eye, Jax flashed a toothy grin. "I know what you're thinkin'. And you're right. But someone else got there way before I did. The cabin was wide open. The door had been torn off its hinges, so I went inside. Just to see if there was anything of interest left behind."

"Uh huh, go on."

"Well, inside looked just as bad off as the door. There was this glass jar on the counter. That's where I found the cash."

"Is there anymore?"

"Might be. That's why I came to get you."

Luca regarded Jax with a suspicious eye. "What ain't you tellin' me?"

"Nothin'. I just figured my favorite cousin might like a cut of the proceeds."

"Bullshit! Favorite cousin my ass! There's somethin' you ain't sayin'."

"Mais la! Couillion! I ain't got time for this!" Jax ran his hand down his face. "You in or no? 'Cause if it's no, then I got others who would jump at the opportunity."

"I didn't say I wasn't interested. I'm just lookin' for the catch."

Jax stared at him, then sighed. "Alright, I need a lookout. I heard some noise while I was out there, and I could use an extra set of eyes to keep watch while I search the cabin. I need you cousin. What do you say? Are you in or no?" He stared with pleading eyes. "Fifty-fifty split of anything we find."

Luca's desire for money waged war against his instincts.

Something wasn't right. He could feel it in his bones. He remembered a conversation he overheard about a week ago between Mr. Primeaux and the Sheriff about recent disappearances in the swamp.

All that aside, if there was a lot of money or other things of value just layin' around, he'd be a fool to pass it up. Indecisiveness took hold, showing no signs of letting up.

Jax released a loud sigh, then he turned to walk over to his rusty old square-body pickup. He watched Luca through the open passenger window as he got in and started the engine.

Luca needed to make up his mind.

Jax revved the engine.

Curiosity overcoming his reluctance, Luca sighed and slid into the passenger seat. Before he could even close the door, they were already at the end of the driveway.

The moon hung heavy against the inky sky as they pulled up to the water's edge. All around them the rhythmic sounds of the swamp filled the air. A deafening chorus of bullfrogs, chirping crickets, and the rustling of unseen creatures. Luca inhaled the warm night air, scented with cypress and damp earth, and was once again reminded why he preferred the beauty of nature to being inside. Yes, the bayou held dangerous creatures, both large and small, but people weren't so different, their hearts just as dark and festering as the swamp itself.

He trailed Jax to the small motorboat and climbed aboard. A moment later, they were coasting along the calm water, toward their destination.

A trio of gators splashed into the tall reeds as they approached. With a wary eye, Luca watched them swim into the boat's wake, their bodies silently disappearing beneath the murky surface, leaving only swirling shadows. He leaned over the edge and peered down just in case any of them were still hanging around.

As old man Guidry's cabin came into view, Jax switched off the engine, allowing the current to carry them smoothly to the dock.

A prickling sensation crawled up Luca's spine as he scanned the area, his unease growing with each passing moment, despite the lack of anything out of the ordinary. He listened intently, but heard nothing. How odd. Dead silence surrounded them.

He stepped out of the boat, marveling over the fact that the old dock was even standing, let alone usable. He stared up at the cabin. The front door was nowhere in sight. So far, it was exactly how Jax described.

A wave of déjà vu washed over Luca as he neared the shack. On the outside, it was practically indistinguishable from the many other bayou cabins he knew. He couldn't decide if the buildings were made of scrap, or if the years of swamp rot and humid air had simply worn them down to that state. Regardless, they all looked and smelled the same.

Luca paused in the doorway and peered inside.

A gaping hole, ragged and uneven, was in the middle of the floor. As he passed, he peered down, startled by the cold, reptilian stare of an alligator that met his own. The air hung heavy with the musky odor of the swamp.

"Come look at these," said Jax, standing over by the tiny kitchen sink.

He moved alongside his cousin and whistled in surprise at a pile of wallets. "There's gotta be a dozen or more. How come you didn't mention you got that cash from these wallets?"

"I didn't," replied Jax. "The money was in that jar over there." He gestured to an empty glass jug on the counter. "I didn't even see these 'till right now."

"I don't like this," said Luca, shaking his head. He stared out the small window above the sink, then scanned the room of the cabin again. "You ain't wonderin' how these all got here?"

Jax shrugged. "Maybe old man Guidry was a serial killer."

Luca scoffed. "Now, I know you ain't serious. That old man could hardly fight off a mosquito, let alone murder a bunch of people."

"It all depends on the age of the victim."

He had to give Jax that one; it was an excellent point. He opened a wallet, found an ID, and read the date of birth. "This fellow was in his thirties." He checked another one. Late twenties. Luca opened another—thirty years old. Every one of them seemed to belong to men, spanning a range of ages from late twenties to early forties. The more he discovered, the more confused he became. "How long you think it's been since anyone's been out here?"

"Old man Guidry passed almost a year ago," said Jax. "He was put in a home about a year before that. So, that would mean he hadn't been out here for at least that long."

Luca stepped into the middle of the room. "So anyone could've been out here doin' all this for a while." His eyes scanned the walls, searching for something—he had no idea what exactly. "Seems kinda odd that someone would be out here robbing men, then bringing the wallets here to dump them. Don't it?"

"I suppose." Jax stared back at him as he pondered the idea briefly and then, shrugging it off, went back to searching the cabin.

A thick layer of dust clung to the edges of the room, a stark contrast to the surprisingly clean center, where even the floorboards looked untouched. Someone had been spending time here. In a dark corner, Luca spotted a small wooden box, poking out from under a musty cot. He walked over and picked it up. With a curious hand, he brushed away the layer of dust from the lid.

"What ya got there?" asked Jax, intrigued. He took a break from searching the kitchen and wandered over.

Luca's fingers trailed over the intricate carvings atop the box. An icy chill ran down his spine, raising goosebumps on his arms, as he recalled the last time he had seen that very box. The memory was sharp, almost painful. It was a cold, damp afternoon in early spring when his mother pulled it out from under her bed. How the hell did it get all the way out here? He wondered. The thief must've ran across her, robbed her and brought back her belongings with the rest of his loot.

It was a straightforward explanation, yet he remained unconvinced. Mainly because it begged the question, what happened to Emmeline? Did whoever stole the box, murder her too? Was that why she never contacted him?

He lifted the lid and gasped. The wooden container was overflowing with rings and jewelry, their intricate details and varied metals catching the moonlight. Beside him, Jax whistled in astonishment as he reached out and scooped up a fistful of items and held them up for inspection.

Luca dug through the box, finding nothing familiar. He knew for certain that his mother didn't own any of those trinkets. The only jewelry item of value she possessed was her grandmother's wedding ring, a precious heirloom that she carried with her everywhere on a fine, golden chain around her neck. She knew all too well that her husband had a habit of pawning anything valuable when they were struggling to pay the bills, so she took precautions to keep it safe.

Jax slapped his shoulder and chuckled. "Hoo lawd! What did I tell ya cousin? I knew there was more."

At that moment, Luca was glad he had come. The money they would fetch for all of this would more than set him up for a few weeks.

Outside, a wolf howled.

"What the hell was that?" he asked, startled.

"Sounded like a wolf."

"I know that couillion. What the hell is a wolf doin' out here in the swamp?"

"It's probably just hunting," said Jax.

Luca stared at his cousin, wondering how the boy could be so stupid. "Fonchock. When have you ever heard of a wolf livin' in the swamp?"

His cousin responded with a shrug. "It's possible."

"Why? Because they're such excellent swimmers?" said Luca sarcastically.

The haunting sound of the wolf's howl echoed through the night once more. The beast was closer now.

A shiver of icy dread ran down Luca's spine; his skin prickled with goosebumps. His gut told him to get the hell out of there. He and Jax quickly stuffed all the jewelry from the box into their pockets, then raced for the dock. His heart plummeted when he saw a pair of glowing eyes malevolently watching him from the open doorway.

What stood before him was no wolf.

The creature's menacing growl, a low, guttural rumble that vibrated through the confined space, preceded each slow, deliberate step. The giant beast towered over Luca. Its head was massive; reminiscent of a wolf's, with a mouth full of the longest, whitest teeth he had ever seen—each a gleaming, wicked point, cold and sharp enough to pierce steel. Or shatter bone. Fear clutched at his heart, making his breath catch in his throat. A wave of scorching heat washed over him from the beast as they glared at each other, its eyes burning into him with an intense, fiery gaze.

Behind him, Jax hollered, "Come on, this way!" Without another word, his cousin turned and sprinted through the backdoor, heading away from the dock and their boat.

With a sudden dash, the creature disregarded Luca, zeroing in on Jax. It charged.

All alone in the cabin, Luca gasped, realizing he'd been holding his breath. His heart pounded in his chest, its frantic beat echoing in his ears, threatening to explode.

Outside, a bone-chilling scream pierced the air. A wave of terror washed over Luca as he burst outside and saw the monster looming over Jax. He needed to do something fast. He ran over and seized his cousin's hand. Engrossed in a wicked game of tug of war, he struggled to stop the monster from dragging them both into the woods.

"Help me!" screamed Jax, with blood dribbling from the corner of his mouth. "Please!"

Luca fought desperately to hold on, but the creature's strength was simply too great. His cousin let out a bloodcurdling scream before disappearing into the shadowy depths of the woods, his anguished cries bouncing off the thick trunks of the trees.

Suddenly, all sound ceased; an unnerving, profound silence blanketed the area.

His heart pounded so loudly in his chest that he could practically hear the rush of blood coursing through his veins. Luca scrambled to his feet, his entire body trembled uncontrollably, the sound of his own ragged breath loud in his ears as he ran back to the cabin. Panic had set in as he frantically searched for a weapon. Much to his dismay, all he could find was a long, rusty scaling knife and a heavy cast-iron frying pan.

A menacing growl erupted from the doorway, filling the room. The creature had returned.

With the pan in one hand and the knife in the other, Luca raced out the back door in a mad dash for the dock and the safety of the tiny boat.

The beast leaped forward, bridging the distance in a single powerful movement. It collided with Luca, sending him crashing to the floor, knocking the air from his lungs. The monster attacked. Its deadly teeth aimed for his throat, but he managed to shield his face with his arm. His screams, raw and filled with terror, echoed through the air as the beast's teeth tore into his flesh, the sounds punctuated by the sickening rip of skin and muscle. Blood gushed from the wound, splattering onto his face and into eyes.

With his other arm, Luca swung the frying pan. It connected with a bone-shattering thud against the beast's head, sending a jarring shock up his arm. The pan slipped from his grasp, leaving him to fumble as he pushed and shoved at the beast's chest, trying to get it off of him.

Suddenly, the beast let go of his arm but stayed hovering above.

He wiped the blood from his eyes and looked up to meet the creature's unwavering stare. Confusion swept over him. What the hell was it doing? Was it readying itself for the final blow?

The knife! A sliver of hope for survival remained. He gripped the knife in his good hand and jammed it forcefully into the beast's neck. Again and again, he stabbed. A torrent of blood, thick and dark, gushed from the monster's neck, splattering his body, soaking his clothes and hair. To his astonishment, the creature didn't fight back; instead; it scurried backward with a pathetic whimper.

He would be damned if he let the beast that killed his cousin go free. With a powerful heave, Luca raised the cast iron pan and brought the weighty skillet down with a loud crash onto the monster's head. Blow after blow landed, each one accompanied by a sickening thud as the creature's life ebbed away.

Overwhelmed by fatigue, his arm gave way, and the heavy pan clattered to the floor. He fell to his knees, his body hitting the ground with a thud. As he looked down at the twisted carcass, he realized it was no longer the fearsome monster he had encountered before. It was a woman. He rolled her over to see who she was, but unfortunately the skillet had done a number on her face, leaving not much left to identify.

His eyes were drawn to something hanging around her neck, glinting in the moonlight. He pulled it off and held it up for inspection.

At first, Luca's mind refused to make sense of what he was seeing. A delicate golden ring, cool to the touch, swung gently from a dainty chain, its smooth surface catching the light. A wedding ring. Memories of his childhood crashed over him as he remembered sitting on his mother's lap, playing with the ring, twirling it on his finger.

A feeling of utter shock and horror shook him to his core. It couldn't be! No! It just wasn't possible! He stared in disbelief, refusing to accept the undeniable truth. This wasn't just any creature —this was his own mother! A Rougarou. Nausea hit him with the force of a physical blow, bile rising from his belly, churning violently until he had no choice but to spin around and expel the contents of his stomach.

He rose to his feet and took a step back. His entire body trembled as he wiped his mouth before collapsing against the wall and slowly sinking to the floor. Huddled in grief, his arms wrapped tightly around his knees, he sat in the pre-dawn gloom; the silence broken only by his ragged sobs as he stared at the lifeless body of his mother.

A dull throbbing ache radiated outward from the wound on his arm. He needed to do something about it, but he couldn't bring himself to move. Deep sorrow seeped into every fiber of his being. He finally understood why his mother hadn't contacted him. Honestly, he'd rather have spent the rest of his life believing she'd left him out of selfishness. This reality was so much worse.

The pain had become unbearable. Summoning every ounce of strength left in his body, he climbed to his feet. With unsteady legs, he made his way to the cabinets in a desperate search for a first-aid kit. A wave of relief washed over him upon discovering the case beneath the sink.

After pouring an entire bottle of peroxide over his arm, Luca worked as well as possible, given the situation, to sew up the wounds and apply clean bandages. Once he finished, he limped to a distant corner of the room and, once again, crumpled to the floor, where he allowed himself to sink into unconsciousness as a fleeting escape from his living nightmare.

Throughout the day and into the night, he wrestled through fevered dreams, only waking for moments at a time.

When his eyes fluttered open the next morning, he was immediately confronted with the same terrifying reality. His arm screamed in pain. The ache was so deep, he couldn't stop himself from wondering if it was infected. Could one get rabies from a Rougarou? Probably not, considering that they were rumored to carry a whole other type of disease. Was it a disease? He pulled off the bandages and stared in shock. The wound was completely healed. The stitches he applied the night before, fell away like tiny particles of dust. All that remained was an angry pink scar, a scorching fever, and the most intense ache he had ever felt in all his days.

After finding some painkillers in the medical case, he set his focus on cleaning things up. He walked over to where his mother's body still lay. A not so small part of him wished she wasn't there, that somehow she got up and wandered off. Or maybe she would be sitting there, ready to tell him what was going on. But there would be no answers. Like everything in his life so far, he was entirely on his own.

The weight of his situation crashed down on him, as he understood that there was no scenario where he could bring either of their bodies home. Folks would have questions—questions he couldn't answer. In light of that, they might just decide to arrest him for murder. After all, who would believe that his mom had been a giant werewolf when he killed her.

As for Jax, due to the unfortunate circumstances of his death, he too was to be interred in the swampy soil alongside Emmeline.

It was nearly noon when he finished digging the two graves.

Once he was finished, he settled down by a bald cypress tree, lighting a cigarette and drinking from a jar of moonshine he'd found in the cabin. It seemed only fitting to say farewell to the only two family members he ever truly cared about, mainly because they were the only two who ever seemed to care about him.

As the sun dipped below the horizon, he steered the boat homeward, oblivious to the horrific events that lay ahead.

THREE

THE WIND WHISPERED through the tall trees as a vista of open road and rolling hills stretched beyond the horizon. Walking alone down the center of the highway, Jewel hummed a cheerful tune, the rhythm matching the steady thump-thump-thump of her boots on the asphalt.

A luminous full moon was suspended in the black sky, its ethereal light bathing the surrounding forest in silver. The air was alive with the chirping of crickets and croaking frogs. From the shadows came the snap of a twig. Peering into the woods, Jewel spotted a mighty buck, its white tail twitching nervously, all the while regarding her with a wary eye. In a flash, he launched into the air, bounding through the trees, followed by two does, their hooves drumming softly on the forest floor. She smiled—venison was not on the menu this evening. Without another thought about the buck and his entourage, she continued to hum her song as she danced along the highway, reveling in the moment's solitude.

Bright headlights appeared in the distance. Here we go, she thought. She took several deep breaths, then ran her fingers through her hair. Getting into character, she hyped herself up to play her part. After all, first impressions were very important.

Country music floated on the breeze as the vehicle glided along the blacktop.

She inhaled, taking in the scents of two men. Based on the level of pheromones in the air, she guessed they were in their late twenties or early thirties. Jewel popped her jaw and stretched her fingers as the car rolled along the deserted road. The distance between them was now less than half a football field. Ready to play, she lifted her hand and stuck her thumb out.

As the vehicle pulled up next to her, she flashed a pleasant smile at the rugged man with a head full of dark brown hair and a thick, bushy beard that peered out at her. His eyes raked over her body before focusing on her face, all the while wearing a predatory grin. "Now, what on earth are you doin' out here, all alone on a night like this?" he said with a distinct country drawl.

"What does it look like silly?" She held her arms out. "I'm just walkin' along, takin' in this beautiful night." She could hear his pulse quicken. Jewel stepped closer and leaned against the door, taking care to lean just enough to give him a good look at her cleavage. "In all honesty," she cooed. "I had a fight with my boyfriend. I didn't wanna ride home with him, so I started walkin'."

A nervous cough escaped the man's lips as he cleared his throat. "Well," he said. "His loss." He glanced up and down the road, then turned his eyes back to her. "You wanna ride with us?"

Jewel smiled at the man, her eyes locked on his as she leaned in, and shifted her gaze the other person inside.

Like his buddy, he wore a thick, bushy beard along his jaw. He gave her a quick, shy nod and smile, then looked away.

Her eyes slid back to the first man. "How kind of you to offer." She licked her lips and leaned close enough to feel his breath on her face. It reeked of weed and greasy food. Why did they always smell so bad when you got close? Struggling to maintain her composure, she said, "I'd love to ride with you."

The driver cleared his throat, interrupting the exchange. "Where are you headed?"

She shrugged. "Where are you going?"

"Anywhere you wanna go," replied the passenger.

"I thought you said you were heading home?" said the driver suspiciously.

Jewel flashed a coy smile and stared directly into his eyes. "I never said I was in a hurry."

The man's gaze faltered under the weight of hers, and he looked away. A delicate dusting of pale red appeared on his neck, spreading slowly upwards.

"My name's John," said the passenger. He jabbed his thumb at the man in the driver's seat. "That there's Cameron."

"Nice to meet you, John." She nodded and returned her attention to Cameron. "Nice to meet you, too. My name's Jewel."

"That's a fitting name for a pretty little thing like you," said John. "Why don't you hop on in."

From the back seat, a faint, almost silent click signaled the lock releasing.

Settling into the soft leather of the back seat, Jewel carefully placed her worn, dusty cowboy boots on the console. "So, where are y'all headed?"

"That depends on wherever it is you want to go," said John with a playful wink.

Cameron's knuckles were bone-white as he gripped the steering wheel.

"Is that so?" she replied. "Well then, I know the perfect place." She pulled her legs back, leaned her elbows on the console and rested her chin atop her hands. Peering up at John with her best doe eyed impression, she said, "You guys wanna party?" She shifted her eyes to Cameron, then back to John.

A quick, almost imperceptible glance passed between the two men.

"That all depends if you're into it," said John.

"I most certainly am." She smiled and pointed out the wind-shield. "See that turnoff up ahead?"

"Yeah, I see it," said Cameron.

She nodded. "Turn down there."

Without another word, Cameron turned off the highway. The tall trees hung over the narrow gravel road, their leaves whispering in the breeze, their branches a shadowy canopy threatening to close in. "Where are we headin'?" he asked anxiously.

Jewel chuckled softly. "There's a cozy parking area just up ahead. It's a perfect little spot for some privacy."

They drove for a little over a mile before Cameron spoke again. "This doesn't look like it goes anywhere."

"Don't be such a chickenshit," chided John. He gestured up the road. "It looks like it opens up there."

Stifling a giggle, Jewel watched as the vehicle passed through the final canopy of trees and entered the clearing. The sound of squeaking brakes filled the air as they rolled to a stop.

Finally, thought Jewel. She hopped out of the back seat and placed her hands on her hips. "Well? Are y'all comin' or what?"

John reacted immediately, jumping from the vehicle in a fraction of a second.

Cameron's pace was much slower. He exited the driver's seat and stood close to the vehicle with the door still open, surveying the surrounding trees with an indecisive eye.

His fear wafted on the air. Jewel breathed in. Such an intoxicating smell. A thrill ran through her, making her whole body vibrate.

John stepped closer, but Jewel moved back, just out of his reach.

She giggled playfully. "Let's play a little game."

"I'm all in," he said excitedly.

Cameron circled the car, then stopped abruptly, gazing into the surrounding darkness. "I don't like this."

Scoffing loudly, John spun around. "Quit being such a pussy!"

While John goaded Cameron, Jewel removed her t-shirt, tossing it on the ground at her feet. She popped her neck and flexed her jaw to make room for her growing teeth, then she kicked off her boots. Tiny hairs sprouted all over her body as she unbuttoned her jeans.

Paralyzed by fear, Cameron watched, transfixed, as Jewel's form shifted and changed right before his eyes. Unable to speak, his hand shot up in a silent gesture, his finger trembling as it pointed.

"Jesus Christ Cam!" shouted John. He turned toward Jewel. His face twisted in a mask of annoyance, then confusion, finally settling into a look of stark terror. He stumbled backward.

With a swift motion, Jewel's claws tore into his belly, the sound of fabric shredding mixed with a wet squelch as she hauled him closer. Blood, dark and thick as motor oil, poured from his mouth, trickling through his facial hair. The metallic scent of iron permeated the air. A strangled sound escaped his lips as he tried to scream.

His face lost all color, becoming pale like chalk, his eyes glazed, and his pulse disappeared.

Jewel released her grip as his body went limp, letting him fall heavily to the ground, his head hitting with a soft thud. With a chilling smile, she licked the lingering warmth and saltiness of the blood from her fingers, her eyes cold as ice as she looked at the petri-fied Cameron. With a light step over the body, she pulled the Trick-ster back, her youthful voice clear and bright as she challenged, "Race ya to the end of the road. If you make it, I'll let you live."

Cameron ran, not saying a word.

Jewel counted from behind. "One, two, three," her voice light and playful. When she reached sixty, she flashed a savage grin and took off, a thrill of exhilaration coursing through her as she pursued her prey.

FOUR

A FULL WEEK of sleepless nights filled with nightmares and fever dreams had passed since the horrifying events at the cabin. Despite the intense throbbing ache in Luca's arm, a small, pale pink scar was the only visible sign of the injury. Though people occasionally inquired about Jax's whereabouts, his disappearances, typically lasting for weeks, were so common that nobody was particularly concerned. As for Emmeline, folks stopped asking about her long ago.

Oblivious to all that had transpired, Luca's father lay fast asleep amidst a pile of empty beer cans in the dimly lit, shabby living room. His snoring, a low rumble that vibrated through the trailer's thin walls, was occasionally punctuated by the metallic clink of shifting cans.

In the solitude of his bedroom, Luca relived what happened that night, idly twisting his mother's ring on his finger. Having grown up in Cajun country, myths and legends were an everyday part of life. He knew exactly what Emmeline was—a Rougarou. He also understood the dangerous consequences a bite from one of those creatures could inflict—would inflict on a man.

His arm tingled with awareness.

Despite the deep, unsettling feeling in his bones, he desperately tried to ignore the truth of what was to come, refusing to face the inevitable. The horror of that night had taken root within him, it became his greatest fear, a chilling dread that haunted him day and night. He could feel it—a crawling sensation creeping its way through his body. It was coming for him. There would be no running from his fate.

A wave of nausea, cold and clammy, washed over him, making his stomach churn violently. He winced as searing white-hot pain exploded in his arm. The sensation was electric, a burning unlike anything he'd ever known. The heat was almost unbearable. He was sure that any moment, he would ignite into a ball of raging flames and burn the whole trailer down.

Little beads of sweat trickled from every pore. A deep, throbbing pain wracked his body; each pulse echoed in his skull—a relentless, agonizing pressure that felt like his very bones were cracking under the strain. It was as if some unseen power was tearing him apart from the inside. The feeling of a million spiders, each leg a needle of ice, crawled across his skin, their tiny movements a writhing, tingling horror. His vision blurred, the world tilting and threatening to disappear as a ragged breath hitched in his throat. His lungs ached with the desperate need for air. A high-pitched ringing filled his ears. His heart pounded a wild rhythm against his ribs, a frantic drum solo of terror as if a horrifying predator were on his trail. A wave of panic washed over him.

Pain, sharp as shattered glass and intense as a thousand burning needles, erupted in every limb, its fiery tendrils spreading like wildfire. In his feverish delirium, he leaped from the bed, leaving behind a damp, dark stain on the sheets. The air was heavy with the smell of sweat. A rush of adrenaline shot through him, his muscles twitched with barely contained energy, and he couldn't fight the urge to run. Carefully, so as not to wake the old man, he eased open the cracked, paint-chipped window, and crawled outside.

The moment the cool night air touched his damp skin, chaos erupted.

Excruciating pain in every limb radiated through his entire body. His insides twisted and turned.

The one thing he knew for certain was that movement would help ease his agony. With a burst of energy, he dashed into the woods; the wind rushed through his sweat soaked hair as he ran at full speed. Never in his life had he felt so much pain. He also never felt so alive and powerful. It was intoxicating.

A sudden, intense stab exploded in his belly, sending him sprawling to his knees as he clutched his stomach. The pain was so profound, he could almost believe he was dying. But he knew better.

His fingers throbbed. He watched in horror as his bones elongated, bending unnaturally, with a series of sickening cracks—a sound like splintering wood accompanied by the horrifying feeling of tearing flesh. Blood gushed from his shredded fingertips. His hands swelled with an unnatural pressure as long, deadly claws emerged. His head pounded with unbearable pain. The pressure of his erupting fangs caused disturbing cracks and pops in his skull, a process he could both hear and feel as his jaw and teeth grew.

Luca screamed, clutching a handful of blond hair that had come loose from his scalp. A forest of short, coarse hairs sprouted all over his body. He blacked out, feeling a peaceful void as his body fell to the ground.

He awakened to a profound feeling of disconnect with his own body.

His slender frame was gone, replaced by a massive, lumbering beast. Each heavy breath sent tremors through his entire body. A surge of strength and energy coursed through him. The pain had vanished, replaced by an overwhelming feeling of raw power.

And a great deal of confusion.

Overwhelmed by hunger, his stomach growled ferociously. His new body cried out for food, teetering on the edge of collapse. When he heard the distinct sound of a small animal scurrying about in the dark, his senses immediately sharpened. He quickly identified the source of the sound—a large, plump possum. Before the creature had a chance to react, it was already in his clutches. Its fate sealed.

It wasn't a great start, but at least he could think clearly.

Wanting to test his strength, he approached a large, sturdy bald cypress tree. His powerful hands gripped the knee protruding from the shallow water, yanking it effortlessly from the earth. It barely took any effort on his part. It was as easy as lifting a toothpick. He tilted his head skyward and unleashed a long, haunting howl.

Luca dashed across the swamp with his newfound strength, his legs driving through the murky water as the cold, slimy mud stuck to his fur covered body. A hungry alligator swam silently toward him, expecting an easy meal, but ended up becoming the prey.

When he had eaten his fill, Luca tossed the gator scraps into the water, causing an explosion of activity as the smaller fish darted for the food.

Exhilarated by the power coursing through him, he pressed onward into the swamp, the sounds of unseen creatures a constant hum around him. He was unstoppable. Nothing could touch him.

The sharp crack of gunfire ripped through the quiet night, followed almost instantly by the deafening echo of another shot.

A sudden impact against Luca's side sent waves of searing pain coursing through him, leaving him momentarily stunned. A piercing yell escaped his lips; then, he looked down to find a trickle of blood oozing from a puncture wound beneath his ribs. He watched in awe as his body expelled the bullet. It fell into the water with a soft plop.

More gunshots.

Fierce anger raged inside him. Who would dare shoot at him? With his supernatural powers, he scanned his surroundings and found a small boat concealed in the reeds. Two men with beer bellies and puffy faces sat inside; one held a rifle, the other binoculars.

Luca charged.

Despite their frantic attempts to escape in their boat, the men were no match for the speed and fury of the enraged Rougarou.

Blind with rage, Luca sent the boat over with a violent heave, the terrified men gasping and struggling in the muddy water. With one hand, he heaved the rifle-wielding man into the air. As he struggled and cried out for help, Luca crushed his skull as though it was merely a fistful of dried leaves. He then turned his attention to the other man, cowering in the knee-deep water beside his boat. There would be no mercy tonight. He descended upon the man, ripping his throat open with his razor-sharp teeth. A rush of warm, metallic blood flooded into his mouth.

The flavor was intoxicating. Eager for more, Luca sank his teeth deeper into the tender flesh. The juicy meat exploded with flavor, feeding his hunger. He savored each bite as though it were a prime delicacy.

When he finished, he nonchalantly disposed of the remains by tossing them into the reeds, then ventured further into the swamp, excited to test his newfound powers.

He awakened the next morning outside his weather-worn trailer, naked, cold, and covered in dried blood, leeches and crusty mud. His memories of the evening returned in disjointed fragments, leaving him confused and disoriented. It was as if a random assortment of movie scenes were playing in his mind.

The men's faces flickered in his memory. He could still taste the iron of the man's blood, a lingering horror that seared the memory into his mind. A sliver of raw, bloody flesh remained lodged in the side of his mouth.

With a violent shudder, Luca spun around, his stomach heaving, and vomited violently. Chunks of the man's remains came up with a sickening wetness. Seeing the reality of it made him throw up a second time.

His body shuddered with weakness as he struggled to stand. His human form paled in strength compared to the primal energy he experienced as a Rougarou.

Luca scanned the yard; his father's truck was missing, meaning he'd already left for work. Nothing unusual there, the old man usually left when it was still dark outside, so it was likely he never even saw his son passed out in the front yard. That was probably a good thing.

Weak and unsteady, he stumbled through the creaking trailer, past the dimly lit living room and cluttered kitchen, collapsing onto his bed in his cramped bedroom and falling into a deep sleep.

His father's furious yelling jolted Luca awake; the old man's rough hands rocked him.

"You stupid fool!" shouted his father. "Get your filthy ass out of bed!"

Luca's anger ignited, a fiery spark that set his blood ablaze. His muscles tensed, and a snarl twisted his lips as the ferocious beast within him was unleashed. With a guttural growl that vibrated through the air like a low rumble of thunder, he delivered a powerful blow that sent the old man sprawling across the room.

Coarse hair sprung out all over his body. Deep inside, Luca understood that if he didn't leave immediately, the furious rage simmering within him would boil over into violence against his father. To avoid harming the man, he pivoted, clearing the window in a single bound, the musty smell of the bayou filling his nostrils as he disappeared into the dense, swampy landscape.

The next morning, he returned, a nervous flutter in his stomach, as he wasn't entirely sure what he would find. Much to his surprise, the old man wasn't in his customary spot on the sofa. He crept down the hall to his bedroom where he found his father sitting on the edge of the bed. Tears streamed down the old man's face, leaving a glistening trail on his weathered cheeks as he gazed up at Luca, his eyes filled with a raw, agonizing pain.

"Take a seat son," he said. "We got some talkin' to do."

Struggling to comprehend the situation, Luca reluctantly obeyed. He was cold and shaking, so he took a soft down blanket and pulled it around his body.

With a heavy sigh, his father's penetrating stare lingered on him for an uncomfortably long time before finally breaking the silence. "I know what you are."

A jolt of shock, sharp and sudden as a lightning strike, ran through Luca, but he bit back his words.

His father ran his hand down his face and raked his beard. "Was it your mama who got to you?"

Unable to speak, Luca's jaw clenched so tightly that a sharp, throbbing pain shot through his teeth. He knew? This whole time, he knew about Emmeline, and he didn't say a damn thing about it. In fact, he was the one who told him the lie that she had just left with no word.

"You knew?" asked Luca, struggling to restrain his bubbling anger.

His father nodded. "She came to me not long after she got bit." He took a swig from the bottle of whiskey in his hand, then placed it down and lit a cigarette. "Do you recall hearing about that tourist family a while back who disappeared in the swamp?"

"The one where they found the girl's arm, but nothing else?"

The old man exhaled a plume of smoke and nodded his head.

"I thought they said that was a gator attack."

"They did, but that was a lie."

Luca watched as his father, with trembling hands, took a long drag from his cigarette. His brow furrowed as he seemed to be struggling to find the words for what he was about to say.

"Emmeline was the one who did that," he said.

The words hung heavy in the room.

When Luca said nothing, the old man continued, "She came to me and confessed. She said she had no control over herself and that she was hardly aware of what she was doing. Before she knew it, she had torn that whole family to pieces."

"How?" choked Luca. "How did she get bit? Who did this to her?"

His father took another long drag, the smoke curling around his head like a hazy halo as he let out a plume of smoke with a sigh. "It ain't no secret that your mother and I hadn't really gotten along for a while now. We were both less than perfect. I'm the first one to admit I was an awful husband and father. To this day I believe you were the only reason she stuck around."

"That still doesn't tell me who did this."

With a quick nod, his father continued, "She slept with another man. Supposedly, he was nobody special to her. None of them were. Either way, while they were in the act, he bit her, and well, you know what happened after."

Luca felt a surge of anger rise within him. The shocking revelation that his mother had been unfaithful to his father sent a jolt of disbelief through him, leaving him breathless and numb. It hurt far more than the whole Rougarou thing. He wanted to shout at the old man and make him tell the truth. Taking everything into account, the only positive aspect he found in this new information was that she cared enough to remain in a loveless relationship with a man she didn't even like, for the sake of her son.

This only deepened the ache in Luca's heart. The person who tragically ended her life was also the one person in the world whom she loved more than anything.

"Was it her who did that to you?" asked his father.

Luca swallowed and nodded slowly.

He shook his head. "I knew I should have gone out to that swamp and put an end to her." Tears welled up in his eyes. "But I couldn't bring myself to do it. Lawd help me, I loved her with my whole heart. If I had done what needed to be done when she first came to me, you wouldn't be in this mess." He glanced around at the floor, then picked up an empty soda can, and stuffed the cigarette butt inside. After placing the can at his feet, he turned his attention back to Luca. "You gotta leave, son. You can't stay here. You're a danger to everyone you care about."

Everyone he cared about. Who exactly would that be? Luca racked his brain, searching desperately for someone besides Jax and his mother who he cared about. A wave of sadness washed over him as he realized his father wasn't even a consideration.

"Is that what you told her?" he asked.

"No. It's what she told me," replied the old man. "She didn't want to hurt anyone she knew or cared about, least of all you. So she left." He swallowed hard. "And I let her."

That was it. Luca's fate was sealed. His father was right, he couldn't stay there. If he did, he would eventually be found out, hunted down, and killed. Even though he wasn't entirely sure how he felt about being a Rougarou, he knew he didn't want to die—not yet, anyway.

But where was he going to go? This tiny hole in the wall town was the only place he had ever known. He didn't know anything about the world out there. He pondered the question, the bitter taste of his mother's betrayal still lingering. Could the man who had bitten her possibly hold the answers he desperately needed?

"What happened to the man who bit her?" he asked.

The old man shook his head. "No idea. He was just some drifter passing through. He spread his infection like an STD and left." He swallowed hard again. "You gotta leave, son. Please. Please don't make it so that I have to kill you. I'm not the best father, but I can't kill my only son. Just leave." He climbed to his feet and headed toward the door. After a long pause in the hallway, he couldn't hold back his emotions any longer and broke down into uncontrollable sobs, begging, "Please." With nothing more to say, the old man shuffled into the living room, leaving Luca alone in his bedroom.

The weight of his father's words settled heavily on him as he sat alone, knowing the old man was right. He couldn't stay. If he did, he would end up killing his father one day. Even though he struggled to feel emotions toward the man, he couldn't bear the thought of murdering yet another one of his parents. He understood why his mother had chosen to leave.

With a deep sigh, he stood up and strolled to his closet where he grabbed the nearest pair of jeans and pulled them on, then found a shirt. His heart heavy with sadness, he carefully packed the few cherished mementos from his past life into his backpack. His last act before leaving the room was to retrieve his grandmother's wedding ring, hanging on the edge of his mirror. He hung it around his neck, then scanned the room one last time.

He found his father sitting in the living room, drinking from a bottle of whiskey. No words were exchanged. A shared grief, thick and suffocating, filled the gulf between them, making any further speech unnecessary.

With nothing more than a nod, Luca walked out of the trailer and mounted his motorcycle. A moment later, he was rolling down the gravel driveway, heading to points unknown, with no clue how the rest of his life would be.

FIVE

AGAINST THE HARSH backdrop of the West Texas mountains, Weston stood alone, his eyes fixed on the small cemetery that stretched out before him. In this barren, rocky soil, generations of his family—the Riggs family—had eked out a living, their struggles carved into the very landscape. He walked by the graves of his older brother Eben and his wife Jenny, then halted at the two most recent additions—those of his nephews, Caleb and Pax.

As he gazed down at Caleb's name etched into the cold, hard stone, he recalled the night, nearly three years ago, when he watched, in icy detachment, as his nephew took his final breath. How similar it was to the night his brother, Eben, did the same. Such a waste. Why was it that the most gifted of their family were also the biggest fools? His brother, unlike him, was always deeply rooted in tradition and reluctant to tap into the immense power their kind possessed.

With their supernatural abilities and cunning, Tricksters could achieve anything they set their minds to. The world was literally at their fingertips. However, most of their kind chose to live in obscurity, surviving on mere scraps. That was fine for them, but it was not how he intended to live his life.

Weston let his mind drift back to the events that unfolded that night. The look of shock on the young man's face; stunned by the betrayal he never saw coming. The warm, thumping sensation of his nephew's heart as it took its last beat, lingered in Weston's hand as he callously tossed it to the ground, alongside the still warm corpse of his oldest nephew.

To this day, he couldn't help but wonder why he felt so little for any of them. After all, wasn't family supposed to be the most important thing in one's life? Something to be cherished and nurtured above everything else? But why? From his perspective, they had never done much for him. He learned at an early age that Eben was the chosen son. The heir. Weston was nothing more than the spare, in case something happened to his older brother.

Who needed family like that? Certainly not he. Weston had created his own family. A loyal group of like-minded individuals who had the same goals—power and money.

Speaking of family, someone was still missing. He glanced around, taking in the grandeur of the mountains that encircled him. Was she up there somewhere, waiting and watching?

During those initial weeks after that fateful night, Weston, Levi, and their men tirelessly combed the area, searching for any sign of his missing niece, Jewel. To no avail. Somehow, amidst the chaos, she and two others had vanished, leaving no trace behind.

He closed his eyes, and the details of that night replayed in his mind.

⸻⸻⸻

Levi was busy barking orders.

One of his most trusted men ran up to them. "Sir!" Sean had been in Weston's employ for several years. Through all the challenging situations he had witnessed the man endure, never had he seen such intense panic reflected in his eyes. "They killed Evans!"

"Who did?" demanded Levi.

Sean licked his lips and stared back at them nervously.

"Show us!" barked Weston.

Without hesitation, Sean guided them around the barn where they came upon dismembered remains scattered about the rocky soil. The smell of blood permeated the air as Weston stared in shock. All around him, the ground was covered in a horrific display of gore and body parts. The man's body lay ripped apart, entrails spilled across the ground.

"Who did this?" asked Weston, somewhat in shock because Evans was by no measure a small man. Whoever did this was extremely powerful. He crouched down beside the severed head, staring in awe at the savagery of the kill.

"The big one," replied Sean.

"Son of a—" shouted Levi. "Where is he now?"

With a nervous swallow, Sean shook his head.

Weston could feel a surge of anger building up within him. "Why are you standing here staring at me like a fool? Go after whoever did this!" He glared. "And where the hell is my niece?"

"She shifted and ran into the cave with another woman," replied Sean. "Two of my best men are on it. When they're finished, they'll bring back her head for proof." Without speaking further, he spun around on his heels and stalked off toward the cave entrance, barking orders to the crew that remained nearby.

"Impressive," said Levi, as he knelt over the pieces of Evans. "This must be one hell of a beast." He stood up and sighed. "Let's go talk to the Sheriff and see what he can tell us about any of this."

Ramirez, in all his inept glory was waiting for them by the front of the barn. The craven man, made Weston's skin crawl. He never really cared much for humans, but there were certain individuals who made his hair stand on end more than most. Ramirez was one of those.

"Alright, Sheriff," said Weston as he approached. "What can you tell us about the Trickster who just killed one of my best men?"

The old man's eyes widened in disbelief. "It had to be the big one," he said. "He and the woman showed up a little over a year ago." He raked his fingers through his sweaty hair. "I don't know much about them other than their names."

Weston waited patiently for that information, when the Sheriff failed to divulge their names, he said, "Are you gonna share that with the rest of us, or do I have to carve it out of you?"

"Bass!" shouted the old man. He took a shaky step backward, as if hoping for a fleeting sense of protection by putting more distance between himself and the situation. "That's the name of the big one. The other one is a woman, her name is Izzy." He cleared his throat. "She's—or she was, Caleb's girlfriend."

"Which family is she from?" asked Weston.

Ramirez shook his head. "Both she and the big one aren't from around here."

"Then where the hell are they from?"

"I don't know," replied the Sheriff. "They never spoke much to anyone outside of Caleb's group. I always got the distinct impression they didn't trust me or any of the townsfolk." His eyes darted around nervously.

Weston had decided he had enough of the repulsive old man. As he pondered the Sheriff's fate, his thoughts were interrupted by a shout that came from the cave. Casting a quick glance at one another, he and Levi marched toward Sean, who was now waiting at the entrance.

"What is it now?" asked Weston.

"They're dead," replied Sean.

At least something was going right, thought Weston. But just to be sure, he asked, "My niece and the woman?"

"No, Sir. Our men."

Like a Molotov cocktail shattering against dried kindling, anger burst forth in a fiery display. "What the hell do you mean?" bellowed Weston.

Levi stepped forward, deftly placing his body between the two men. "Show us."

Sean led them into the dank tunnel.

Weston, already intimately familiar with the terrain, needed no guide. The scent of rich, dark soil and the metallic tang of generations of blood filled his nostrils as he breathed in, instantly bringing forth the vivid memory of his first turning.

Up ahead, Sean came to a stop in the main chamber.

Fresh gore was everywhere; sticky, wet, and glistening in the dim light. It clung to the ceiling like grotesque stalactites, dripping and oozing down the walls. Intestines, blood, and organs were strewn across the floor, like discarded children's toys on a beach at night. Limbs were scattered haphazardly, like broken branches after a storm. The whole cavern looked as though a bomb had gone off.

"Am I supposed to believe a woman and child did this?" asked Levi.

"We don't know, sir," said Sean, shifting his weight anxiously.

Weston scanned the chamber and stared down the exit tunnel, knowing full well whoever did this had escaped out the other side of the mountain. He spun around and kicked a leg across the floor. "It was the big one," he said. "He must have come in here, following the girls."

"If he can do this to two of our best men, then we need to proceed with caution," said Levi.

Struggling to contain his anger, Weston leered into Sean's eyes. "We need to find out who they are and where they went. Get the rest of your men together and find them. I want their heads by morning, or I'll take yours in exchange."

In a seething rage, he pivoted and stormed out of the cave.

Three years had passed, and the search across the region had yielded nothing—not a single trace of his niece or her companions. Wherever they had gone, it was nowhere close. He had no way to be certain, but it seemed likely that they had gone far beyond the state's boundaries. Smart. It would be wise for them to stay away, never to return.

The sound of an eagle's cry echoed through the hills as it gracefully soared overhead. Weston squinted against the sun's harsh glare unable to tear his eyes away from the magnificent bird gliding effortlessly through the sky.

As he watched, the bird gave out a final cry, then tilted its body and soared over the mountain ridge out of sight. Once again, he shifted his attention to the graves all around him. The annual visit had ended. It was time to head back to civilization. To the world, he preferred.

"Goodbye brother," he said, strolling past Eben's grave. "Happy birthday! Tell the family I said hello. Oh, and don't worry, I'm still working on bringing your daughter home." A wicked smirk spread across his face as he sauntered through the iron gates and climbed into his truck. With a last glance around the desert-scape, he sped down the gravel road, leaving behind his past, making his way back to Austin.

SIX

"PIQUET-TOI!" Luca shouted angrily, flipping his middle finger in the air at the semi rushing past, blaring its horn. A powerful gust of hot air, thick with the acrid smell of diesel exhaust, hit him in the face. Disheartened, he turned his attention back to his motorcycle, giving the ground a frustrated kick. "Fils Putain," he muttered quietly, his voice laced with frustration. What the hell was he gonna do?

Six months had passed since he struck out on his own. His initial plan was to ride his bike across the country. He had no particular place to go, so he chose to wander and see where he ended up. It worked out well at first, taking him west, then north. Winter's arrival made him realize he disliked cold weather, prompting a return south. And now, here he was, smack dab in butt crack nowhere, Arkansas.

He scanned the horizon. After nearly an hour without seeing a single vehicle, spotting that big rig felt like a minor victory. Only to have it dashed when the truck driver refused to stop. It had been so long since he'd seen a gas station, he could scarcely remember seeing any. Calling someone for help wasn't really an option. He had no one to turn to.

Luca let out a heavy sigh, pushing his hair back from his face with a weak gesture. It was just one of many annoyances at the moment. "Come on, Luca," he muttered, willing his mind to focus. He eyed the surrounding woods. Exactly how far was the nearest town from where he stood? While it didn't personally bother him to have to walk, he worried about his bike being left out here for so long. Being his most prized possession, he was reluctant to leave it unattended in a place where it could easily be stolen or seized.

On the horizon, a red pickup truck emerged. Luca perked up and watched as it coasted along the highway, heading straight toward him. He ran his fingers through his hair and wiped his hands on his jeans while silently praying for the driver's mercy.

The vehicle slowed to a stop beside him, the smell of exhaust briefly filling the air. The driver's window rolled down, revealing a young man wearing a sun-bleached baseball cap, who looked about his own age. In the passenger seat sat a young woman, her long brown hair cascading down her shoulders. A sneer crossed her face as she briefly met Luca's eyes before looking away.

Luca flashed his most friendly smile to the driver.

"Hey there," said the young man. "You look like you could use some help." Without waiting for a reply, he jumped out of his truck and reached out his hand. "My name's Tyler. Friends call me Ty."

"Luca."

"Nice to meet you, Luca." Ty pointed to the young woman. "That's Emily." He turned his focus to the motorcycle. "What seems to be the problem?"

"It's the steering head," replied Luca. "At least, that's what I think it is."

Tyler scanned the horizon. "You from around here?"

"No. I was just passin' through. I was hopin' I'd make it some-place I could get her fixed before it all went to shit."

"Looks like it didn't quite work out that way."

"That it does. That it does."

"Well, I don't have a way to fix it for you," said Ty. "But I've got a set of ramps in the back of my truck." He gestured toward the bike. "We could push it up into the bed and I can drive you to the nearest station."

"That would be great," replied Luca. "I appreciate it."

Working together, they wrestled the bike into the truck bed, settling it in place with a thud, before securing it with several tie-down straps to prevent movement during the drive. By the time they had finished, the sky was painted with hues of yellow, orange and pink as the sun began its descent behind the tree line.

Luca quickly jumped into the back seat. He smiled at Emily and, using his best country boy tone said, "Sorry to interrupt your afternoon, Ma'am."

Noisily chewing her gum, she sneered at him then glared at her boyfriend. "Are we done helping every drifter we stumble upon?"

Her words dripped with disdain, casting an icy chill on the vibe. Luca decided he didn't like her.

"Now come on, Babe," said Tyler. "You know it ain't good to leave someone in need on the side of the road." He winked at Luca. "I mean, what if a serial killer comes along?"

"Valid point," replied Luca, barely able to contain a snicker. "Ain't no tellin' who might roll up on you out here."

As Emily popped the gum in her mouth, she glanced back at him, rolling her eyes.

A moment later, they were heading down the road. Uncomfortable silence hung in the cab's air like a damp, heavy blanket. Luca didn't mind too much; he was lost in his twisted thoughts, envisioning the various ways he could carve up Emily into tiny, unidentifiable pieces. As for Tyler, however, it was clear from the concerned look in his eyes that he genuinely cared about the girl's opinion.

"So, how long have y'all been together?" asked Luca.

"Six months," said Tyler, puffing out his chest and flashing a cheery grin.

Emily shot him a glare that could freeze lava.

Pauvre bête, thought Luca. Tyler had no clue that his feelings weren't reciprocated. While she might like him, she sure as hell wasn't as enthralled with him to the extent that he was with her. The poor guy seemed more of a placeholder. This made Luca dislike her even more.

For nearly half an hour, things continued in this manner. Every time Emily rolled her eyes or popped her gum, Luca felt the urge to end her life, a terrifying precipice he almost tumbled over more than once, but for the sake of Tyler, he held back.

As they rolled into the first gas station, the last streaks of pink and orange faded from the sky, replaced by a soft purple and blue dusk, the air noticeably cooler than before.

"Well, shit," said Tyler. "Looks like they're closed." He turned to glance back at Luca. "Looks like you ain't getting any help here. Where is it you were heading?"

As his options dwindled, Luca felt a heavy, hopeless feeling settle in his chest. Once again, the crushing weight of his solitary existence bore down on him. He had nowhere to go.

"Maybe we could keep searching until we find a place that's open," said Tyler.

"Ugh!" scoffed Emily. "I am not sitting here while you drive this dirty road trash around like a chauffer."

The woman had a unique way of grating on Luca's last nerve.

"Tell you what," said Ty. He adjusted his baseball cap on his head. "There's a town about ten miles up the road. If you want, we can take you there. I'm not sure there's anyplace open right now, but you might find somewhere to sleep for the night."

Out of options, Luca reluctantly agreed.

As they rolled away from the gas station, all he could think about was how the hell he was going to get someone to give him the parts he needed. He knew from personal experience that parts were expensive, and he had no money.

The squealing of the truck's brakes pulled him out of his thoughts. He glanced up and found himself staring at a beautiful young woman standing in the middle of the road.

Slender of frame, with long, sandy blonde hair flowing down her back nearly to her waist, she appeared barely older than nineteen.

She waited until the truck came to a full stop, then sauntered casually over and rested her arms on the window. "Howdy," she said with a smile. Her eyes locked onto Tyler, then slid over to Emily. A slight smirk played at the corners of her lips. She moved her gaze to the backseat where her pale blue eyes settled on him.

A flush of warmth spread throughout his body; Luca quickly looked away.

"Why are we stopping?" demanded Emily, followed by the annoying sound of popping gum.

With a predatory intensity, the young woman's gaze settled once again on Emily; a silent threat hung in the air.

Tyler cleared his throat and asked, "Did your car breakdown or something?"

From the backseat, Luca scanned the horizon, but there was no sign of any vehicle; just an empty expanse of road stretching before him. Something in the way the girl carried herself, a certain spark in her eyes, intrigued him. On a deep, instinctual level, he sensed danger, but for the life of him, he couldn't figure out why. From his perspective, the girl, small and seemingly harmless, posed no threat. He returned his attention to the conversation.

"No," said the girl. "I had a fight with my friend." She stood up straight and sighed. "Needless to say, I'm left to walkin' back home."

"Well, that won't do," said Tyler. He turned his attention to Luca. "Do you mind if we take a brief detour?"

"Not at all."

Emily gasped, then folded her arms and stared angrily out her window.

"I was taught to never leave a lady to struggle on her own," said Tyler. "Hop on in, and we'll take you home."

"That's incredibly sweet of you," said the girl. "Are you sure?"

Tyler nodded.

The door to the backseat swung open, and the girl climbed inside, her eyes locked on Luca the entire time.

"My name's Jewel."

"Hello Jewel. I'm Tyler, and this is Emily. That there is Luca. We're giving him a ride, too."

She stared at him with eyes that seemed to shimmer with ethereal light. "Hello Luca." She flashed a smile, revealing tiny sharp fangs.

Luca pinched his eyes. Surely, he was seeing things. When he looked back, the girl appeared completely normal; her face was calm, her eyes clear and bright. That is, aside from the eerie way she continued to stare at him.

"I want to go home," said Emily. "Now!"

A look of worry appeared on Ty's face. Without a sound, he turned back onto the road.

Heavy silence hung in the air. With each passing moment, it felt more intense; the pressure mounted as Luca struggled to break the stillness.

Jewel cleared her throat. "So, where's everybody from?"

Jumping at the opportunity, Luca replied, "Louisiana."

"I've always wanted to go there." She scooted close enough that their thighs touched.

Scorching heat radiated through his body, making his ears burn and his skin feel like it was on fire. His pulse quickened. A subtle, musky fragrance, uniquely hers, filled the air. It was intoxicating. He wanted to close his eyes and simply breathe it in.

"What's it like?"

Startled, Luca's breath hitched as their eyes met. They were glowing. He wasn't imaging any of this. He glanced over at the front seat where Tyler was busy staring at the road, while Emily pouted and stared out her window.

"Well?" asked Jewel.

"Huh?" said Luca, before he could stop himself.

"What's it like in Louisiana?"

He cleared his throat. "It's um, it's nice." *It's nice! What in the world was that for a response?* He could hardly contain the cringey feeling that swept over him.

Jewel giggled. "You're funny. I like that."

"So, Jewel," said Tyler from the front seat. "Where are we taking you?"

She winked at Luca, then turned to lock eyes with Tyler through the rearview mirror. "There's a road about a mile or so from here. If you could just scoot off up there, I can make it the rest of the way."

Just as she had described, the turnoff appeared out of nowhere, a ribbon of gravel snaking through the trees. With a jolt and a cloud of dust, the truck turned off the highway and bumped onto the washboard road.

Tall trees, their leaves rustling in the breeze, lined the road, their branches reaching out to one another as if to embrace the path.

"You can stop anywhere along here," said Jewel. She reached for the door handle.

Panic seized Luca. She can't leave. He needed to find out who she was and why she was so different. He opened his mouth to speak; the words forming on his lips, when Tyler's voice cut through the quiet.

"I can't let you out here," he said. "It ain't right. Let me drive you all the way home."

Emily gasped and popped her gum.

Luca said a silent prayer that she would accept.

"Okay," replied Jewel, as she pulled her hand away from the door. "If you insist." She smiled and winked at Luca.

A moment later, they continued down the ever-darkening country road.

SEVEN

WHY WERE humans so easy to manipulate? Wondered Jewel.

The road narrowed to a single lane path; the scent of damp earth and pine needles filling the air. She wondered how long it would be before someone mentioned that it looked like they were going the wrong way.

Tyler leaned forward and peered up at the trees. "It sure is pretty out here," he said.

"Pretty desolate," scoffed Emily. Pop! Slurp.

Jewel almost felt pity for Tyler. As for Emily, she could hardly wait to rip the flesh from her bones. The incessant snap, snap, snap of her chewing gum was the most irritating thing she'd endured in ages.

As for Luca—from the corner of her eye, she studied the strange young man, his clothes oddly patched and his hair unkempt, wondering what exactly he was. It was obvious that he wasn't entirely human. But having little experience with other supernaturals, she had no idea what category he fell into.

His mesmerizing blue eyes met hers, peering from a tangled mass of unruly pale blond hair.

She smiled.

A flush of light pink spread across his face from his ears. He glanced away, pretending to be interested in the blurry green of the scrolling trees outside his window.

"How much farther?" asked Emily. Her superior facade was beginning to crack.

"Almost there," replied Jewel. She pointed ahead. "See that turn up there?"

Tyler nodded.

"Take that."

The truck's tires crunched on the dirt road as it turned—the narrow track barely wide enough for the vehicle. The trees were so thick, their branches intertwined like a shadowy ceiling, giving the impression of a long, dark tunnel.

"Oh, come on!" shouted Emily. "Do we have to drive down here?" She turned to Tyler. "I don't wanna go any farther. Stop here and let her out."

"We're almost there," said Tyler.

"I don't care! I want her out now!"

"Now, Em..."

"Get her out now!"

Tyler continued to drive.

"Now! Or I'm gonna jump out right here!"

The truck came to an abrupt stop. "Babe," said Tyler.

Jewel had reached her limit with the girl. She couldn't take any more of the wretched woman's whining or gum popping. With a wicked grin, she extended her long, sharp nails, and reached into the front seat, reveling in the sensation as her claws raked across the girl's throat.

The windshield was drenched in a gush of thick, red blood, splattering Tyler as he looked on, utterly speechless with terror.

As a warm stream of blood flowed freely from her neck, Emily's breath hitched in ragged gasps, her eyes reflecting shock and terror. With a final, shuddering sigh, the girl's arm dropped; her eyes remained locked in a vacant stare, the horrifying expression forever imprinted on her face.

While she was glad she didn't have to listen to that awful woman any longer, Jewel kind of regretted doing it so quickly. A big part of her wanted to make her suffer.

The driver's side door flew open with a loud screech, and Tyler tumbled out onto the dirt road. Covered in the blood of his lady, he scurried backward, away from the truck.

Jewel climbed out. She stood tall before him, ready to end the young man's life, when she felt a firm hand on her shoulder. She wheeled around and found herself staring up at an enormous, wolf-like beast, its fur the color of bright morning sunlight, eyes glowing like stars in the midnight sky.

On the ground, Tyler let out a terrified scream, scrambling to his feet before sprinting away.

With a snarl of irritation, she wrenched herself away from the beast, tearing her shirt and skin. She pulled her Trickster forward and growled with bared teeth directly into his face.

The beast stood firm, its muscles tense, a low growl rumbling in its chest.

There would be time to deal with him later. She turned and set her sights on Tyler, who was already at the bend in the road. Just as she was about to spring forward, the wolf-man's powerful grasp seized her again.

A visceral rage filled her belly. She lashed out, her claws sinking deep into his flesh. Long, angry red welts appeared, only to vanish instantly, leaving a trail of warmth on her claws and a faint scent of his blood in the air. This only made her angrier. Saliva flew as she lunged forward, jaws snapping shut just inches from her target.

His long arms kept her at bay, much to her dismay, as his strength and reach far surpassed hers. Much to her surprise, he didn't attack; his only action was to restrain her, his intent clear—to protect Tyler from her.

The more she struggled, the more ridiculous she felt. The fire in her eyes cooled to a simmer of annoyance, which then burst into peals of laughter at the absurdity of it all.

He too succumbed to the silliness of the situation, a chuckle escaping his lips as his grip loosened.

Jewel looked up at Luca and said, "I knew you were something!"

The tall, slender man came forward through the beastly appearance. "And I just knew you were too," he said. He stepped back and studied her. "Are you some kind of Rougarou too?"

Rougarou. Jewel had heard that name before, but for the life of her, she couldn't recall where. She moved her head from side to side. "I'm what's called a Trickster."

"Well," he said. "I can see I got a lot more to learn. I had no idea that was a thing."

As she stared up at Luca, something in her memory clicked, suddenly recalling what she had been taught about Rougarou. They were made not born. In order for one to be made, they had to first survive an attack from one. That was no small feat if they were all as big and strong as he was when he shifted. "Luca," she said. "How long have you been turning?"

"Turning? Oh! You mean, how long have I been able to turn into a werewolf?"

"Yes. How long ago were you bitten?"

He rubbed his chin. "It's been about half a year, give or take."

"Six months," she said aloud.

"Is that a problem?"

Jewel could sense him bristling at her questions. Not wanting to hurt his feelings, she decided to change the discussion. She pointed to the bike in the truck bed, a sly grin on her face. "Is your motorcycle really broken, or was it a ploy?"

"A ploy?" He shook his head. "Nah, unfortunately the bike really is broken. Tyler didn't have to stop and help me, but he did. That's why I didn't want you to hurt him. I didn't mind what you did to Emily. I've been fighting that urge myself ever since they picked me up."

With the wind whistling past her ears, Jewel stared down the long, empty road. She figured Tyler was probably halfway to the highway by now. It would be in their best interest to leave the area. Judging by the reverent tone in Luca's voice when he spoke of his motorcycle, there was no way he would leave that behind.

"Looks like we're takin' the truck," she said.

"You wanna drive? Or would you rather I do?"

She grinned and climbed into the driver's seat.

While Luca pulled Emily's body into the woods, Jewel rummaged around for a cloth of some sort to clean the windshield. The only thing she could find was the girl's sweater. She held it up to get a better look at it. Soft and feminine, she wondered if she wanted to keep it. With a quick shrug, she decided it wasn't really her style, then used it to wipe away the blood from the glass and tossed it in the back seat.

"Alright, Jewel," said Luca as he climbed into the passenger seat. "Where to?"

"Well, we gotta get rid of this truck. So I say we figure out a way to fix your bike, and then we can move on from there. What do you say?"

"Sounds like a plan." He smiled and then quickly stopped. "Boudreaux."

"Huh?"

"My last name's Boudreaux."

She smiled warmly. "Pleased to meet you, Luca Boudreaux. My name's Jewel Riggs."

EIGHT

THE NOISE from the tires rumbling along the road punctuated the silence that hung heavy like a shroud over them. From the corner of his eye, Luca studied the young woman, attempting to be discreet. A Trickster. He'd never heard of that before. What should have been an answer only ended up adding more questions. He was curious how many other types of shapeshifter beings there were out there. Not wanting to sound like an ignorant fool, he kept his questions to himself.

A subtle smirk appeared at the corners of Jewel's lips. "You look like a man with lots of questions," she said, all the while her eyes never left the road.

"What exactly is a Trickster?"

She turned her head and met his gaze, sending a flash of heat from his belly to his ears. "Like you, we're shapeshifters. Unlike you, we are not made, we're born."

"Born? Like you could do this as a baby?"

Jewel let out a laugh that sounded like the most beautiful music he had ever heard. When she smiled, he couldn't stop himself from

51

smiling back. The intensity in her eyes ignited something within him, a fiery sensation unlike anything he'd ever felt before.

"We may be born like this, but it's not something we can do until we reach a certain age. Up until that time comes, we're just like everyone else I suppose."

Luca was trying to wrap his brain around what the beautiful girl was telling him. Paying attention never was one of his strong suits, this time though, it was made much more difficult because of the way she made him feel.

"So, how old were you when you first turned?"

A solemn look spread across her face. "Sixteen," she replied. "A little over three years ago."

The somber inflection of her voice sparked a sudden, intense anger that vibrated through his very being. He'd just met her, but the fierce protectiveness he felt was already a burning coal in his chest; he'd hurt anyone who threatened her. Heavy silence descended once again, filled with unspoken words, prompting him subtly to shift the conversation to safer territory.

"Well, you got about two and a half years on me," he said wistfully.

"How about you?" she asked. "How did you get bitten?"

Now, there was a story he wasn't quite ready to divulge. To even consider reliving those memories felt impossible; the pain was still too raw—the images too vivid. He sighed and stared out the windshield. "My cousin and I were messin' around in the swamp. We came up against one and, well, the rest is history."

"Why do I feel you're leaving some details out?"

"A guy can't divulge all his secrets at first glance," he said, trying to play coy. "I don't wanna be too much of an open book." He grinned. "Gotta save somethin' for later days."

"Later days, huh?" she said, wearing a soft smile on her face. "That's mighty presumptuous of you."

A cold sweat washed over him. Why did he say that? He swallowed against the lump in his throat. "I-I um—"

Jewel chuckled playfully, then pointed at a sign up the road. "Zeke's garage," she said aloud. "Think they'd have what you need?"

Thankful for the change of topic, he replied, "It's worth a try."

When they rolled up to the old station, the crumbling brick and faded paint sent a wave of defeat through Luca. The run-down building and stack of old tires along the side gave him little hope that he might find anything he could use there.

Jewel steered the old truck around the back and cut the engine.

Though highly unlikely, based on the condition of the area, Luca scanned the building for cameras or any sort of security system.

He climbed out of the vehicle and followed Jewel as she whistled a jaunty tune, strolling around casually, as if she wasn't about to break into the garage.

The sharp ratcheting sound of a shotgun loading sliced through the air.

Luca stopped in his tracks and spun around to find himself staring down the barrel of a gun. At the other end stood an old man, his head a cloud of white hair, his beard a thick, shaggy curtain along his jaw, his posture firm and unwavering.

"Stay right there," said the old man. "And put your goddamn hands up where I can see them."

To buy time, Luca slowly raised his hands, the silence amplifying the frantic thump of his own heartbeat. He cursed himself for missing the dilapidated trailer its mossy, moldy exterior blending seamlessly with the dark green trees.

"Stop right there," warned the old man. "Make no mistake, I will shoot you."

Something dark and fast, a mere blur, zipped past Luca. He heard a low growl coming from behind the old man, followed by a strange, wet sound.

A bright flash of fire erupted from the gun, and the smell of gunpowder filled the air. With a desperate dive, Luca avoided a deadly spray of buckshot, the impact of the ground jarred him.

The old man gurgled, and dark red blood welled up past his lips.

His expression was one of utter bewilderment as his eyes fell upon the crimson colored hand protruding from his chest, gripping his heart. It was still beating. He collapsed to his knees, his eyes rolling back in his head as he hit the ground.

With the organ in her hand, Jewel stood over the dead man. A viscous sneer twisted her lips as she ran her tongue along the heart's edge before dropping it on the ground. Eyes locked on Luca; she sucked the blood from her fingers while stepping over the body as if it were worthless trash.

Luca stood transfixed, unsure if he was terrified or aroused, as Jewel walked to the door and tore it open with a single, powerful tug.

"Well?" she said. "You comin' or not?"

Turned on—that's what he was. This woman was by far the most interesting person he had ever met. He laughed to himself and sighed, then followed her into the garage.

The scent of oil and grease permeated the air. Tools and parts lay askew all over the place, making him wonder how the hell the old man could get anything done. He put on a good act of searching, despite battling a feeling of hopelessness.

"Think it might be in here?" said Jewel, standing in an open doorway.

He went over to her, reached in, and turned on the light. A humming, buzzing sound accompanied the artificial, gloomy light of the fluorescent bulbs illuminating the neatly stocked boxes. A cursory glance told Luca that these were all parts. Joy washed over him.

"What are we looking for?" asked Jewel as she sauntered alongside him, gazing up at the shelves.

Luca's eyes landed on the exact part he needed. He grinned broadly as he picked up the box, then faced her. "This." He could hardly believe his luck.

Together, the duo rolled the bike off the truck and inside the bay of the garage. While Luca got to work, Jewel took the time to clean up the mess she made with the old man and the truck. After all, once the bike was up and running, they no longer needed it.

When she finished, she joined him in the garage, where she pulled up a chair and chatted away as though she was just a typical young woman. As though she hadn't just ripped the heart from an old man's chest.

Strangely enough, he too had no difficulty in forgetting the entire ordeal.

"Alright, I'll give you that one," said Luca. "But riddle me this, someone who is all-knowing would know everything. Wouldn't you agree?"

Jewel bobbed her head up and down. "Yes."

"So, if they knew everything, then there ain't any mysteries to them. They would know how someone was going to react. And that just solidifies my point, that they would already know what you were gonna do before you do it."

The bike repair was taking far longer than if Luca had done it alone, but he didn't mind. He found the company intriguing; he particularly liked the sound of her laugh and her smile set off a flurry of butterflies in his belly. He rather liked the sensation.

Jewel giggled. "It's called free will for a reason. An omnipotent being would know all the possible choices, but free will is the wild card. They have no idea which path would be chosen."

"Then how are they omnipotent if they don't know something. I mean, if they're omnipotent, then they would know everything. Anything less would only make them wise elders."

"Well, they do know everything," said Jewel. "They know all the potential paths." She shrugged. "They just don't know which will be chosen."

Luca sighed and moved his head from side to side. "Woman, you make my head hurt."

Her smile filled his heart with immense joy. He was smiling like such a fool; his face was beginning to hurt. Like a gust of wind, this girl breathed life into an otherwise mundane existence.

A restless spirit, he'd always been captivated by the allure of the unknown, constantly yearning for new adventures. His new situation provided him with the freedom to explore without boundaries; to hit the road and live the life of adventure and excitement he always dreamed about. What was the point of having all this power if all you were gonna do was settle down in the woods and eek out a simple existence? Why on earth would anyone stay in one place until they died? He just couldn't wrap his brain around it.

He remembered what it was like back home in southern Louisiana. The oppressive, sweltering heat of summer and the frigid cold and dampness of winter. He never minded the weather too much. The small, outdated single-wide trailer he grew up in was far from cozy, but he learned to navigate the challenging weather from a young age. After all, the temperature outside was hardly a concern for him, compared to the goings-on inside.

His family was known far and wide in the county, but not for good reasons. Given his circumstances, social advancement was impossible. The dark shadow cast by his own kin loomed over him from birth, making it impossible to break free and forge his own identity. With no other options, he leaned into it and fully embraced his Boudreaux heritage, just like generations before him.

To put it simply, Luca always felt like an outsider, never truly fitting in anywhere. But now, due to a chain of circumstances even he would find difficult to believe, here he was, spending time with the most beautiful and intriguing woman he had ever met. Not only were they talking, but she even seemed to be enjoying his company as much as he was enjoying hers.

Maybe being a Rougarou wasn't a curse after all.

NINE

JEWEL WAS HAVING SO much fun bantering back and forth with Luca, she lost all track of time. This strange young man with the curious way of speaking was fascinating. Time moved so quickly that by the time she even took notice, he was wiping his hands with a soiled cloth.

"Alright, here goes," said Luca. He hopped onto the bike, dug the keys out of his pocket and dangled them in the air. "The moment of truth is at hand. Cross your fingers and toes."

Jewel dramatically inhaled, puffing out her cheeks like a blowfish, then held her hands aloft, fingers tightly crossed, making a big show of it.

"Woman, what are you doin'?"

She exhaled. "I'm holding my breath and crossing my fingers and toes."

Luca chuckled. "Well, don't be doin' that. You could pass out from lack of oxygen." He grinned. "Especially if it don't start."

Jewel shrugged. "Okay, if you say so." She held up her hands to show her fingers were still crossed.

With a playful wink of his eye, Luca stomped down on the pedal and the bike roared to life. "Woo-hoo!" he shouted. "Hell yeah! We're back in business, yo!" He leaned down and stroked the tank adoringly. "I told you Daddy was gonna make it all okay."

"Ahem," said Jewel, clearing her throat. "Should I leave you two alone?" She giggled.

A flash of bright red bloomed across his face. He sat upright. "Come on," he said, gesturing with his head. "Climb on board, let's go for a ride."

She held up her hand. "I've got one more thing to do before we leave," she said. "I'll meet you out front." Without waiting for a response, she spun around on her heels and walked out of the garage.

The pickup truck sat idle; the old man's body propped up against the steering wheel. She went to the door of the camper, where earlier she had placed three propane bottles. With a hiss of escaping gas, she opened the valves, stepped back, and went to the truck where she turned on the ignition and placed a cinder block on the gas pedal, listening to the engine roar. Thrilled to see the outcome, she shifted the transmission, hopped back, and let the truck speed off.

As the truck crashed head-on into the camper, a grinding, metallic shriek ripped through the surrounding quiet. Sparks flew, then came a fiery explosion of bright light and intense heat.

She stepped back and admired her handiwork.

Gazing down at her feet, she used her boot to cover the bloodstain with sand, effectively burying it. The heart remained on the ground, so she picked that up and tossed it into the fire.

With a swipe of her hand, she brushed off the grime, then circled the garage to find Luca waiting.

As he slipped on a pair of leather gloves, Jewel climbed onto the bike, and frantically searched for something to hold on to. The motorcycle provided no proper handholds for a passenger, leaving her no choice but to wrap her arms around his waist for support. Her unexpected embrace made him startle in surprise. His body stiffened. She could feel his heart-beat faster. For a moment, she thought she should withdraw her arms and find another way to hold on, but then he relaxed. She let her body melt against his, reveling in the musky, earthy scent that emanated from him.

A deep rumble shook the bike beneath her, the powerful vibrations a physical manifestation of the adrenaline coursing through her veins. Images of sun-drenched roads and the feeling of freedom flooded back as she thought about her rides with her father. The rumbling was so intense she felt the vibrations in her bones for days after the ride. Amid her happiness, thoughts of her father and family surged forward in her mind, threatening to derail the moment of bliss and fill her heart with sorrow. Inhaling deeply, she swallowed her emotions, clearing her mind to focus on the present.

Luca rolled the bike forward, then sped out onto the road.

With excitement coursing through her, Jewel held on tightly to his waist, leaning in close to feel the warmth of his body, breathing in his scent.

The first rays of the morning sun, golden and warm, peeked over the trees, illuminating the forest with a gentle light. She tilted her head, gazing up at the waning moon, its pale shape barely visible in the brightening sky.

Trees blurred past her in a frenzied rush, their deep green hues blending together with occasional bursts of brown. Now and then, the noise from the motorcycle would startle a group of deer, causing them to dart out from their hiding spots and quickly vanish deeper into the woods. The road unfurled before them, a vast expanse of blacktop; the yellow dashed lines snaked endlessly, punctuated by the occasional weathered mile marker.

Jewel lifted her chin and breathed in the fresh air. She pulled the Trickster forward just enough to analyze each scent. The world was alive with a sense of enchantment. In that moment, she experienced a sense of weightlessness, as if the burdens of the world had been lifted off her shoulders. She extended her arms, feeling the rush of wind as they sliced through the air.

The asphalt blurred beneath them as they rolled down the highway. Hours passed as they rode, and it dawned on Jewel that she was completely clueless about their location. To be honest, she realized she didn't care. She was happy and for some strange reason; she felt perfectly safe with Luca.

It was noon when she realized her stomach was empty, causing her to wonder whether food would be on the itinerary. As her hunger grew, she couldn't help but fantasize about pulling off the road and hunting a deer, just to satisfy her appetite before continuing on their journey.

On the horizon, an old retro diner emerged, its neon lights barely visible in the afternoon sun. Hunger gnawed at her belly, she tugged at Luca's arm and pointed to the shabby building. He nodded in understanding.

"Sorry about that," he said, climbing off the bike. "When I ride, I tend to forget about everything." He patted his belly. "Come to think of it, I could use something to eat myself."

She smoothed her hair with her fingers and followed him to the door that he dutifully held open for her. Opting for privacy, they chose a booth in a quiet corner, away from the prying eyes of the other customers.

Their waitress, Juli, was a pleasant woman in her middle age, with streaks of gray hair blending into her long, dark brown locks, tied up in a messy bun. She spoke with a deep Southern accent, leaving Jewel to once again wonder where they were. As soon as Juli left them alone, Jewel scanned the menu for a location. Broken Bow, Oklahoma; she didn't recall seeing any state line signs on their ride, but since they took small, country roads, it made sense.

The door to the diner swung open, and five young adults, three men and two women, entered the diner, their laughter filling the air as they settled into a booth.

Luca peered over his shoulder and watched the group, he turned and exchanged a quick, knowing glance with Jewel, then quickly abandoned his seat and settled down beside her on the bench, giving him a comfortable vantage point to observe the entourage.

Jewel felt a powerful surge of warmth spreading through her

body, making her skin tingle. His proximity sent a rush of sensations surging through her, catching her off guard. The captivating scent that radiated from him seemed to have an irresistible pull, drawing her in without explanation. Overwhelmed by self-consciousness, she clumsily fumbled with the menu, desperately hoping to divert attention away from herself.

She looked over at Luca and realized her efforts were unnecessary as his eyes were locked on the group of young people. He stared at them, his jaw tense, and his eyes filled with calculating intensity. She had seen that stare before; it was eerily similar to the way that her older brother would study his prey.

The mere thought of Caleb brought a sharp pang of sorrow that stabbed at her heart. Not now, she told herself, and then quickly stuffed away those emotions.

"So, what'll it be?" asked Juli as she pulled out a pen and held up her pad.

"Oh," said Jewel. "Um, I don't know." She glanced over at Luca who was still staring at the group. She nudged him.

His trance broken, he blinked and turned his head to look at Jewel. For a moment, it appeared as though he had forgotten all about her, at least that was what his expression told her. The confused look on his face gave way to a charismatic smile. "Let the lady order whatever she wants," he said with a wink.

A rush of warmth flooded her chest, traveling up to her ears, creating a gentle warmth on her cheeks. She quickly scanned the menu. "Um, I'll have a burger. Please," she said.

After writing in her pad, Juli took the menu from Jewel, then set her focus to Luca. "And you?"

He handed the menu back to the waitress. "I'll have the same."

Juli nodded and scribbled something on the pad in her hand. She turned to Jewel. "How do you want that cooked?"

"Rare."

The woman gave her a quick nod and cast a suspicious glance over her shoulder before heading toward the order window where she carefully placed the slip on the counter, ensuring that the cook would notice it.

As Luca studied the group of young adults, he was lost in his own thoughts, oblivious to his surroundings. Jewel moved her gaze over to them.

For the most part, they appeared to be a pretty run-of-the-mill group. All dressed in clean, well-fitting clothes with neat hairstyles. Two of the young men were clearly together, the taller one had his arm wrapped around the shorter one. The third young man sat opposite them, scrunched together on the bench between the two women, his arm wrapped around the shoulder of the pretty ash blonde, while her friend sat pressed up against the window.

The group laughed and teased one another, occasionally breaking into bouts of loud chuckles and playful banter.

As Jewel watched them, she felt a slight tinge of jealously over how at ease they seemed to be. For people like them the world was a beautiful place filled with hope and fun. Envy washed over her like a wave of ice-cold ocean water. She hated them.

"Now, what's going on in that pretty little head of yours?" asked Luca.

"Huh?" Jewel shook her head and turned to face him. "What?"

He smiled. "Are you thinkin' what I'm thinkin'?" He tilted his head toward the group of friends at the other table, then leaned close and whispered conspiratorially, "You up for some fun?"

Jewel breathed in, feeling a tingly sensation in her limbs. She flashed a toothy grin. "Absolutely. Whatchya got in mind?"

Luca winked at her, a mischievous glint in his eyes that accompanied his sly grin.

When Juli returned with the burger, Jewel was suddenly not very hungry. Her tastebuds craved something more savory than a ground up patty of overcooked beef. Still, she needed something to tide her over, so, with the help of Luca, they managed to devour most of the food that was on their plates, leaving behind the buns and vegetables.

The group of young travelers paid their bill, then made a big production of gathering their things and heading out the door.

As soon as they were outside, Luca tossed a twenty-dollar bill on the table and rose to his feet. "Come on," he said, holding out his hand.

"Y'all have a nice day," Julie called out as they left the diner. "Stay safe on that motorcycle."

Jewel flashed an innocent smile and waved goodbye to the older woman, then strolled through the door that Luca held open. Eyes glued to their target, they silently mounted the motorcycle, waiting for the other vehicle to pull out of the parking lot.

TEN

LUCA FIRED UP THE ENGINE; the powerful sound reverberated in his ears as he donned his leather gloves while Jewel climbed on the back. With a swoop of his leg, he raised the kickstand and glided forward.

He glared at his target: a car full of the people he despised—wealthy, snobbish, entitled idiots who thought they were better than everyone else. He'd always disliked people like these, not surprisingly, those feelings were tenfold ever since the bite. For that matter, every emotion seemed to be more intense these days.

From behind, Jewel's arms, warm and soft, encircled his waist, her scent filling the air around him. A jolt of electricity shot through him as her inner thighs brushed against his; he could feel his pulse pounding in his ears. He was acutely aware of the feather-light rise and fall of her breathing. The thudding of his heart, a loud rhythm in his chest, had him wondering: was it the thrill of the hunt, or was it her?

He shadowed the vehicle for around twenty miles, keeping a safe distance. The journey took them past the edge of the small town and deeper into a densely wooded area. He could hardly imagine a better setting. So far, this was going well.

The vehicle turned off the main road and slowly made its way down a long, narrow driveway, disappearing behind a screen of thick, towering trees.

Luca rolled to a stop and studied the property. A wall of trees was all that was visible from the road, their thick trunks and heavy foliage completely blocking any sight of the house. Even though he couldn't see the building, he just knew it was excessive, since individuals of their kind always inhabited opulent houses. You'd never catch them living in a trailer in the swamp.

With a quick, sweeping glance, he scanned the area, taking in every detail of his surroundings. To the best of his knowledge, the nearest neighbor was situated half a mile in the opposite direction. Perfect. He drove a little farther up the road, then stopped.

"So, what's the plan?" asked Jewel.

It suddenly occurred to Luca that he had no clue. He hadn't really considered what exactly they would do when they got to this point. He pondered their next move. "We're gonna hide the bike in there," he said, gesturing into the trees.

Jewel needed no prodding. She climbed off the bike and stepped back, allowing him to roll it into the woods, following him close behind.

As he took pains to find the perfect spot, making sure the bike was secure, Jewel removed her t-shirt, leaving only a lacy white bra.

"What are you doin'?" he asked, suddenly keenly aware of how soft and pink her skin appeared against the delicate fabric. Overwhelmed by the desire to touch her, he struggled to resist reaching out.

"I'm shifting," she said nonchalantly. She kicked off her boots and unbuttoned the top button of her jeans.

He quickly glanced away. When he heard the soft sound of her jeans falling to the ground, a flash of heat exploded in his belly and rushed throughout his body. He was sure that at any moment he would spontaneously combust. "It's too early," he said, barely maintaining his composure. "We can't go walkin' up there when there's still daylight." He peered up at the sky through the trees. "We probably got another hour or so."

Jewel giggled. "That's why I'm shifting. A human would be noticed right away, but a coyote is a totally different thing. I'll just look like any other wildlife out here. They won't even notice me."

"And if they do?" he asked, struggling to control his tone. A sense of resentment welled up inside him, but he fought to keep it at bay. Truth was, it frustrated him greatly that she could change completely, while the best he could muster was a giant, man-like wolf creature. Granted, he was huge when he transformed, much larger than her, but the ability to change into a whole other animal was not something he could ever do. And this, for some irrational reason, irritated him.

"Luca Boudreaux are you worried about me?"

"Would that be such a bad thing?"

She approached him and halted, leaving inches of space between them. He was so close to her that he could feel the warmth radiating from her half-naked body, or maybe it was his own body heat, he couldn't distinguish anymore. The beast inside willed him to spin around and take her in his arms. The human side of him fought against the urge. "I-I'm responsible for you."

"I can take care of myself," she said defiantly.

His mouth was dry; his throat tight and scratchy. He wanted to say something, but couldn't remember any words. Unable to move, all he could do was stand there with his back to her, and listen as she shifted. The sounds of tearing flesh, stretching tendons and breaking bones resonated off the trees that surrounded them. One would think that would be enough to quell his desire, but it seemed to have the opposite effect. It felt like forever as the Rougarou battled his human self internally.

Silence descended upon the area. He breathed a sigh of relief, hoping the shift was complete. Luca turned around, taking in the large, pale blue-eyed coyote that stood before him. She huffed as she proudly strolled past him, whipping her tail, then after a quick nod of her head, she bounded off into the trees, disappearing from his sight.

ELEVEN

JEWEL STALKED THROUGH THE TREES, quickly reaching the edge of the clearing. The massive log cabin loomed before her. In the driveway stood the vehicle they followed from the diner.

She lifted her head and inhaled. A sudden shift in the wind carried Luca's scent to her. She closed her eyes and breathed it in, feeling that now familiar, tingly sensation in her belly.

Now was not the time for any of that. She needed to maintain her focus.

With her head low, she crept around the perimeter of the property, observing every detail. Loud music, laughter, and the sound of clinking glasses filled the house. From her vantage point, she watched a man and woman dancing seductively; their bodies moving against one another in perfect rhythm with the music, while their friends were busy playing some sort of board game.

Satisfied that she had gained all the knowledge she needed, she turned and made her way through the trees and back to Luca.

She strolled past him to where her clothes lay scattered on the ground. This time, shifting right before his eyes, deliberately holding his gaze the entire time. As soon as her human form came into full view, his face turned scarlet red and he quickly glanced away, staring at the ground. A smirk played on her lips. She wanted to tease him, but the poor man was breathing so fast, she feared he might pass out. So, she simply donned her shirt and jeans.

"Okay, you can turn around now."

"What did you see?" he asked.

"I think the house is one of those vacation rentals." She pulled her long hair back into a ponytail. "It's a big, beautiful cabin. I heard one of them mention something about the owners leaving snacks out for them."

"Good. Vacationers. They won't be familiar with the terrain."

Jewel nodded her head in agreement. "So, have you come up with a plan yet?"

"Good question." He tapped his chin and stared off into the woods toward the house. "Well, for starters, we wait 'till nightfall."

"Brilliant! I like it so far," she prodded.

The moment seemed to drag on with Luca repeatedly glancing up at the sky, and Jewel unable to do much more than watch him. If she were alone, she would spend this time daydreaming of all the ways she would tear those people apart. But she had company this time—company she liked a lot more than she cared to admit to herself. There was something about Luca. He seemed like a messy, clever rogue on the outside, but inwardly, she knew he was incredibly cunning.

While her savagery lay hidden beneath a mask of innocence, his true prowess was cleverly disguised by his foolish, country boy facade. The combination of his funny way of speaking and unassuming nature made him more fascinating to her than anyone she had ever met before. She could hardly wait to see his inner beast rear its glorious head, allowing her a glimpse into his true self.

Daylight waned, and before long the moon emerged from behind the trees, shining amongst the dazzling stars in the night sky. With excitement buzzing through her body, Jewel shifted alongside Luca.

This time, she chose a more humanoid version of her Trickster form rather than a complete transformation to better align herself with him. The Rougarou towered over her. He stood well over seven feet tall, with long, muscular arms, razor-sharp claws, and robust, sturdy legs. In contrast, when her kind were partially transformed, they kept their human height. If they were short, then their humanoid form would also be short, same as if they were tall.

Together, they took off through the woods, running full tilt toward the cabin.

They stood in the shadows, their eyes carefully scanning the surroundings. Based on what could be seen, the occupants were all inside, milling around in the brightly lit living room, blissfully unaware that this would be their last night.

The sound of a screen door swinging open and slamming closed with a loud thwack, startled Jewel.

She glanced over, her eyes locking on a single man who was busy collecting an armful of firewood. Perfect timing, she was ready for some action. Her body buzzed with anticipation.

A solemn howl from Luca set the scene; then he dashed toward the house, too fast for the unwitting human to see clearly. He sprinted past, causing the man to whirl around in confusion.

Jewel ran past from the other side.

Luca circled the man one more time, only this time as he passed, he knocked him to the ground.

The air was filled with the scent of fear as their prey struggled to regain his footing. Jewel lunged at him from the opposite direction, striking him with enough force to knock the air from his lungs as he fell to his knees.

He tried to get his friends' attention by shouting, but his voice was drowned out by the sound of their laughter and the loud music.

With slow, deliberate steps, Jewel wandered up to stand in front of him. He gasped in terror. He was so terrified he didn't even notice Luca as he crept up from behind.

The man turned to flee only to collide, head first, into the massive beast. He bounced off of Luca, stumbling backward as though he had hit a brick wall. A guttural scream was trapped in his throat as he tripped over a tree root, crashing to the ground. Paralyzed in fear, all he could do was stare wide-eyed in terror at the wolf-man standing before him.

With a deep, low rumble in his chest, Luca snarled, his face so close to the terrified man, they nearly touched.

Desperate to escape, the man scurried backward, bumping into Jewel. She extended her clawed hand and gently ran her fingers through his hair, all the while breathing in deeply, relishing the savory scent of his fear.

She wanted to play a little longer, but there were four more people inside to play with. Unfortunately for this man, his time on this earth had come to an end.

With one of his massive hands, Luca gripped the trembling man by the head, lifting him slowly. A pathetic whimper filled the air.

The Rougarou growled, exposing his sharp, deadly teeth. He wrapped his other hand around the man's throat and pulled. Bones snapped, and flesh tore.

A crimson torrent of blood poured from his neck, soaking the ground. One last tug, and the head came loose in Luca's hand. He dropped the body, watching it collapse at his feet; then, with a proud flourish, he raised the severed head, its spinal cord still attached, dangling like a grotesque chandelier.

It was the perfect start to what promised to be an evening filled with entertainment.

Luca tossed the head to the ground with a soft thud. Then, shifted his attention to the occupants inside the cabin.

Her body abuzz with anticipation, Jewel kept pace as the Rougarou, moving cautiously, approached the basement door.

The rickety screen door was no match for his strength. Without intending to, he ripped it completely off its hinges, flinging it to the side. Upstairs, on the main floor of the house, the joyful laughter of the clueless revelers filled the air, a sharp contrast to the somber reality of their friend's untimely end.

In true gentlemanly fashion, Luca stood back to let Jewel through. With stealth in mind, she moved slowly to the foot of the stairs where she paused momentarily while she debated how she wanted to go about the kill this time. In the end, she decided on full scale terror. Go in snarling and growling for maximum shock, then pick them off one by one as they try to escape.

She charged up the stairs, bursting through the door, creating a storm of flying wood splinters. The group of friends were so stunned by the commotion, they hardly registered what was happening when Luca rushed past her, descending upon the nearest human. He lashed out with one of his powerful claws and ripped a fist-sized hole through the man's throat, then stepped back and watched him crumple to the floor.

Maybe it was the bloodlust, maybe it was something much deeper, but Jewel found herself aroused by simply watching the Rougarou in the heat of a kill.

Movement in the corner of her eye caught her attention. She bolted off, charging at full speed after the other man. She pounced and landed on top of him, lifting his head high, she slashed his throat open.

The women ran screaming, their footsteps pounding on the hard floor, before throwing themselves into a bedroom and locking the door.

Jewel snickered. Pathetic humans. Such fools to believe a flimsy sheet of wood could keep them safe. With no need to rush, she followed Luca down the hall, dragging a single claw along the wall, leaving a deep gash in the drywall.

She could hear faint whimpers coming from the room. The familiar sound of a rifle cocking met her ears. She laughed. No weapon would save their lives.

Luca reached down and turned the knob. A single shot rang out, followed immediately by an explosion of wood fragments all around him. Thousands of tiny droplets of blood erupted all over his body. He stumbled backward. But the beast was already healing itself. As the final bits of wood and metal fell to the floor, he looked down at the large, crimson stain that covered his fur, then with a malevolent growl, he moved his gaze back to the woman standing in the center of the room, holding the weapon.

With a deafening roar that shook the very foundations of the building, he burst into the room. What remained of the door fell away like kindling. He gripped the barrel of the gun and wrenched it out of the woman's trembling hands, tossing it aside. It clattered to the floor like a child's toy.

The woman screamed and tried to run for the open window, but she was simply not fast enough. Luca gripped her by the nape of the neck and flung her across the room.

Her friend, having already climbed out of the window, was scurrying her way across the metal roof in a futile attempt to make her way to the ground.

Jewel dashed past Luca and out the window, following the woman's path with the skill of a ballerina. The woman didn't have a chance.

Eyes locked on her prey; she moved with a laser-like focus across the cool metal roof. She was in no hurry; she wanted to take her time —to revel in this kill. With her sharp claws, she slashed and gored the woman, leaving gaping wounds all over her body.

Playtime had ended.

With a single swipe, Jewel's claw found its mark, severing the woman's spine just below the rib cage. She folded in on herself like a puppet with broken strings. Jewel stepped closer, relishing the moment as she toyed with her incapacitated prey. She licked her claws clean, savoring the flavor of the fear infused blood, then hoisted her catch over her shoulder and made her way back inside.

She returned through the window, holding her prize, the air thick with the smell of blood. With no regard, she dropped her victim onto the floor, as if the person was just a useless rag doll. Despite her broken body, the woman, terrified and in pain, whimpered as she rolled over and desperately crawled across the floor, trying to get away.

Like a cat playing with a mouse, Jewel patiently followed her prey, cooing and poking at her, enjoying every moment. Her eyes flicked to Luca; the woman who had fired the gun at him was suspended in his hand. Still alive, she clawed at his arm, struggling to ease his grip from her throat, gasping for breath. All the while her feet kicked and flailed wildly beneath her.

The Rougarou pulled her close. His eyes bore into hers, a deep, menacing growl emanating from his chest. The woman cried out in terror. Her eyes bulged from their sockets—her face was scarlet red. The room filled with the telltale snap of bone, then her body went limp, but she was still alive. He tossed her onto the floor, where she gasped and sputtered, but lay completely still, watching in horror, unable to scream or move.

His actions held Jewel's attention so completely that she lost interest in her own prey, still dragging herself across the floor in a hopeless attempt to escape. In a stroke of evil delight, she strolled over to the woman and lifted her into the air. Now what to do with her? A buck's head suspended on the wall caught her eye. With a vicious chuckle, she impaled the woman on the long, sharp antlers.

She stepped back and took a moment to admire her handiwork. That will do nicely, she thought, then she turned her attention back to Luca.

His inner beast pulled back as his body became more human. Seeing his transformation, she too allowed her beast to subside. She flashed a mischievous grin.

He reached out, pulling her close until their lips met in a kiss that set her body on fire. A kaleidoscope of sensations coursed through every fiber of her being. The taste of warm blood on his lips only further ignited her lust as they fell onto the bed wrapped in each other's arms. Amidst the haunting sounds of their prey's moans and sobs, with the music still playing in the living room, they explored every inch of one another's bodies.

TWELVE

THE SOFT MATTRESS yielded beneath Luca's body as he lay entwined with Jewel, the warmth and softness of her skin an extreme contrast to the carnage that surrounded them. With the utmost tenderness, he leaned in and gently pressed his lips to her forehead. "You have an evil streak, Sha." he said with a grin.

She kissed him lightly on the lips. "Is that a problem?"

He chuckled. "It might be. It seems to have an unexpected effect on me." He pressed his body against hers. "We'll have to make sure it doesn't get out of hand."

"Mhm," she sighed. "We wouldn't want it to get out of hand." She smiled up at him, sending a shiver of delight down his spine.

A serious look swept over her face. "How did it happen?"

"What?" he asked.

"Rougarou are made. You managed to wriggle out of telling me the story of the bite earlier." She flashed a sly grin. "Don't think I didn't notice. But now I wanna know all the details."

The memories of that fateful night came rushing back, crashing through his mind like a torrent of muddy water. He rolled over and stared up at the ceiling, then released a weary sigh. With his head nestled against the cozy pillow, he allowed his mind to wander back to that unforgettable night. The memory of the nightmare was painful to revisit. After all, who would want to remember every fine detail of murdering their own mother?

Jewel rested her head on his chest and fiddled with the chain that held his mother's wedding ring, idly twirling the golden band on the tip of her finger.

Silence filled the space between them as she waited patiently for him to begin.

He pinched his eyes, trying desperately to push aside the gruesome image of his dead mother from his mind. As he struggled to contain his emotions, he slowly told the story of that dreadful evening. This time in the retelling, not a single detail was left out.

Jewel listened intently—never once interrupting him.

When he finished, a long, uncomfortable pause followed.

Anxious, he waited for her to speak. Anything would be better than her silence as she pondered all the information he just dumped on her.

"That's awful," she said, then leaned up on her elbow and kissed him softly on the cheek. "I'm so sorry." She rested her head against his chest.

The gentleness of her touch, coupled with the sadness in her voice did little to quell his anxiety over reliving his worst nightmare.

As he lay there, breathing in her scent while softly stroking her hair, he realized, had none of that ever happened, he wouldn't have met Jewel. In a cruel twist of fate, the single worst thing that ever happened in his life led to something far more wonderful than he ever imagined possible.

The simple act of just being with her made him feel calm.

He realized that he knew almost nothing about this woman who had stolen his heart. "Okay Sha," he said. "Now it's your turn. Time to come clean. What was it like for you?"

She sat up in the bed. A subtle shadow of sorrow came over her face. "Scary at first, but I had my brothers with me. I also knew what was happening. Did you know what was happening?"

"Lawd no," he replied. "I mean, I grew up with all the stories, so I suppose I kinda knew something. But when it hit, I was fully unprepared. It was terrifying and painful. I thought I was dying."

Jewel placed a soft hand on his arm and delicately caressed the muscle, sending a shiver down his spine. "It had to have been scary, not knowing what was happening," she said. She leaned in, her lips meeting his.

That was the end of the discussion. They spent the remainder of the night intertwined in bed, their whispered conversations a soft murmur against the gentle rhythm of their breaths and the touch of their hands. This new and unfamiliar feeling toward a woman both frightened and thrilled Luca like never before. As for Jewel, she seemed to feel the same way. At least, that was what he chose to believe.

As the first rays of dawn beamed in through the window, they reluctantly left their warm bed. Sometime during the night, the woman hanging from the buck had succumbed to her injuries. Her friend, on the other hand, had the unfortunate distinction of being the lone survivor. In her current state, she could only bear witness in terror as Jewel savagely devoured her organs for breakfast.

The sight of her feeding made Luca uneasy. Enthralled by his budding relationship with the girl, he brushed his apprehension aside, after all, she wasn't really human. Who was he to judge?

Leaving her to her meal, he took a quick shower. As he stood under the warm water, he stared down at the red flakes of blood swirling at his feet, disappearing down the drain. Shouldn't he feel some sort of remorse? This wasn't his first kill; it wouldn't be his last. Was it the Rougarou or was it something broken deep inside of him that made it so he felt no regret?

He ran his finger over the red blotch on his chest, that was all that remained of the gaping hole created by the shotgun. Anger and hatred simmered in his heart. "Fuck that bitch," he muttered. Given the chance, she would have felt no remorse if he was dead. She got what she deserved. In this world, you were predator or prey. And he was at the top of the food chain.

As he stepped out of the shower, Jewel sauntered into the room, wearing nothing more than a playful grin, her face smeared with the deep red blood of her victim. She giggled like a happy schoolgirl, then blew him a kiss and climbed into the shower.

While she cleaned up, Luca found himself a set of clean clothes, then wandered around the cabin, collecting anything of value.

In the kitchen, he placed several candles on the counter beside the stove, then rummaged around in search of a lighter.

Jewel's giddy voice floated out from one of the bedrooms. "You would think that with all their money, these women would have better taste in clothes." She popped into the hallway wearing a tank top and jeans with a flannel shirt tied around her waist. "I suppose this will do. What do you think?"

"On you? I lean heavily toward the absence of clothes." He winked. "But if you're asking for my honest opinion on your current ensemble, Mon Sha, I think you could make a trash bag look sexy."

With a playful giggle and a flick of her damp hair, she joined him in the kitchen, holding up a book of matches. "Looking for these?"

"What would I do without you?"

"Well, for one, you'd still be searching for something to light those candles."

Fighting the urge to wrap his arms around her, he set his mind to the task at hand. There was no telling how much time they had before someone came by.

While Jewel lit the candles, he pulled the stove away from the wall and, with a forceful kick, disconnected the gas line, instantly filling the room with the subtle aroma of natural gas.

It was time to go.

After jumping out of the window, they hurried through the woods, the sound of twigs breaking under their feet echoing as they ran back to the motorcycle.

As he hastily pulled on his boots, his anticipation grew—any moment now.

The explosion shattered the calm of the forest. The ground beneath his feet shook as debris from the cabin flew into the air like fireworks on the Fourth of July. The towering flames licked at the sky, their intense heat radiating toward the couple hiding among the trees, as they took it all in. They stood there in silence and watched the flames for a moment, then Luca walked his bike out of the woods and onto the road, where they climbed on and rode away.

THIRTEEN

"HEY," said Theo, snapping his fingers at Wyatt before roughly yanking off his headphones, pulling some hair out in the process. "Earth to loser boy."

Through a curtain of overgrown, dark brown hair, Wyatt's hatred for the bully seethed. The image of Theo's throat, torn and bleeding —a remnant from his most recent nightmare, filled his mind, along with the sight of his mindless buddies meeting a similar fate.

The nightmares had become a regular occurrence for Wyatt. Ever since his last birthday, he couldn't close his eyes without them. Night after night, his subconscious mind played hellish scenes of a feral beast slaughtering everyone in its path. Was he the beast? He wasn't sure, but he could almost taste the blood. Deep inside, he knew he should feel repulsed by the grotesque, swirling visions, but instead he felt a grim satisfaction, cold and hard like winter ice.

"I don't care if you're getting dropped off first, move your ass," said Theo. "No one wants you sitting anywhere near them. You smell bad." He wrinkled his nose for emphasis and gestured to the backseat. "Go sit in your regular spot, freak." A wicked grin spread across the boy's face. "Away from the normal folks."

From the moment Wyatt arrived at his new foster home, Theo, Blaze, and Carter set out to bully him. Their taunts and jeers were relentless. At every opportunity, they would push or trip him, always resulting in Wyatt being scolded when he would try to fight back.

The only bright spot of the entire house was Elian, an older boy who also lived in the home when he first arrived. Large and bulked up from weightlifting, he was the only person who managed to keep their bullying in check; the trio only dared to go after Wyatt when Elian was out of hearing range. He told Wyatt that he didn't care much for Theo and his crew, so when they turned their focus on the newcomer, he placed himself between them and stood firm. As long as he was around, Wyatt was off limits.

That all changed a little over two months ago, when Elian aged out of the system. The day after his eighteenth birthday, he was made to pack up his belongings and leave the home.

From that moment on, Wyatt was fair game. And Theo and his crew took full advantage.

At six foot three, Wyatt was by no means a pathetic wimp. His time in foster care taught him the importance of self-defense from an early age. However, in this house the bullies had an added advantage —Ellen, the foster mother who ran the whole shit show.

The moment he entered the house, her beady, rat-like eyes glared at him from behind her thick glasses, letting him know in no uncertain terms that she did not approve of her new ward. Within the first half hour of meeting him, she unleashed a string of insults about his clothing, mannerisms, and personal hygiene. All of it cleverly masked as helpful criticism. Her husband, Corey wasn't much better. The man was almost never home, yet he always seemed to materialize whenever Ellen was about to go off on one of her tirades.

Wyatt learned quickly that Ellen had a clear favorite—Theo. The boy walked around the house as though he owned it. If something was broken, he would quickly blame Wyatt, then step back and grin while Ellen berated him. Her words were always cruel. For the life of him, he had no idea why she disliked him so. One more thing that made his life suck.

Any time he would try to stand up on his own behalf, she would be there with her pointed face and rat-like eyes, ready to unleash swift and harsh punishment. He couldn't cower and hide—there was no place to go. No one to turn to for help. He was alone. His only choice was to endure, waiting for the day when he, like Elain, finally aged out of the system and could leave.

And so it went, day after day. He tried hard to stay away from the trio, yet they always seemed to track him down. The only solace he had was the few hours a week when he got to trade the prison of the foster home for a shift at the old gas station at the edge of town. The job wasn't anything exciting, if anything it was downright boring, but at least it gave him a chance to get away from Theo and his goons. The extra cash wasn't too bad either.

"Well?" said Theo. "What are you waiting for?" He shoved Wyatt, then made a show of wiping his hands off in disgust. "Freak."

As Wyatt moved past Blaze, the boy made a point of shoving him. "Come on, move it. Take your stink over there," he chided. A round of malicious laughter erupted.

Throughout his childhood, Wyatt was shuffled between various foster homes. So many in fact, they all blurred together. Unlike most of the other kids, he knew nothing about his family. All he had ever been told about his early years was that he was found by a young woman who lost her mind and ended up being admitted into a state institution. As far as he knew, she was not his mother, and she never disclosed who might be.

He gazed out the window, the scrolling landscape calming his mind. His seventeenth birthday had come and gone a little over two months ago, which meant that he only had to endure the foster system for another nine and half months. Wyatt didn't care where he would go after that, truth be told, the thought of being homeless paled compared to the life he lived so far. Sleeping under a bridge would be a cakewalk. He actually looked forward to it.

He stared out at the surrounding forest, imagining what it would be like to live freely in the woods. No people to make him miserable. And most of all, no Theo.

The acrid smell of burning wood and smoke filled his nostrils. He scanned the horizon just above the trees, searching the sky for a plume of grey smoke rising against a backdrop of fluffy white clouds. Nothing. How strange, he was sure he could smell a fire. He turned around and stared out at the sky behind them. A thin, barely visible, bluish wisp of smoke, like a ribbon, unfurled above the trees. He inhaled, shocked that he could smell the fire from so far away. How was that even possible?

A motorcycle's engine rumbled in the distance. He scanned the road, surprised to see it empty. The sound grew louder. Wyatt watched and waited, knowing that any moment, a motorcycle would crest the hill behind them.

One, two, three, four. Five seconds passed before the bike carrying two riders appeared. A man with pale blond hair and a young woman with a head full of wild, sandy blonde hair, billowing in the wind, barreled down the road.

With a rumble and roar of the engine, they rapidly caught up, moving much faster than the van. Wyatt stared at the couple with envy. How he wished he could ride away on a motorcycle.

Daydreams swirling in his mind, he was startled to see the young woman's intense, curious stare as she peered out from behind the man. A strange feeling settled in his stomach. Looking back at her through the window, a deep sense of unease washed over him. Was it unease? Or was it something else?

With a roar and a jerk of the handlebars, the driver sped up, then crossed over into the other lane. As they passed, the girl held Wyatt's gaze, her eyes unwavering.

The bike's motor revved louder, then the duo passed the van and whizzed on down the road, leaving Wyatt behind.

As he watched them disappear on the horizon, a strange feeling descended upon him. Something bad was coming, he could feel it in his bones. He turned his focus back to the scrolling trees and let his mind wander.

FOURTEEN

THE ROAD OPENED BEFORE THEM. Jewel, with a full stomach and warm sunshine on her face, leaned against Luca's shoulder, wrapping her arms around his waist. The rumble of the motorcycle beneath her, coupled with the range of emotions she felt for this strange new addition to her life made her feel happier than she had in years. The wind swirled around her, carrying with it his musky scent. She inhaled, feeling the heat rise in her body. Is this what it's like to fall in love?

After cresting a small hill, they stumbled upon the first vehicle they had seen in miles. Jewel perked up her head and gazed into the windows at the occupants only to find a peculiar boy gazing back out. They locked eyes. Trickster? If he was, he would be from another pack she never met before. Intrigued, she studied the other occupants of the van. As far as she could see, they were all human. How odd. Confused and wondering if she misinterpreted things, she returned her attention to the boy. He stared back with eyes hidden behind a greasy mop of dark brown hair. A strange sense of familiarity washed over her.

The motorcycle picked up speed and passed the van. As the

vehicle faded in the distance, she let her thoughts wander back to the moment. She hugged Luca tightly and smiled.

Several miles up the road, they rolled into a small country gas station.

With only two rusty pumps out front, the tiny establishment wasn't much to behold. Then again, in this part of the country, they were lucky to have a gas station at all. Most had closed long ago, leaving nothing but the bones of what remained of someone else's hopes and dreams.

She climbed off the bike, and then, stretching her arms high above her head, brought them down to encircle Luca's neck in a warm embrace. He leaned forward, his breath warm on her skin, and kissed her slowly; then, pulling away, a blissful smile spread across his face.

The van with the young Trickster boy rolled into the station, its tires triggering the bell as it rolled over the long hose spread along the ground.

Jewel stepped away from Luca and watched with a cautious eye as the side door slid open.

"Don't touch me!" shouted a boy inside the van. "I swear to God, if you spread your stink on me, I'm gonna—"

The boy's words and tone were cruel. Jewel decided she didn't like him. She watched a lone figure make his way past the other occupants and climb out of the van. The Trickster boy. She watched him move as she breathed in deeply, but the air was blowing the wrong way, so she couldn't get a good lock on his scent.

With slumped shoulders, the boy entered the gas station. The van door slammed closed, and the vehicle rolled out onto the road, disappearing from sight shortly after.

As she stood there, pondering this curious development, the shop's door swung open. The teenage boy stepped out carrying two bags of deer feed, one on each shoulder. He stacked them onto a wooden pallet, then turned and momentarily locked eyes with Jewel.

She smiled and waved.

A flash of red appeared on his face, then he spun around and went back inside.

There was something about him, a certain glint in his eye and the peculiar way he tilted his head, that struck her as oddly familiar. She needed to know more about him. She turned to Luca, who was filling the tank, and said, "Um, I'm gonna go inside for a minute." Not waiting for a response, she strolled away.

The bell above the door chimed as she entered, alerting the dire looking woman who was sitting behind the counter. She peered up through a pair of reading glasses.

Jewel nodded in greeting, then strolled down the aisle, searching for the young man.

The backroom door burst open, and he walked out, nearly colliding with her.

"Sorry," he blurted, then averted his gaze and scooted around her.

Beyond the smell of pubescent sweat that clung to him like cheap, skunky perfume, a subtle, more familiar scent permeated the air around him. The boy was definitely a member of her kind, more importantly, he was a Trickster on the cusp of his first turning.

"Don't just stand around," shouted the woman. "I don't pay you for nothin'. Get over there and refill the water bottles in the cooler."

The boy nodded; his eyes fixed on the worn wooden floor as he shuffled across the dimly lit shop.

There was something deeply sad about this boy. The way he carried himself told Jewel that he had very low self-esteem. He seemed to be doing everything in his power to be small and unnoticeable. Not an easy task considering how tall he was.

Out of the corner of her eye, she kept a close watch on him while pretending to examine the candy bars. One more sniff of the air confirmed her suspicion. The boy was a Trickster—but the woman wasn't.

How odd, thought Jewel.

She moved closer to get a better look at his face, feigning surprise when she bumped directly into him.

The boy startled and stepped back quickly. "I-I'm sorry," he stammered.

"No worries. I should be the one to apologize." She flashed a warm smile, hoping to get him to relax.

He stared down at the floor.

"What's your name?"

The boy glanced up, his amber-brown eyes peered back at her, shimmering with the faintest glint of budding supernatural light.

Once again, that odd sensation that she had seen him somewhere before washed over her. She opened her mouth to speak again.

"I hope you're not messin' around back there," shouted the wretched woman. "Leave the customers alone and do your job."

Images of tearing the woman to shreds played out in Jewel's mind. She brushed them aside, choosing instead to focus on this strange boy.

"My name's Jewel." She leaned close and said conspiratorially, "Is she always like this or is it just because of me?"

He smiled timidly.

It was a start.

"You know it's only proper etiquette when a young woman tells you her name, that you return the favor."

"Wyatt," he whispered. His face flushed a deep crimson, then drained to a ghostly, pallid whitish-green, the change was so rapid it was almost imperceptible. His eyes glossed over, then he clasped his hand over his mouth and ran off for the restroom, slamming the door closed behind him.

The bell chimed and Luca stepped inside, his height allowing him to see across the aisles. With a gentle smile, Luca approached, and snaked his arms around her waist.

The old woman glared at them with eyes as sharp as daggers. "You two gonna buy something?"

Once again, Jewel's thoughts played out various methods of torture for the wretched woman.

"Come on," whispered Luca in her ear. "Let's hit the road." He pressed his body against hers.

Jewel melted into his embrace, feeling the warmth, relishing the sensation. With one last glance over her shoulder at the closed bathroom door, she allowed Luca to lead her back outside into the bright sun.

FIFTEEN

TINY BEADS of sweat popped out all over his body. Hot and slick it trickled down Wyatt's skin, soaking through his already damp clothes, leaving him clammy and uncomfortable. The waves of nausea grew stronger, each one longer than the last. The lingering smell of disinfectant mixed with urine stung his nostrils as he waited for the wave to pass, rocking back and forth while sitting on the cold, damp restroom floor. "Please, please, please, stop," he muttered. His legs trembled as he struggled to stand, the mirror reflecting a face so pale and drawn it was almost unfamiliar.

He was hungry. A sharp, agonizing pang shot through his stomach; the hunger was almost unbearable. But whenever he tried to put a morsel of food against his lips, he wanted to vomit. He couldn't even come close to describing the way he felt, which only made things worse with all the adults in his life who seemed determined to believe he was faking it.

Truth be told, he wasn't sure what was wrong with him. In all of his seventeen years, he couldn't recall ever feeling this bad. His entire body ached; a searing, relentless pain that would periodically wrack him, forcing him to double over, gasping for breath, until the wave subsided. He had such sharp pain in his teeth; he was forced to go to Ellen and ask to see a dentist, positive he would need a tooth extraction. But when the dentist found nothing—not even a cavity—Ellen responded with pure malevolent anger, warning him to never waste her time like that again.

Half the time, he was drenched in sweat, his fever burning, while the other half, he was shivering uncontrollably, his teeth chattering.

Between the random, physical ailments and the violent nightmares, it was hard to decide which was worse.

Fearful that he would find himself locked up in a home for the criminally insane, Wyatt kept his hellish visions to himself. He spent many waking hours researching the meanings behind his nightmares, desperately hoping to find one person, one book, anything that would tell him he wasn't some hopeless psychopath or losing his mind. He didn't ask for any of this, all he ever wanted was to be a normal boy.

The weakness in his limbs subsided. He splashed cold water over his face and took a moment to inspect his teeth, then turned and walked back out to the shop floor. The strange, pretty woman was gone. He was both relieved and saddened by this.

"Well?" said Molly, his manager. "Did you hear me? Stop dawdling, I don't pay you to take long breaks in the restroom. Those coolers ain't gonna restock themselves."

Startled out of his thoughts by her voice, Wyatt turned to see the woman emerge from behind the counter, realizing she'd been talking to him the whole time. But he had no idea what she was saying.

She stepped close, her eyes narrowed, and glared at him, her lips curling into a sneer as she opened her mouth to unleash another torrent of insults.

Not wanting to sit through another round of "Wyatt is a loser." from yet another person in his life, he turned around, doing his best to ignore the sudden wave of nausea that crashed over him. He shoved bottle after bottle onto the racks, the refrigerated air a welcome contrast to his flushed skin. Behind him, he could hear Molly talking, but his brain refused to process it.

Please stop, he willed his body. A seesaw of hot and cold swept through him as undulating waves of nausea crested and crashed, leaving him drenched in a cold sweat. The room spun around him. Pain shot through his jaw. The feeling of a thousand tiny thorns pricking him all at once was excruciating; he doubled over, a low groan escaping his lips. He could hold it in no longer. With a shuddering heave, he expelled the remnants of his morning breakfast onto the dusty floor, a sour smell filling the air.

Molly yelped and jumped backward, just barely in enough time to avoid the splatter. Her face flashed from confused to enraged. "What the hell is the matter with you?"

"I-I'm sorry," he muttered between gags.

"You're sorry?" she shouted. "I swear to god Wyatt, if you get me sick with whatever the hell it is you have, you're done. I only gave you this job as a favor to Ellen."

Unable to speak, he collapsed to his knees. A torrent of sweat poured from his body, dripping to the floor where it mingled with the fetid liquid he purged a moment ago.

"That's it, I'm calling Ellen," said Molly. "I'm gonna have her pick you up. And don't even think about coming back here unless you have a doctor's note." Without another word, she hurried away to the front of the shop.

A sudden, agonizing pain shot through his abdomen like a hot poker. He cried out and struggled to catch his breath. Darkness seeped into the edges of his vision. The world was turning upside down. His final conscious thought was, this must be what it feels like to die.

SIXTEEN

UNDER THE COVER of a copse of trees, Jewel watched the gas station while Luca whittled away at a thin branch with his hunting knife. It didn't take much convincing to get him to stick around, one thing she knew above all others was that Luca would do whatever she asked. Even if he didn't want to.

As she kept her eyes on the shop, a sense of foreboding settled over her. She recalled the first moment she set eyes on Wyatt through the window of the van. She thought she saw a tiny spark in his eyes, then she told herself it was probably just the sunlight hitting the glass just right. But after seeing him up close, she no longer had any doubt.

She had so many questions. The first, and most important, being what the hell a young Trickster so close to his first turning was doing out here with a mismatched group of teens, surrounded by adults who didn't seem to care much for any of them.

Recalling her own experience, her heart ached for the boy. The memories of the night of her first transformation were forever etched deep in her mind. The pain, the sickness and the absolute loss of self-control. Her mind reeled with thoughts of the many ways the next twenty-four hours of that young boy's life would change irrevocably.

Her thoughts were interrupted by the metallic screech of brakes as the gray van lurched to a stop at the gas station. How odd that it would return so abruptly. From the shadows, Jewel watched as a grim-faced woman jumped out of the vehicle and ran inside.

Something was afoot.

She heard nothing despite straining her ears to listen intently.

As she grappled with the idea of going inside the establishment, the door opened.

"You better not be sick, boy," said the driver of the van as she shoved Wyatt, causing him to stumble forward and nearly fall.

Anger rising in her belly, Jewel watched as the boy climbed shakily into the vehicle. Barely able to hold himself up, he collapsed onto the rear seat. His first turning was close. A wicked grin played across her lips as she realized there would be nothing left of that woman when the boy was done. Perhaps that was for the best.

As the van pulled out onto the road, Jewel turned to Luca. "Come on."

He peered up at her with a look of confusion. "Where to?"

"We're gonna follow them."

"Who?"

"The van. More importantly, Wyatt; the boy that's in the van."

He scoffed. "What's the draw to that kid?"

"Luca Boudreaux," she said sauntering close, pressing her body against his. "Do I detect a slight sound of jealousy in your voice?" His body tensed, telling her that she was correct in her assumption.

"Nah, I ain't jealous," he said unconvincingly.

Jewel smiled and planted a kiss on his cheek then stepped away and began walking toward the bike.

"You're serious, ain't you?" said Luca as he moved to follow her, then stopped dead in his tracks and crossed his arms. "I'm gonna need an explanation before I go along."

"I already told you, the boy is a Trickster," blurted Jewel, growing anxious over the wasted time. If she was going to help Wyatt, they needed to get back on the road while the scent was still strong enough to follow. As much as it boosted her ego, she didn't have time for Luca's jealousy.

"How do you know?"

She glared at him.

"Right," he said, as though the answer had just occurred to him. "So, what does that have to do with you? With us? Ain't that something his people would deal with?"

Jewel thought about that. He was right, ordinarily, the boy's clan would be the ones to help him. But why did it seem as though he didn't have one?

Precious time was ticking away. "Luca, I need you to listen to me. I can't answer your questions because I have a whole bunch of my own. All I can say is that something in my gut is telling me that boy is alone in the world. I know without a doubt that he's about to turn for the first time, and something is telling me he has no idea. You, of all people should be able to relate to what that's like." She reached out her hand. "Now please, can we go?"

His shoulders slumped, and he gave out a long sigh, then climbed onto his bike. With hardly another word, he waited while she got situated behind him, then turned on the engine.

As they rolled out onto the road, Jewel pulled her inner beast forward and inhaled, following the unmistakable scent of the boy mingled with the exhaust from the van. Her mind swirled with memories of the one time she had witnessed the unfortunate outcome when a youngling turned in an unsecure space.

The cool blue moon cast an eerie, silvery light across the night, its presence dominating the star-studded sky. Unable to sleep, eight-year-old Jewel tossed and turned, her sheets tangled around her legs, the silence of the night amplifying her restlessness. She climbed out of her bed and stared out the window at the billions of twinkling stars overhead just in time to see the truck barreling down the driveway at breakneck speed.

She recognized it as Mr. Garza's, a member of their clan who lived on the other side of the mountain. His family had been in these parts for longer than the Riggs family, in fact, the Garza's have long been touted as the original family of Tricksters to settle these parts. But that was long ago, many generations in fact.

A flurry of activity erupted on the front porch, punctuated by the rapid footsteps of Jewel's father, Eben, and her mom, Jenny running out onto the gravel driveway.

Mr. Garza's truck came to a grinding halt, kicking up a cloud of dust and debris. He burst out of the driver's seat and ran around to the passenger side.

"Teo," shouted Eben. "What the hell is going on?"

"Ava! She got out!" came the rapid reply. He pulled open the passenger door.

Something in the older man's tone set off alarm bells in Jewel. She had known Mr. Garza her entire life, and never had she heard him sound so scared. A sense of foreboding settled upon her.

Mrs. Garza jumped out; her clothes were covered in deep red stains. She moved aside and let her husband reach back into the truck.

Due to the glow of the porch lights, Jewel noticed the blood that was all over Mr. Garza's shirt and arms.

Her bedroom door opened then closed quietly. Pax crept up to the window and sat down beside her. "What's happening?" he asked, observing the spectacle below.

"Not sure. Mr. Garza sounds scared."

Teo stepped back, in his arms he cradled the limp body of his son, Ezra.

Both Jewel and Pax gasped in shock.

The front door swung open once again, this time it was Caleb who charged out, coming to a skittering halt in front of the adults.

At fourteen years old, Caleb was already nearly as tall as his father. "Ezra!" he shouted. "What happened?"

"Quickly," said their mother. "Get him inside."

Jewel and Pax raced to the top of the stairs. With bated breath, they watched as Mr. Garza carried Ezra into the living room and placed him softly on the sofa.

"Caleb!" shouted their mother. "I need you to get my medicine case."

Seemingly locked in some sort of a trance, Caleb didn't even flinch as he stared wide eyed at his best friend laying on the sofa, so close to death.

Ezra moaned as he swiveled his head. Deep red blood oozed out of the ugly wound that stretched from the side of his face down to his throat, soaking the cushions and dripping to the floor.

"Son!" boomed their father. "Do what your Mama says. Now!"

Caleb shook his head and ran off into the kitchen.

"Dammit, Teo!" cursed Eben. "I thought you said you were gonna repair the chamber."

"She turned before we could get to it."

Mrs. Garza shook her head slowly. "It happened so fast," she said with a quavering voice. She peered down at her son with tear-filled eyes and stroked his wet hair.

Caleb returned carrying their mom's medical case. He handed it over to her then joined the older men.

From her perch at the head of the stairs, Jewel watched as Caleb assumed an equal position with the grown-ups. She admired her oldest brother. He never seemed to be plagued by a sense of not belonging, rather, he was born knowing his position in life, and he was proud of it.

She moved her gaze over to the sofa and watched as her mother and Mrs. Garza worked on poor Ezra.

Born on the same day, Ezra and Caleb had been inseparable since before they could even crawl. The boys were two halves to one whole. So much so that Jewel considered Ezra a brother, and he, in turn, behaved as such.

Somewhere in the hills a lone coyote called out.

Every adult in the room paused. The air was thick with tension.

Silent and furious, Eben and Teo charged toward the front door, Caleb right on their heels.

"Where are you going?" asked Eben, placing a firm hand against his son's chest.

"With you."

Their father shook his head. "This ain't nothing for you to deal with."

"He's my best friend."

"Which is why you're gonna stay here safe with the others."

"I wanna help!"

"Son," said Eben. "You're years from your first turning. If she ran into you, you would end up exactly like Ezra. Or worse." He gestured to the sofa. "The last thing we need is another casualty." The older man stepped through the door. "You're staying here." The conversation was over. Eben pulled the door closed behind him.

Caleb seethed, glaring at the closed door. He spun around on his heels and locked eyes with Jewel, then Pax, who recoiled at the glare, then he stormed into the living room.

─────

Jewel remembered every tiny detail of that night. The fear in the adult's hearts was so palpable, she could almost taste it.

Of course, Ezra survived, with a lifelong reminder of that awful night. As for his sister, Ava, sometime just before dawn, Eben and Teo returned with her. Sobbing and begging for forgiveness, she collapsed to her knees beside the sofa and waited for her brother to awaken.

No one held any ill will toward her. Instinctively, they all understood. Even Ezra.

SEVENTEEN

"YOU, *of all people should be able to relate to what that's like.*" The sting of Jewel's words reverberated in Luca's head, like a worm burrowing deep into his self-esteem.

The way those words rolled off her tongue hurt. She didn't sound hateful, but the condescension was clear.

Mais la! Stop it! He scolded himself. She wasn't trying to slight you. Quit readin' more into things.

He did his best to focus on the road ahead, driving blind, following Jewels directions. He was annoyed; her superior sense of smell enabled her to track something he could not see. His emotions threatened to overwhelm him. Why couldn't he detect the scent? When they caught up to this van, what the hell were they gonna do? And what was with her attraction to this kid?

He was jealous. The realization struck Luca suddenly—in all his years, the thought of possessing any woman, or even feeling a twinge of jealousy, had never crossed his mind. This was uncharted territory. He couldn't figure out if this was the Boudreaux in him or was it because of his new biology—that was also, now, very much a part of him.

Confusion reigned supreme. The one thing he was certain of was that he didn't like anything about this whole situation.

Jewel tapped his shoulder and pointed.

Luca slowed the bike and halted at the end of a narrow driveway. Finally, there it was—the van they had been tailing, parked before a tidy little garage. He nodded, truly impressed by Jewel's ability.

Now that they knew where the kid was, they needed to find a place to stow the bike. After all, two strangers rolling up to the house probably wouldn't go over very well. It might even get them shot.

He glanced around at the surrounding trees, then coasted about a half mile up the road, and glided into the dense overgrowth.

"Please tell me you have a plan," he said as he climbed off his motorcycle.

Jewel stared off through the forest, no doubt deep in thought. She spun around. "Truthfully, I'm not sure what to do next."

Since this was obviously important to her, Luca reluctantly pushed aside his growing irritation over the whole side quest. "Well, let's start with the first turning. What makes you so sure he's about to pop?"

Her lips curled into the slightest of smiles. "You have a way with words."

"I just say it like it is, Sha," he replied.

She sauntered close enough to press her body against his. "And that is just one of the many things I adore about you." Standing on her tiptoes, she planted a kiss on his cheek.

He put his arms around her and breathed in, letting her scent flood his senses.

"Let's try to stay on track," she said as she dropped out of his arms and took a step back. "We're here for a reason."

"Right, right, your underage boyfriend over there and his impending lifelong upheaval."

A slow sigh escaped Jewel's lips, a sound heavy with unspoken words, as she shook her head. Her face registered genuine concern for the boy.

Luca felt ashamed. He was acting like a jealous boyfriend. The kid was just a gangly teen; he was no threat to him at all. But then again, Luca wasn't much more than a gangly young man himself. The one thing he had on the kid was that his first turning was well behind him. And of course, he met Jewel first.

He stared at her and finally realized how silly he'd been. "So, tell me why you think this kid doesn't have people."

"I'm not sure," she replied. "The only thing I know for sure is that he's right on the cusp of his first turning." She paused. "And he's very confused. It's as though he doesn't even know what's happening to his body."

"Now, how would you know that? Did you read his mind or something?"

She shook her head. "I just know."

"How sure are you that he don't have family?"

"Because it's obvious that he's about to change. Even a new Trickster could smell it on him. His kin wouldn't let him out to wander in his condition. It's not how my kind does things." She halted, as though she realized the bite in her words.

Deep inside, every time she pointed out how different they were, it was like a stab to his gut.

"I'm sorry," she blurted. Once again, she strolled up to him and put her arms around his neck. "I don't mean to sound judgmental or cruel. I'm just trying to grasp all of this myself."

He was being stupid. Luca released the tension in his shoulders, a sigh escaping his lips, then gently kissed her forehead before letting her go. "I'll stop being such a couillion." He gazed off toward the house. "So, it's obvious by the scent that he's about to change, and that he's surrounded by folks who have no idea."

"It looks as though somehow he ended up separated from his clan."

"Does that happen often?"

"I've honestly never heard of it happening before." She nibbled at her bottom lip. "I'm worried for him."

"I get that," he replied. "What I don't understand is why."

Jewel turned her eyes to him. "I've told you about my first turning, but I didn't tell you everything." She took him by the hand. "A few years ago, I was a stupid, terrified kid who was in the same place as he is." She glanced down at the ground. "Well, sorta."

Luca took a seat on the soft ground and waited for her to get comfortable beside him. When she was ready, she began.

"I told you about how I grew up in a close-knit clan from the West Texas mountains. My family had been there for generations. I knew exactly who and what I was from birth. My mom and dad taught me and my brothers to be proud of who we are."

"Not long after my thirteenth birthday, my mom and dad got into a horrible accident and died, leaving me and my brother Pax in the care of my oldest brother, Caleb."

Her lips curved into a melancholic smile, a faint tremor in her voice as she whispered the names. Her chin trembled, her lower lip quivering, threatening to unleash a torrent of tears.

"At first, my brother Caleb hated being thrown into the role of adult. He spent so much time away from Pax and me. Every night, he would wander out alone, only to return home in the early hours of dawn reeking of alcohol and blood."

"I'm not gonna lie, I hated him. In my stupid, pubescent mind, I blamed him for all my misery. My only solace was Pax."

She reached into her jeans and pulled out a lighter. Holding it in her hand, she ran her thumb across the surface, tracing what appeared to be a rune or something. Luca wanted a better look, but didn't want to interrupt her story.

Jewel put the lighter away and pinched the tears from her eyes.

Seeing her this way broke his heart. He took her hand, and she forced a smile.

"For a while, Pax was the only person who was always there for me. He was my best friend. And then, he had his first turning and, just like that, he was a younger Caleb."

"It felt like when I lost my mom and dad all over again, only this time I was totally alone."

She stared out through the trees. "One day, Caleb came back with this woman. Her name was Izzy. Like us, she was a Trickster, but she wasn't from our clan."

"Izzy was okay, I suppose. She was nice to me, and she wasn't afraid to stand her own against Caleb."

"Her twin brother Bass moved onto the ranch to live with us."

"Not long after, Caleb moved himself and Izzy into my mom and dad's bedroom. That was when I moved upstairs to the attic. I couldn't stand hearing them laugh in that room. I was so mad at him."

Jewel wiped her cheeks and cleared her throat. "By this point, I hated them all. Caleb was busy being the big man in town. He was strong willed, cunning and handsome, so he got away with a lot. As for Pax, all he ever did anymore was try to prove himself to Caleb. It drove me crazy watching him bend over and twist himself up in knots in an attempt to show Caleb he was every bit as strong as he was."

"I didn't want to be like them. All I wanted to do was run away. We had an uncle who lived in Austin. I hadn't seen him since the funeral, but I convinced myself that if I could get to him, he would let me stay and I wouldn't have to be around Caleb anymore."

"The night I finally made a run for it was also the night of my first turning."

"I had a feeling it was happening, but I was in complete denial. I didn't want to be anything like my brothers. I had seen how profoundly they had changed, and I didn't want that to happen to me."

A melancholy smile spread across her face. "Needless to say, I was wrong. When it mattered most, my brothers were there for me. Both of them. And I wouldn't have it any other way."

She looked up at Luca with plaintive eyes. "I know what it's like to be scared and alone when you first turn. When I looked at that boy, I literally felt his loneliness and confusion. It was damn near identical to the way I felt that first time. I can't leave him alone like that."

The pieces clicked into place, a sudden rush of understanding washing over him. Luca scolded himself for being so self-centered. Here she was processing serious trauma and reaching out to someone else to help them through, and all he could think of was himself. He was such a fool. It was time for him to step up and be the type of man who deserves a woman like Jewel in his life.

He pulled her close against his chest; he could feel her heart beating. "We won't let that happen, Sha. I promise." He kissed the top of her head.

EIGHTEEN

THE PAIN WAS A RELENTLESS TIDE, surging and receding, each agonizing crest threatening to overwhelm Wyatt before subsiding into a dull, throbbing misery.

As if the searing pain wasn't bad enough, the smells were even worse. From Theo's B.O. to Blaze's chronic bad breath, it was all so potent. Wyatt swore he could even smell dust.

His entire body trembling, he sat on the edge of his bed, rocking back and forth, hugging his knees to his chest in a feeble attempt to ignore the bone-deep, paralyzing ache that pulsed with each breath. His guts churned and groaned, making him wonder if they weren't tying themselves into knots.

His clothes were soaked through with sweat; the damp fabric stuck to his skin, causing a cold, chafing sensation. It felt like burlap or sandpaper—scratchy, uncomfortable, and irritating against his overly sensitive skin. He wanted to tear them off.

The sound of hip hop playing from Theo's bedroom down the hall assaulted his ears, causing a loud ringing that seemed to get more intense with each beat. It was impossible that the music was as loud as he thought it was. Ellen and Corey had hard and fast rules when it came to music—if they could hear it, it was too loud. Even Theo, as arrogant and defiant as he was, wouldn't dare push that boundary.

The smell of burning garlic and overcooked onions wafted from the kitchen, making his stomach flip. If there was anything left in his belly, he would have purged it by now.

Unable to take it any longer, he pulled his t-shirt off. It was soaked; so much so that it coated his hands in sweat. After taking a deep breath, relishing the cool air, his body was suddenly seized by a spasm. He clenched his chest. Is this what a heart attack feels like? Terror grew inside him. Am I dying?

A searing, stinging pain, like a swarm of yellow jackets gnawing away at his flesh, exploded across the top of his finger; the sharp agony made him gasp. He watched in shock as the nail slowly pushed its way free from the nail-bed; he could feel the pressure, the tearing, and see the tiny, glistening drops of blood forming. It toppled to the floor.

"This isn't real," he muttered.

Dark red blood oozed from the wound. The throbbing intensified, a painful counterpoint to the heavy bass vibrating from Theo's room. His eyes widened in horror as a bone-white shard, like a tiny, jagged tooth, burst from his fingertip. Before he could comprehend the nightmare that he was witnessing, his middle finger began its own transformation.

What's happening? Tears exploded from his eyes.

An itchy, crawling sensation, like millions of tiny bugs, spread across his skin. Tiny, coarse hairs, like the bristles of a brush, erupted all over. He retched violently, what little remained of the contents of his stomach churned and roiled, working its way up. He clamped his hand over his mouth, then sprinted from his bedroom, into the bathroom, slamming and locking the door behind him with a resounding thud.

Water. He needed water. He turned on the faucet and shoved his face under the cool stream. With each desperate gulp, the liquid barely touched the intense heat that seared his insides, leaving him gasping for relief.

Hot tears of terror mingled with the cold sweat that poured from his face, stinging his eyes. He peered into the mirror and cried out at the vision that stood before him.

His eyes shimmered with electric amber light. His face, covered in a fine layer of short, bristly hairs, mirrored the same fuzz that now coated his entire body. A trickle of blood, warm and metallic, escaped his lips, trickling down his chin. A shiver went down his spine as he ran his finger along his gums; each tooth felt unnervingly loose, moving all on their own with a sickening, grating sound. One by one, they tumbled into the sink.

He wanted to scream in terror, but feared Ellen's wrath.

Unable to mask the pain any longer, Wyatt cried out in horror as he watched long, sharp fang-like teeth fill the gaping holes. Dog teeth! He was growing dog teeth in his mouth!

"I'm hallucinating. This isn't real. This isn't real," he muttered, shaking his head violently. As though his body were answering him, the sound of snapping bones—sharp, brittle, and horrifying—filled his ears.

Someone was pounding on the door.

"What're you up to in there, loser?" shouted Blaze from the other side.

Pure, unbridled rage ignited in his mind. A crimson haze filled his vision as his world turned blood red. He could smell Blaze through the door. His belly growled, a hollow ache that sent a trickle of saliva down his parched lips. He swallowed. The blood-infused flesh called to him; he needed to taste its rich, iron-like flavor. That would make the gnawing hunger subside.

Blaze's furious pounding on the door continued, punctuated by his increasingly vicious insults.

Wyatt gazed at his reflection in the mirror. The meek boy was gone, replaced by a ferocious beast; its hunger a palpable thing, a wildness that snarled and snapped, ready to tear flesh from bone with savage delight. The beast ripped the door open with so much force that it came free in his hand. He flung it aside, then grabbed his prey and bit into his throat before the boy could scream.

A savory explosion of blood filled the beast's mouth, the hot, metallic liquid rushing down his throat, calming the unrest in his belly. That was it. He needed to feed.

"What the fuck?" shouted Carter, in the hallway, his face a mask of shock and terror.

Feed!

The beast released the dead flesh in its hands and lunged forward, tackling its new prey. The tender flesh parted easily under the weight of his deadly claws, a spray of blood misting the air as they sliced and tore. The boy opened his mouth, but the only thing that came out was a gurgling sound. His eyes rolled up in the back of his head as his heartbeat slowed, then stopped altogether.

"What the hell are you boys doing up there?" demanded Ellen from the bottom of the stairs.

The beast swung its head toward the sound of its next prey.

"Shit!" screamed Theo, standing in the doorway of his bedroom. He slammed the door closed and clicked the lock into place.

"That is it!" said Ellen.

Each footfall, heavy and angry, echoed in the beast's ears as she pounded up the stairs. He inhaled, breathing in her scent. His blood-soaked maw dripped with saliva. When the top of her head appeared, the monster lunged.

His claws sank into her skull, a sickening crunch accompanying the abrupt end to her screams as he yanked her head back, severing it completely from her body. A crimson explosion of blood coated the walls, its sticky texture seeping into the cracks in the drywall, flooding down the stairs.

Feed!

The beast tore the soft flesh from the bone, savoring each delicious mouthful.

The air vibrated with the sharp crack of a gunshot; the sound bounced off the walls, leaving a lingering smell of gunpowder.

Before the beast could react, another shot was fired.

The searing pain of hot molten metal invading the beast's body was immediate; a wave of intense heat that felt like a thousand burning needles. He reared up and howled in rage. Then his eyes locked onto the man standing in the stairwell, holding the shotgun with trembling hands.

When he realized the beast was coming for him, he tossed the useless weapon aside and ran down the stairs, taking them two at a time. With a desperate scramble, he skittered to the door and managed to fling it open right before the beast caught up with him and pulled him back inside the house.

High-pitched screams pierced the air as the beast reveled in the taste of the warm, savory meat, a bloody feast.

Silence descended.

He stared down at Corey's remains—and felt nothing. The air hung heavy with the silence of death. A sense of clarity washed over him; he felt comfortable in his own skin. He was fully himself.

A frantic scratching and scuffling on the roof above reached his ears, followed by the soft thud of feet landing on the ground. There was still one loose end to take care of.

He stepped over the remains, and out onto the porch then peered up at the night sky. His body was electric, tingling with a sudden surge of adrenaline. Every muscle vibrated with power and energy. The trees pulsed with a life he'd never seen before, their branches reaching toward the sky like grasping arms, their leaves shimmering with an ethereal glow. A myriad of scents—pine, damp earth, and decaying leaves—floated on the air, filling his nostrils with their earthy perfume.

He scanned the treeline, searching for his quarry.

The branches swayed—something large and dark moved between the trees. Wyatt stared into the shadows. A strange odor tickled his nose; something unfamiliar, yet familiar at the same time. He listened intently, picking up the subtle sound of hurried footsteps on the forest floor.

The sound of Theo crying out in pain bounced off the trees.

He swiveled his head back and forth to discern the direction of the sound. Wyatt took a tentative step forward to the edge of the trees and inhaled. Theo's scent mingled with something else. Someone else.

Slow footsteps and shuffling feet moved closer.

It looked at first as though Theo had burst from the trees—his head hanging down, his movements jerky and unnatural. His eyes stared blindly; his face was frozen in a mask of perpetual terror. He was dead.

Behind what remained of his foster sibling, a hulking wolf-like creature stood, its shadow stretching long and ominous in the dim light. It dangled the lifeless body in its massive hands.

With a soft thud, the beast dropped Theo to the ground and then stepped over his remains, coming to a stop, towering over Wyatt.

The air vibrated with a low growl from behind the wolfman; the smell of musky fur heavy in the air, and then another stepped into view. This one was much smaller. A female.

She placed her body between Wyatt and the wolfman, then slowly shifted before his eyes.

As the animalistic features receded, revealing smooth skin, her vibrant blue eyes glowed, and her face transformed into that of the young woman he'd seen earlier. She stepped forward and reached out with a slender hand, gently touching Wyatt's chest. "It's okay, my brother," she said with a soothing soft voice.

NINETEEN

WHEN THE SOUND of gun fire ripped through the quiet woods, Jewel ran, releasing the Trickster as she raced toward the horrifying sounds, already knowing what awaited her.

Luca, a giant compared to her, sped ahead, his footsteps thudding heavily on the forest floor, the sound echoing through the trees.

By the time she caught up with him, he had already dispatched one member of the house. A low growl, rumbling like distant thunder, emanated from deep within his chest, the sound thick with menace as he stood before the young Trickster.

A knot of anxiety, cold and tight, clenched in her stomach as she stepped forward, driven by instinct, to soothe the boy. A palpable heat filled the air, his confusion and terror clear in his wide, darting eyes and shallow, rapid breaths. Having never done this before, she relied on her intuition.

The moment she showed herself to the boy, he calmed.

His heart gradually eased into a slower rhythm. The Trickster subsided, giving way to the body of a confused teenage boy. He crumpled to his knees before her, his breaths hitching in ragged gasps as his body wracked with uncontrollable sobs.

The sight of the poor boy filled her with sadness. Jewel wrapped her arms around him and waited for him to calm. When he was ready, she guided him back inside the house, past all the carnage on the stairs, and into his bedroom.

While he cleaned himself up, she helped herself to a new set of clothes. As she dug around in the woman's closet, she couldn't help but gripe under breath over the fact that they never seemed to stumble upon victims with good taste.

In the hallway, she heard Luca shout, "Whoo Lawd! This boy fucked these people up!" It took all her resolve to contain a chuckle. He appeared in the doorway, wearing an old T-shirt and a pair of jeans that didn't quite fit right, dangling a length of bloody intestines in his hand. "We gotta burn it all down." He clucked his tongue and shook his head and then spun around. As he wandered off, he muttered, "There ain't a mop in this world that could clean this shit up. Hell, I don't think there's an industrial vacuum that could do this job."

While Luca carried out the clean-up task of gathering what remained of Wyatt's victims, Jewel helped the boy collect his things. The air was thick with a heavy silence, punctuated by the occasional morbid joke from Luca as he methodically collected the remains into mounds of gore throughout the house.

With slow, deliberate movements, Wyatt collected clothes and a small bundle of treasured items, the only sound was the soft rustle of fabric in the otherwise still room. His expression was emotionless. The whole time, he uttered not a single word. At the top of the stairs, he paused, gazing up at the ominous dark red stain along the wall. He hesitated, as though a word was caught in his throat, then exhaled, the sound echoing slightly in the stairwell as he started down.

Luca waited for them at the base of the stairs. In his hands, he held a candle and a lighter. As Wyatt walked past, he gave a curt nod, his eyes following the boy out the door. As Jewel passed, they shared a single glance of understanding, then he wandered off toward the kitchen.

Realizing the motorcycle couldn't accommodate all three of them, Jewel took charge of driving the van. Luca would have to follow them on his bike. She helped Wyatt place his things into the vehicle and get seated, then climbed in behind the steering wheel. In the side mirror, she watched as Luca ran from the house and mounted his motorcycle. He gave her a thumbs up and winked.

"You ready?" she asked.

Wyatt clipped his seatbelt into place and nodded.

"Let's get you out of here," she said as she rolled down the driveway.

They were nearly a half mile up the road when the explosion rocked the earth, sending a shockwave they could feel in the vehicle. The scent of burning wood wafted on the breeze.

In her rearview mirror, she watched the bright orange and yellow flames dance against the pale morning sky; the heat radiating off them even from that distance.

Exhausted from the ordeal and lulled by the rhythmic rumble of the van and the soft, calming melodies drifting from the radio, Wyatt fell asleep.

As she focused on the road ahead, Jewel shot the occasional glance at the boy. Where the hell did he come from? It was an unheard-of situation: a Trickster child somehow left to be raised by humans. How did this happen? Trickster mothers are notoriously protective of their young.

Try as she might, she couldn't imagine a scenario where a mother would abandon her child—let alone hand him over to the humans. It made no sense.

Beside her, Wyatt continued to sleep steadily. Behind them, Luca rolled along on his motorcycle. She glanced at him through the side mirror and smiled as she wondered what was going through his mind.

TWENTY

THE VAN HIT a pothole-ridden section of road, the jarring jolt snapping Wyatt awake. Startled, he jumped upright and glanced around nervously. Was it all just a bad dream?

"Sorry about that," said Jewel. "I guess you could say I suck at driving. My brother Caleb used to say, if there was a pothole in the road, I was sure to hit it." She flashed a smile that seemed a little sad.

He rubbed his eyes, feeling the grit of sleep crust in the corners. Images flashed forward in his memory—a horrifying montage of blood-soaked scenes and screaming faces, like a terrifying horror movie trailer on fast-forward. It was real. It was all real. Despair, cold and heavy like a physical weight, washed over him. A cold sweat slicked his skin as his breath came in short, panicked bursts; his heart beat wildly in his chest. He tried to swallow, but his mouth was too dry. Something foreign was lodged between his teeth. With a tentative poke of his tongue, the slightly warm, oddly smooth texture sent a shock of horror through him; it was a sliver of flesh. His stomach lurched violently, a sour taste rising in his throat, as he gagged and desperately grasped the door handle.

The van screeched to a halt, throwing him forward, just in time for him to lean out and vomit violently onto the dusty ground. Red. It was all deep dark red with large and small chunks of flesh mixed in. He squeezed his eyes shut against the grotesque pool below and retched.

A soft, gentle hand reached out and rested on his shoulder. "It's okay," said Jewel. "It's gonna be okay."

"How?" he croaked, his throat felt like sandpaper. "I murdered them." He licked his lips, the tang of iron and bile lingered in his mouth. "I—I." He couldn't bring himself to say the words out loud.

With a soft touch, Jewel cupped his chin and tilted his face to look into his eyes. "It's okay," she said. "You're with us now. You're okay."

The motorcycle rolled up alongside the truck as Luca peered into the cab. "Everything good?" he asked warily.

"Yeah, we're fine," said Jewel.

Luca's eyes narrowed and fixed on Wyatt. He had seen that look his entire life. It was the glare of a person who didn't care for him at all.

Jewel's voice broke the silence. "I realize this is probably bad timing." She smiled sheepishly. "I don't know about y'all, but I'm starving."

Wyatt's stomach did somersaults at the mere thought of food; a cold sweat and queasy feeling washed over him.

"I'm pretty hungry too," said Luca. "Though our boy here might not agree." He flashed a wild grin at Wyatt. "What do you say, man-eater? Now that you purged your midnight snack, you got any room in there for a little lunch?" He paused momentarily, then tapped his teeth. "Speaking of which, you got a little somethin' right there."

Wyatt poked his tongue along his teeth, discovering yet another tiny piece of flesh embedded between them. His stomach flipped, the bile burning a path up his esophagus. He lurched out of the vehicle, barely containing the eruption, the acrid spray hitting the ground where it mingled with all the rest. To his left, he could hear Luca laughing heartily.

"Luca Boudreaux!" scolded Jewel. She slapped him playfully.

Wyatt leaned back and wiped his mouth with his sleeve. He wanted to say something, but found no words. A heavy silence descended upon them.

The grin vanished from Luca's face as his eyes fell to the ground, the playful light in them dimming. "She's right," he sighed. "That was uncalled for." He locked eyes with Wyatt. "You been through enough. You don't need me makin' it worse."

"Thank you," said Jewel.

Luca smiled warmly at her. "The sign back there said there was a town a few miles up the road. We can check it out and see if there's anything to eat there."

"Yeah," said Jewel. "Let's do that. What do you think Wyatt?"

Startled by the sound of his name, he peered up at her, his sweat-matted hair falling over his eyes, then glanced at Luca and gave a quick, almost imperceptible nod.

"Alright then!" said Luca as he tapped the van with his hand. "I'll lead. Don't take this the wrong way, but I can't do another mile staring at your ass end."

"I thought you liked my ass end," said Jewel flirtatiously.

"Mon Sha," he replied with a playful grin. "Never doubt how much I love your ass end."

Jewel giggled like a schoolgirl as she pressed her lips against his.

Sitting in the presence of the two lovebirds, Wyatt couldn't help but feel as though he was in the way. In an effort to make himself small, he pressed his back against the seat. Thankfully, their playfulness ended, and Luca left to go back over to his bike.

The motorcycle's engine roared to life, the sound vibrating through the air as it rumbled forward. Following his lead, Jewel turned back onto the road.

The town wasn't much to speak of, but his new companions managed to find a little shop that made sandwiches. After securing the food, they found a shaded spot on a barren road and settled beneath the gnarled branches of an ancient oak tree.

With the sun warm on his face and a gentle breeze whispering through the leaves, Wyatt felt almost normal.

"You should try to eat something," said Jewel.

The sandwich sat before him, a monument to his lack of appetite. He stared at the mayonnaise, its sharp, vinegary scent making his stomach churn, unable to bring himself to touch it. There was no way he would even try to put it against his lips. He may never eat again.

"If you ain't gonna eat it," said Luca through a mouthful of partially chewed bread and lunch meat, "mind if I take it?"

A wave of warmth rose from Wyatt's belly. With a nod, he pushed the sandwich toward Luca, who grabbed it. His eyes shining with hunger, he tore into it immediately.

Jewel climbed to her feet, brushed her hands off, and winked. "Gotta go take care of business," she said, then wandered across the road and disappeared behind a cluster of shrubs.

The sound of Luca's chewing filled the area, overpowering the rustling leaves and occasional twitter of birds in the trees. The sound was maddening. Each wet chew felt like a tiny pinprick, a dull throbbing pain that echoed in Wyatt's head with every repetitive sound. Irrational anger grew inside him. He squeezed his eyes shut and did his best to focus on the gentle whisper of leaves rustling in the breeze, but all he could hear was the slosh and squish of saliva in Luca's mouth.

"Okay Wyatt," said Jewel, as she made her way back over to the shady spot. "We haven't done much talking since last night. Do you feel up for answering some questions?"

"Yeah, I guess so," he replied, thankful for the ability to focus on something else.

Jewel crossed her ankles and sat down, the rich scent of fertile earth rose like a plume, mingling with the dry, almost brittle smell of the grass.

"Let's start with you," she said. "You have to have questions."

A torrent of thoughts, each one a wave crashing against the next, rushed forward. Unable to contain himself, he blurted, "What happened? Am I a monster? Why is this happening to me?"

"Let's start small," said Jewel. "First, you were born this way. You're a Trickster." She sat upright. "Like me." Her face became serious. "You are not a monster. What happened to you was just your first turning. It's a scary time, even for those of us who know it's coming. I can't even imagine how terrifying it had to be not having any idea what was going on."

"I can," said Luca.

"The first time?" said Wyatt. "Does that mean it's gonna happen again? A wave of despair washed over him as he pictured the previous night's horrors repeating themselves with another group of hapless victims.

"You'll get it under control pretty quickly," said Jewel. She flashed a gentle smile. "In no time at all, you'll see what a gift it is. Promise."

"Or you'll come to terms with the curse," added Luca.

"Are you a Trickster, too?" asked Wyatt.

Luca sighed and shook his head. "I'm something else entirely," he said. "Like you, it came out of nowhere. However, not like you, had I made different choices, I wouldn't be here right now." He pointed at Wyatt. "You would be in this situation no matter what you did. So, don't be so hard on yourself. You're just a kid who was put into a shitty situation."

"He's right," said Jewel. "This sort of brings me to a question I have. How did you end up with those people? Where is your family?"

That was a question Wyatt had pondered for years, a nagging thought that echoed in the quiet moments until he finally found peace by letting it go. He shrugged.

"Do you have any recollection of them?"

"The only memories I have are living with one foster family after another. I never had any family come visit," said Wyatt. "Never had any mention of family come up." He scanned his memory in search of even the slightest kernel of information that might be a clue. "In my last home—the one before this one, I asked my foster mother about it. She came back a week later with some story about a woman who appeared one night in an emergency room, hysterical, covered in blood and rambling. She was carrying me. Apparently, she ended up locked away in an institution somewhere, and I ended up a ward of the state."

"What are the odds that's his mother?" asked Luca.

"Slim," replied Jewel. "But we won't know unless we find her." She turned to Wyatt. "Did your foster mother ever say anything more?"

"Two weeks later, I was shipped off to Ellen and Corey. I never heard anything else, nor did I ask."

"Well, if your foster mother could get that info, there must be a file about you somewhere," said Luca. "I'm gonna bet your caseworker has it." With a mischievous glint in his eyes, he turned to Jewel. "You thinkin' what I'm thinkin'?"

"That we go find that caseworker?"

He bobbed his head up and down, grinning wildly.

"Wait, what?" asked Wyatt.

"We're gonna go see if your caseworker has a file on you. If there is one, there might be some info about where you came from," said Jewel.

"It'd be a start," said Luca. "What do you say? Wanna go see if we can find some answers?"

The thought of finally uncovering his true identity and origins sent a shiver down Wyatt's spine, a feeling he hadn't allowed himself to acknowledge in years. What if his family intentionally gave him away? What if they didn't want him? There was a high likelihood that the answers he found would hurt far more than not knowing. Even so, burning curiosity compelled him to find out. He needed answers. If they turned out to be more painful than not knowing, he would at least be able to move on. He glanced at Luca, then Jewel and nodded. "Okay."

TWENTY-ONE

THE OFFICE BUILDING loomed large before him. As Luca stared up at the impressive edifice, he wondered why the hell he offered to get himself into this whole mess. His entire life, he had gone out of his way to avoid authorities of any kind, and now here he was, about to break into one of their fortresses. Did they have security? Were there alarms? What the hell was he thinking?

"So, what are you thinking?" asked Jewel, as she snaked her slender arms around his waist.

He leaned against her body. "I think we've lost our minds."

"Besides that," she said. "How are we doing this?"

"We?"

"Yes." She withdrew her arms and moved to face him. "We."

Her fiery spirit was one of the many things he adored about her. Like a moth to a flame, he felt an irresistible pull toward her, a force that transcended logic and reason. He hooked his fingers in her belt loops and tugged her close, leaning in to kiss her.

Jewel pulled back and smiled. "Not now, we have to be serious."

"Right. Serious." Luca released her and shifted his attention to the building, once again wondering how he got himself into this. He glanced around the empty street, at the parking lot with no vehicles—thank God for weekends—then over to Wyatt who was seated beneath a shade tree. "First of all, he ain't comin' with us. He looks about as gray as the concrete on that building."

"He can stay right where he is," said Jewel. She turned to Wyatt. "Can you whistle or anything?"

The boy peered up at her and shrugged.

"That's okay, he don't need to do anything," said Luca. "He'd be more of a liability, anyway. I got enough on my plate keeping you out of trouble."

She scoffed and placed her hands on her hips. "My good sir, I assure you I am perfectly capable of taking care of myself."

Of this, he was completely certain. Jewel could definitely take care of herself. She already made that clear.

Luca tilted his chin up to the sky. "The good thing is that it's a weekend and nightfall will be soon."

"So, we wait 'til then?"

He nodded. "It'll give me some time to take a good look around."

"I'm coming."

"No, you're staying with man-eater over there. Keep an eye out for security or something. I'll be right back." Without waiting for a response, Luca turned and strolled off.

The bland, sterile architecture of government buildings never ceased to amaze him. With all that tax money, you would think they could hire an architect with some sort of creativity or imagination.

He estimated that there were several doors that could provide entry—the first being the front door. But that was where the armed security guard was stationed. No need to get into that mess if they didn't have to. Their best course of action would be to sneak into one of the side doors, then slip quietly through the building to the office, get what they needed, and leave. Best-case scenario, they could pull it all off in minutes without alerting the guard. Worst-case scenario—well, it was best if things didn't get to that point.

Just for the hell of it, he tugged on the nearest door handle. It didn't budge. He put a little more beast into it and pulled again. The door swung open; the handle coming off in his hand. He paused, standing dead still, listening for the sound of an alarm or hurried footsteps.

"Ahem," came a female voice behind him.

Luca glanced over his shoulder and found himself staring at Jewel, her arms folded.

"I thought we were gonna wait," she said.

"I was." He shrugged. "At least that's what I intended to do at first. I guess I suck at following my own plans."

"Mhm."

"Where's Wyatt?"

"I left him by the tree. He's fine." She stepped to the door. "We ready to do this now?"

"I suppose there's no time like the present," he said. "Did you happen to see the security guard on your way back here?"

"Last I saw him he was eating and staring down at his phone at the front desk."

"Alright then," said Luca. "No time like the present." He held the door open and gestured. "My lady."

Jewel giggled and curtsied playfully. "Why thank you, kind sir," she said as she passed him and slipped through the doorway.

The air thrummed with the high-pitched buzz of fluorescent lights reflecting harshly off the gleaming, cold marble walls and floor. The smell of pine scented cleaner lingered in the air.

Before moving on, Luca turned to Jewel with his hands up and pressed a finger to his lips, then he paused and listened for any sound out of the ordinary. Confident that the coast was clear, he allowed himself to relax a little. Now, all he had to do was figure out which direction they needed to go. He turned to check on Jewel, but she was nowhere in sight. Panic swelled in his chest as he spun around, glancing down the empty corridor like a worried parent whose toddler had run off.

A proud grin illuminated her face as she appeared at the corner, her hands gesturing excitedly for him to follow.

His inner adult wanted to scold her, but he understood this was not the time and it would do no good. Jewel was gonna do what Jewel wanted to do. So, instead he followed her lead.

They stopped in front of a building directory, and she pointed. Sarah Knowles, fifth floor.

Now that they knew where they needed to go, they just had to figure out how to get there. Before he could do anything, Jewel made a bee-line for the elevator. Luca raced after her, taking hold of her arm. He wiggled his finger to tell her no.

She responded by shaking her head and raising her shoulders, demanding to know how else they would get to the upper levels.

He had no clue, but rather than divulge this, he pretended as though he was in control and knew what they were doing. Something in Jewel's demeanor told him she wasn't buying it.

Luca glanced up at the exit sign hanging from the ceiling, then shifted his gaze in the opposite direction. Surely there would be stairs somewhere nearby. Still holding tight to Jewel's wrist, he dragged her along unable to explain his thinking to her due to the need for silence. Thankfully, she didn't struggle or try to do her own thing, but allowed herself to be guided by him.

The sign in front of them read stairs.

With a triumphant grin, Luca pointed, then pushed the metal door and held it open for her.

She gave a quick nod, then strolled into the stairwell.

As he quietly closed the door, he held his finger to his lips once again, and said, "Shh."

Jewel nodded.

Slowly, they climbed the steps, pausing to listen at each floor. By the time they reached the fifth floor, Luca was ready to rip the damn thing from its hinges, but he knew that was the last thing he should do. They managed to come this far without being detected; it was best to get through the rest of this the same way.

Mold green carpet tiles covered the floor, its color made even more ugly with the overhead fluorescent lights. A seemingly endless expanse of identical cubicles stood before them. How the hell did people come to a depressing place like this every day and not want to end it all? He'd take the swamp any day over this.

Thanks to the directory, they knew Sarah had an office of her own. Moving swiftly, they followed the outside wall, reading the name placards attached to each door until they finally came to one with her name on it.

Luca tried the handle, but it was locked. He tried it again, with a little more beast, and it came open as though it were never locked.

Jewel gave him a congratulatory air clap to celebrate.

While he went to the file cabinets, she inspected the files and papers on the desk.

He scanned the letters on the drawers, searching for the letter C, for Conroe. After discovering nothing in the first cabinet, Luca pulled open the top drawer of the second. With a triumphant smile, he lifted Wyatt's folder into the air.

Once again, Jewel celebrated with a round of gleeful air claps.

Time was of the essence. They had what they came for; it was now time to leave. Luca stuffed the folder into the back of his jeans and pulled his shirt over it, then he quickly guided Jewel back over to the stairs.

This time they didn't worry too much about stealth, rather their focus was speed. In a fraction of the time it took them to get upstairs, they were already at the door, heading back outside.

Not a single alert or alarm was sounded. And no sign whatsoever of the guard.

Fueled by adrenaline and the thrill of having pulled the whole thing off without a hitch, Jewel and Luca sprinted around the building toward Wyatt.

TWENTY-TWO

"DO you think that's a good idea?" asked Wyatt, sitting in the van with the file open on his lap.

"I do," said Jewel. "It's the only way to get some real answers."

Lost in thought, Luca chewed on his nails, his gaze fixed on an unseen point in the distance. After what seemed to be a long time, he glanced up at Wyatt and nodded his head. "She's right. I don't see any other way to get more info than what's in that folder."

Wyatt stared down at the papers. They contained nothing of any value. He wasn't quite sure what he expected to find, but he certainly wasn't expecting the nothing there was. No original surname, kin, or even a birth location—nothing. Just a single sheet stating his assumed age, sex and overall health, followed by page after page of all the homes he had been put into—along with every tiny detail of how he never seemed to fit in. As he read through the file, he was overcome by a deep sense of defeat over it all.

"Well?" prodded Jewel. "What do you think?"

He flipped the pages. "I guess we have nothing to lose. I mean, we can't get any less than nothing."

"That's my boy," said Luca as he clapped a firm hand on his shoulder.

"Okay then," said Jewel. "Where does the file say the woman is living?"

Wyatt glanced at her, confused.

"The first page. There's mention of the home she was placed in. Where is it?"

"What if she's not there anymore?"

"One thing at a time, son," said Luca.

He was right. No sense in accepting defeat when they hadn't even begun yet. He flipped to the page in question and read the name aloud, "Griffin Memorial in Oklahoma City."

"Oklahoma City it is!" said Jewel.

With a grunt, Luca hauled himself from the van, then glanced back at Wyatt and Jewel. "I'm takin' the lead." He grinned and planted a peck on Jewel's cheek and sauntered off to his motorcycle. A moment later, the air filled with the loud rumble of his engine.

"What are the odds that she's still there?" asked Wyatt.

Jewel shrugged. "As good as any. At least it's a start."

She had a point. He made an effort to be more upbeat about it all, but no matter how hard he tried he couldn't overcome his natural sense of defeat. In his world, hope was scarce. He had no reason to have any. A quiet sense of self-loathing washed over him. Why was he so pathetic? Maybe Theo was right all along, he was a loser and would always be a loser.

The drive to Oklahoma City was uneventful.

He and Jewel mostly sat in silence, their minds elsewhere, punctuated only by inconsequential small talk. Up ahead, Luca rumbled along. Wyatt was starting to like the odd speaking stranger. He wished he could be as upbeat and carefree as Luca. It seemed to him that the ability to take things in stride was probably the most important skill one could have in life.

Welcome to Oklahoma City, read the sign up ahead.

Wyatt perked up. A shock of energy coursed through his body.

This is it. He was either gonna find some answers, or it would be another dead end. In many ways, that too would be an answer. Regardless, this was a pivotal moment.

As the van rolled to a slow stop in the parking lot, Wyatt stared out at the unimpressive building with its flat, red brick walls. What a depressing place.

Luca leaned into the driver's side window. "Okay, we're here. What now?"

"Well, we should go in," said Jewel. She looked over at Wyatt. "Please don't take this the wrong way, but I don't think you should do this on your own. You might not be able to control your reactions. Do you mind if I come with you?"

"Could you?" blurted Wyatt. He really didn't want to walk into that facility alone.

"Absolutely."

"I'll just wait out here with the vehicles," said Luca. He stepped back and pulled open the door for Jewel. "I'll be out here listenin', just in case anything goes down."

With trembling legs, Wyatt made the trip across the parking lot to the front door. His breath hitched in his throat, his heart thrumming away like a trapped bird fluttering wildly against his ribs.

"Relax," said Jewel. "We're here to visit your aunt." She winked. "Margot."

"Maggie," said Wyatt.

His throat was so dry it hurt to swallow. With a sweaty hand, he pulled the door handle and entered the building.

A rush of frigid, sterile air, smelling faintly of antiseptic and metal, hit him immediately. The floors and walls gleamed with a drab, shiny tile, reflecting the dim light. Instrumental music poured out of hidden speakers, providing the final surreal touch to the facility.

"Can I help you?" asked a severe-looking woman behind the front desk. She stared at Wyatt, then Jewel, her eyes showing no emotion.

He opened his mouth to speak, but couldn't utter a word. Thankfully, Jewel intervened.

"We're here to see his aunt, Maggie."

"Mhm," replied the woman. "Maggie who?"

Jewel glanced over at Wyatt. She didn't know. Oh god! Thought Wyatt. He swallowed, cleared his throat and then croaked, "Lawler."

A volley of clicking keys filled the air as the woman glanced at her computer monitor, her eyes scanning the words on the screen. She paused and stared at Wyatt over the rim of her glasses. "Ms. Lawler's never had a visitor before."

This time it was Jewel who interjected. "That's because Wyatt here just recently got his license and is finally able to come visit."

"I'm going to need to see that license," said the woman, her eyes piercing through him.

He didn't have a license. When he turned sixteen, he was afraid to ask his foster parents if he could take driving lessons. They never brought it up either, so he just went without. The only thing he had was an ID card. Unable to think of anything to say, he glanced over, helpless, at Jewel.

"That's right!" Jewel snapped her fingers. "I just remembered." She turned to the woman. "His license hasn't come in the mail yet." She flashed an innocent smile. "We're still waiting on it to arrive.

The woman regarded Wyatt with a suspicious gaze. "That's fine. The paper from the DMV will do."

Paralyzed with fear, Wyatt swallowed as he struggled to keep his body from trembling. "I-I don't have it on me," he croaked.

"You know, you shouldn't be out here driving without one."

"We were just so excited to come and visit," said Jewel. "You know, her never having any family members come visit before and all. We sorta got ahead of ourselves."

There was a long, uncomfortable pause as the woman studied Jewel. She looked to Wyatt. Her expression grew soft, then she cleared her throat. "Well, then," she said. "I understand. My oldest did the same thing when he first got his license. I had to fold the paper and put it into his wallet myself." She smiled. "Let me see your ID."

Wyatt handed the card to the woman, who scanned it with practiced efficiency.

A sudden rush of icy fear shot through him as he realized the system might cough up an arrest warrant, his heart pounding a frantic rhythm against his ribs. After all, he did just eat his entire foster family. He stole a glance at Jewel, her eyes sharp and observant as she followed the woman's every move, completely composed.

"Hm," said the woman. "You don't have the same last name."

"Wyatt's mom was Maggie's sister," blurted Jewel.

The woman's gaze lingered on the pair, an unsettling silence stretching between them before a subtle smile curved her lips. She wordlessly gave back his license. "Okay, Wyatt, let me tell the staff that Ms. Lawler's nephew is here for a visit. Oh, and when you get home, make sure you fold that paper and put it in your wallet. Don't be driving around without it." She picked up the phone and dialed. "You two take a seat over there. Someone will be out shortly."

The wait was excruciating. The cheap plastic chairs offered no comfort as Wyatt sat, his thoughts and emotions a chaotic storm, his legs twitching like restless insects.

Jewel reached out and took his hand in hers.

He was thankful for the gesture, but it did nothing to calm his nerves.

The sound of a buzzer erupted, then a heavy gray door swung open with a whoosh. A tall, muscular man with a thick beard stepped out, flashed a pleasant smile, and said, "Wyatt?"

Unable to speak, he nodded.

"Come with me," said the man. He stepped back and held the door open.

Wyatt's body refused to move. After all that twitching, his legs sat there as though they were paralyzed. A cold sweat seeped through his pores. He could feel the hair on his scalp growing damp.

"Come on," whispered Jewel. She squeezed his hand and stood

up, pulling him gently behind her. "He's a little nervous," she said to the man. "He hasn't seen his aunt since he was a baby."

The man's face wore an empathetic expression as he nodded in understanding.

Once he crossed the threshold, the large doors swung closed with a loud click. Wyatt's anxiety was through the roof. His body trembled uncontrollably; his teeth chattered, and his hands shook like leaves in a storm. A kaleidoscope of incomprehensible thoughts swirled in his head.

All the while, Jewel bantered calmly with the big man as though this was just a typical family visit.

They stopped in front of a metal door with a single tiny window. "For obvious reasons, we don't do visits in the resident's room," said the man. "Take a seat in here and I'll bring her right out." With a swipe of his keycard, he unlocked the door and pushed it open.

The walls and floor were covered in the same ugly tile. The only furniture was a set of four padded, living room style chairs. At least they weren't plastic, thought Wyatt. He took a seat and breathed in deeply, trying to calm his nerves.

A tiny electronic buzzer sounded, then a metallic click announced the opening lock, and the door swung inward with a gentle sigh.

"Alright," said the RN. "Come on, Maggie." He guided a slender woman into the room. Once she was seated, the man nodded to Wyatt and Jewel and said, "I'll be right outside if you need me. When you're finished, just give the door a tap." With a final nod, he left the room.

Uncomfortable quiet filled the air. Where to begin? Wyatt had no clue.

Maggie stared down at the floor, her long, dark hair streaked with silver, falling like a curtain down her shoulders. Her hands folded in her lap.

The sound of the fluorescent lights humming was deafening. Wyatt was sure everyone could hear his heartbeat.

"Who are you?" asked Maggie, her voice low and subtle. She peered up at the duo with hollow eyes. "I have no sister." Her eyes locked onto Wyatt. "So, I have no nephew." Her expression melted into a malevolent glare. "Who are you?"

"I—I," choked Wyatt.

"I guess we should just cut to the chase," said Jewel. "Fifteen years ago, you found a toddler."

The woman's eyes grew wide. Her expression softened as her hands fluttered to her throat, then to her mouth. "It's you!" Her eyes welled with tears that spilled onto her cheeks as a trembling hand reached for Wyatt. "I saved you!"

"From what?" said Wyatt, his voice finally returning.

The woman's body trembled as her eyes grew dark with fear. "The monsters of course."

"Monsters?" said Jewel.

Maggie jerked her head to face Jewel. "Coyote people! Shapeshifters!" Tears streamed down her cheeks, dripping to her lap. "They murdered everyone in that awful barn! Ate them!" She chomped her jaws, then laughed maniacally. Her eyes flitted over to Wyatt. "My brother James gave his life so we could escape. I found you locked away in a filthy bedroom in that old farmhouse." A wistful smile tugged at the corners of her lips. "You were scared and all alone. I couldn't just leave you there. So, I scooped you up in my arms and ran through the woods." She leaned close and whispered conspiratorially, "They must have murdered your mother. But you're safe now, because of James."

Wyatt shot a quick glance at Jewel, her expression unreadable, making him uneasy. He wondered what she was thinking. Confusion churned in his thoughts. This was all too much to take in.

"Maggie," said Jewel. "Where was this farmhouse?"

"In the woods!" shouted the woman, her voice rising. Something in her countenance shifted. "You don't believe me! No one does!" Her body trembled. "No one wants to believe that there is a cult of coyote shapeshifters out there. They all think I'm crazy!" She tapped the side of her head. "But I'm not! I know what I saw." She slid her eyes to Wyatt. "What we saw."

"They ate them all! Every one of them! I saw them! They eat people! Those evil, disgusting things!"

The energy in the room shifted. Wyatt turned to Jewel; a chilling sneer twisted her lips, revealing sharp teeth that seemed to gleam with a predatory hunger as she stared at the woman. Her eyes shimmered with hate. "Watch your language woman," she said. "You aren't as safe as you think you are within these walls."

Maggie screamed and jumped to her feet. "You're one of them!" She flung herself at Jewel.

A primal urge inside Wyatt took over. He stepped between Jewel and Maggie and grabbed the woman's arm. "Enough!" he bellowed. His voice was so deep and menacing, he almost thought it came from someone else.

The woman stared up at him, her eyes filled with terror. "No!" she screamed.

He released his grip on her arm.

She backed away until she hit the wall. "You're one of them!" she shouted, pointing at Wyatt. "What did I do?" Screaming and crying out, she crumpled to the floor, banging her head against the wall.

The door flung open, and the big man entered. "Visit's over," he announced as he tried to calm the hysterical woman.

Without another word, Jewel and Wyatt slipped from the room, their footsteps hushed as they hurried toward the exit. As they waited for the door to the waiting room to open, a new fear washed over him. What if they don't let them out? A sigh of relief escaped his lips when he heard the telltale click, followed by the whoosh of the door opening. They quickly passed the woman at the counter and then left the building. As soon as the sun hit his face, he felt much better.

A sense of calm washed over him as they pulled out of the parking lot, leaving the sterile smell and harsh fluorescent lights of the dreary little hospital behind.

TWENTY-THREE

JEWEL'S HEAD throbbed as the woman's crazed insults, sharp and spiteful, ricocheted within her mind. How dare she speak of Tricksters like that? If they weren't in that tomb of a hospital, she would have torn the wretched woman's heart from her chest right then and there. A fairly large part of her wanted to go back and do just that.

She glanced over at Wyatt, his face like stone—unreadable.

Her anger subsided. Now was not the moment to indulge her emotions.

After the encounter at the hospital, she had a pretty good idea where Wyatt came from—who his family really was. Why hadn't the truth of it all occurred to her before? In hindsight, it was painfully obvious.

There was only one group of Tricksters that hunted the woods in eastern Oklahoma. Led by Raye, one of the strongest female elders Jewel had ever met. The odds were extremely high that Wyatt's mother was a member of that clan.

But what if she hauled him all the way there only to find another dead end?

Maggie clearly said she found him in a small room in an old farmhouse. Jewel knew that farmhouse. She also knew the barn too. Maggie didn't rescue Wyatt—the wretched woman kidnapped him.

A fresh wave of anger and frustration washed over her. She sighed and commanded herself to focus on the poor kid sitting next to her.

Would Raye and the others welcome Wyatt?

A gentle smile spread across her lips as she thought about the older woman and the feral clan she led, followed immediately by an overwhelming sense of loss and heartache over the circumstances that led to her arrival at the compound.

Jewel brushed aside her creeping despair. Of course, Raye would welcome Wyatt. He was a Trickster, and for all she knew; he was a member of Raye's clan. But why had she never heard of a missing boy? She had lived among the members of the clan for almost three years. Why did no one even mention it? Whatever the reason, the questions they sought could only be found in Kosoma.

She hit the horn and pulled off to the shoulder.

Luca swerved around and pulled up alongside the van. "What gives?"

"I know," breathed Jewel. She sighed and calmed her nerves. "I mean, I think I know where Wyatt's family is. At least his clan." She glanced over at the boy, taking note of the conflicted expression in his eyes.

"What do you mean?" he asked.

"I mean, I know a feral clan that lives in a compound with the old farmhouse Maggie mentioned." She waited for him to process the information.

"That would've been valuable information to know a couple of days ago," said Luca.

"Until Maggie mentioned the farmhouse, I didn't think it was relevant."

"Wait. There's a whole clan somewhere nearby?" asked Wyatt, stunned.

Jewel nodded. "We can take you there. Now." She shifted her

gaze to Luca. His expression was unfamiliar to her. Was he angry? She couldn't tell.

"Okay," said Wyatt. "Let's go."

"Hold up," said Luca. "You used the word feral to describe this clan. How are they gonna take a bunch of strangers rollin' up on 'em out of nowhere?"

"We're not strangers," she said. "At least I'm not. I have family there, too."

"I thought you grew up in West Texas?" said Luca.

"I did."

"And that your whole family is dead."

"They are. At least my mom, dad and brothers are."

"You're being vague."

Luca's tone was harsh and cold. Jewel could sense his anger rising, and she could hardly blame him. She reached out to touch his arm, but he pulled away. It hurt to see him act this way toward her. She pushed open the door and climbed out of the vehicle.

"Luca, I never said anything about the clan because I didn't think it was necessary," she said.

"Mais la!" he shouted. "You know, I can't help but wonder what other information you might think is unnecessary to share." His jaw flexed as he stared at her with narrowed eyes. "And when we ran into Wyatt, it never occurred to you that somehow he might be a part of that clan?"

Hearing him say it out loud, she realized he was right. She was wrong for not saying anything sooner. She was also a fool for not even considering that they might be Wyatt's lost kin.

"You're right," she said. "I'm a fool for not considering any of that. Had I spoken sooner, we could already have the answers Wyatt needs." She turned to the boy. "I'm sorry."

"It's okay," said Wyatt, his voice small and broken.

Jewel turned to Luca. "I'm sorry."

His shoulders relaxed. He reached out, hooked his fingers into the belt loops of her jeans, and pulled her close.

She leaned her head against his chest and listened to his heartbeat. "I'm sorry. I didn't think of saying anything before. Please don't hate me."

He inhaled and whispered in her ear, "Mon Sha, I could never hate you. Nor could I be mad at you for long. I love you too much."

Those words sent a shiver down her spine—her heart fluttered with a mixture of giddy excitement and nervousness. The air around her filled with his scent. She looked up into his eyes and smiled. "I love you, too."

The horn blasted. "Can we go now?" asked Wyatt from the van.

TWENTY-FOUR

"SNAP OUT OF IT!"

Weston's eyes flew open. At first confused about his surroundings, he quickly realized, upon glancing around the moonlit space, that he was in his bedroom and not at the ranch in Sierra Diablo. It was only a dream. The same one that haunted his sleep all too frequently. Studying his hand in the dark, he marveled over the fact that, even now, three years later, he could still feel the sensation of his nephew's heart pulsating in his hand.

He lay back against the soft cotton of his pillow, a sense of quiet satisfaction settling over him as he scoured his feelings for regret, finding none. Why should he? After all, Caleb wasn't his offspring. He had no genuine bond with the young man other than sharing the Riggs family name. Once you got past that minor detail, the only thing you were left with was the fact that the kid was a royal pain in the ass. Still, he couldn't help but feel as though it was a monstrous waste. Among Eben's three children, Caleb was the one who showed the most promise. He was also the one who could be the biggest threat to Weston and his ambitions.

The words of his father came wafting back in his memory like a shadow from the past, "In this world there is no greater bond or oblig-ation than kin."

Weston scoffed and sat up. Since childhood, he had been taught that nothing held greater importance than the bonds of family. That the most important thing he could do was to procreate and continue the Riggs lineage. He never found that appealing. In fact, he could scarcely recall a moment in all his years when he even considered he might want to even give it a try. The thought of being surrounded by smelly little crotch goblins made his skin crawl.

He remembered when Caleb was first born. It took Weston five months before he could even bring himself to go out there and visit. Not because he was too busy, but because the idea of driving such a long distance for no other reason than to gaze upon a wrinkly, screaming rug-rat was wildly unappealing. Children were a distrac-tion. A resource and wealth devouring parasite. They were filthy, annoying, and they smelled bad.

The sound of soft breathing reached his ears. He turned his gaze over to the woman sleeping blissfully beside him, wondering what it would be like to rip her throat open and watch her blood explode all over the dark ceiling. What sort of design would it create?

The daughter of a well-known kingmaker in Texas political groups, Elyse was an interesting addition to his life. One that he was quite sure that he didn't want, but could tolerate as long as she stayed out of his way and played her role. Prior to meeting her, the idea of marriage had never even crossed his mind. The mere thought of spending his entire life with one person didn't sit well with him. It still didn't. But he acknowledged that if marrying this thin woman with the cold eyes and severe facial expression was the price to pay for reaching his desired station in life, he would do it. Though if he were being honest, he found her presence repulsive on a deep, primal level.

As though she could sense his thoughts, she sighed and rolled over on her side, facing away from him.

Weston didn't want to awaken the woman. Not because he cared about her sleep, but more so because he preferred not to spend any more time with her than he already had to.

As stealthily as possible, he climbed out of bed, pulled on a pair of pajama bottoms, and quietly left the room.

The house was empty and silent, just the way he liked it. As he made his way down the hall, he reveled in the cool sensation of the tile floor against his bare feet. In the kitchen, he paused long enough to pour himself a glass of whiskey, then made his way outside onto the concrete patio.

The scent of change was all around him. Weston looked up at the dark sky, where a tapestry of shimmering stars painted the black canvas above him. All around him, the night was filled with a symphony of sounds as tiny creatures continued about their business.

Once again, his thoughts went back to his brother's children. Well, in particular, one child—Jewel.

Whatever happened to his niece? He wondered. Did her life come to a tragic end because of some unfortunate event? Could he be so fortunate? Or was she still out there somewhere, watching, waiting for the chance to seek revenge?

His lips curled into a sly grin. She would need to possess an extraordinary level of intelligence in order to succeed at that. Many have tried; all have failed. Her father—Westons's own brother, Eben —among them. In fact, her own brother, Caleb, as cunning as he was, proved powerless in the end. What skill could a female child possibly have that would provide any advantage over him. No, she was wise to stay away.

Even before that fateful night, he hadn't laid eyes on the girl in a long time. The image that remained with him was of her as a child, quietly mourning the loss of her mother and father. At the funeral, she spent the entire time sobbing and cowering behind her brother Pax.

The uncertainty lingered in his mind, making him question whether he would recognize her, even if she were standing right in front of him. If he were being completely honest, he never paid much attention to Eben's children. The only reason he even knew Caleb was because he was older, which meant he spent more time with the adults of the pack. Pax and Jewel blended in so well with the other children that it was hard for him to single them out.

And what of the two mystery Tricksters? The giant beast who had managed to outmaneuver and slaughter several of his best men, and the cunning woman who knew enough to stay in the shadows. Was the girl with them? Who were they?

Ramirez was less than useless. The only skill he appeared to possess was the ability to pour a drink. The only information he managed to get from the old man about the mysterious duo was that they appeared one day, with no explanation of where they had come from. First the woman, then, not long after, the beast.

Weston knew that there were countless other clans occupying various regions across the country. Most of them chose to lead independent lives, detached from other packs. They trusted only a handful of individuals and were hesitant to form connections with anyone beyond their own group. There was no way for him to pry into their affairs or dig up any information, as he had no connection with them. Truth be told, he wouldn't even know where to look. Even if he knew their general locations, venturing into the heart of a compound occupied by Tricksters without permission was a foolhardy decision that could result in a swift and fatal end.

Unfortunately, the West Texas pack was less than amenable to his enquiries. In fact, they all but shunned him. Ezra's family was so devastated by his passing, they refused to listen to anything Weston tried to say. He made every effort to convince them it was an unfortunate happenstance; that Ezra, along with Caleb and Pax, were the victims of some cabal of humans, seeking revenge for their long, lost loved ones. On the surface, it seemed as though they bought his story, but their cold shoulder told him he was on thin ice. Levi dismissed it as insignificant, but Weston, being intimately familiar with the strength of family ties, knew better. Ezra's family would watch him with keen eyes. They no longer trusted him, as was clear when he inquired about the woman and the beast, every single pack member proclaimed ignorance.

He was at an impasse.

The mere thought of the woman and the giant beast somewhere out there sent a nervous chill down his spine. He had a deep aversion to loose strings, finding them incredibly bothersome. Whoever they were, wherever they went, they were a potential problem waiting in the shadows.

Of course, there was always the slight chance that they took off for wherever the hell it was that they came from, never to return. One could only hope. It was the most plausible explanation, after all, they had no genuine connection to the area.

Should any of them ever have the audacity to come back and seek retribution, he would be ready to defend himself. The world belonged to the powerful—the ones who were relentless in their pursuit of their goals, no matter the cost. There was no room for those with integrity or morals. Those were relics of a time long past.

Taking things for granted was never Weston's style. His current level of success was not achieved by taking chances; he carefully calculated every move. Three years on, most would have forgotten about the potential threat, believing that the girl and her friends had moved on. But deep in his bones, he knew better. His niece was out there somewhere, along with the woman Izzy, and her brother Bass. The thought of three cunning Tricksters capable of ambushing him filled him with a sense of foreboding.

With no images to go off for the woman or the big man, he had no way of knowing who they were. This made him almost paranoid when meeting new people. How would he even know if he were to come face to face with either of them? He couldn't trust anyone he didn't already know. After the events of Sierra Diablo, he decided to narrow down his circle even more, fearing that, at any moment, the man or the woman could be hiding among any group—human or otherwise.

He hated that he could be so affected by some wayward beasts.

Someday he would find them, and he would make them pay for every moment they stole from him.

"Such a waste," he muttered. A Trickster as big as Bass would be quite handy to have around.

In his mind, he recalled another young man who would have been of great use to him—Caleb.

Oh well, he thought, accepting the situation with a shrug. It was all for the best. There was no chance the young man would bow down to Weston; his excessive pride practically guaranteed an inevitable confrontation. As for Pax, being the second son, Weston should have felt some sort of connection with the boy, but he didn't. He was far too enthralled with his older brother to be of any use. Loyal to a fault.

Weston downed what remained of his whiskey, then wandered back inside. The thought of crawling back into bed next to Elyse was unappealing, so he made his way to his office where he clicked on the computer screen and did what he always did when he couldn't sleep —scrolled the news for any mention of himself.

Of course, his email inbox was full, the tiny number in the red circle showed he had well over eighty-six messages to go through. He clicked on the bubble and scanned the messages, choosing to peruse the subject lines to see if any were truly worth his bother at this hour of the night.

A message from Levi caught his attention. The subject line read; Thought you'd want to see this. Call me in the morning so we can talk about it.

Weston opened the email; at first, the headline seemed nothing out of the ordinary.

"Oklahoma Family Massacre Has Authorities Scratching Their Heads."
Two days ago, the quiet of the rural countryside was shattered by a massive explosion from a ruptured gas

line in a home, resulting in the tragic loss of an entire family. At first, authorities believed there was nothing suspicious. But based on the coroner's findings, questions need to be answered.

In a shocking twist, the day after the fire, there was a burglary at the local government building. Thieves broke in and stole a single file from the office of Sarah Knowles, the CPS caseworker who was in charge of overseeing the teenagers in the home.

Foul play is now suspected.

Authorities are urgently asking anyone with information that could lead to the identification of the two individuals seen on security footage breaking into the office. If anyone has information that could lead to their identities, please call the number.

Below the article was a video. He hit the play button.

On the screen, a tall young man with unkempt hair, broke the handle of the back door with hardly any effort at all.

Intrigued, Weston sat upright, then a slender female came into frame.

A wicked grin played at the edges of his lips. He paused the video and stared at the face of his niece. Could he be so lucky? Fate was certainly on his side.

He leaned back in his leather chair and stared at the computer screen. At first light of dawn, he would have to get with his men and organize a little trip north into Oklahoma.

TWENTY-FIVE

IZZY AWAKENED to the rumbling sound of a motorcycle, its engine a deep thrum that vibrated through the trees outside. Exhausted and irritable from another restless night, she stared up at the ceiling, silently berating herself for allowing herself to sleep in, though she knew she needed the rest. Based on the hue of the sun beaming through the windows, it was almost noon.

She lay there in solitude, feeling every ache in her body. When was the last time she slept through the morning? She wondered. Then again, when was the last time she had a full night's restful sleep?

Since leaving Sierra Diablo, she'd been plagued by troubled thoughts and sleepless nights, but the recent insomnia was particularly brutal, leaving her exhausted. She knew why. With each passing day, the third anniversary of that horrific night drew nearer, its shadow stretching long and ominous.

Three years.

For three years, she and her children remained hidden while Weston and his entourage lived large, cloaked in luxury and power.

The boys.

She scanned the tiny trailer any sign of the twins. Caleb and Pax, named for their father and uncle, were gone, leaving only silence in their wake. Her eyes darted to Jewel's empty bed in the dimly lit corner, searching for any sign of her return, but a heavy sigh escaped her lips as she acknowledged the futility of such hope.

It wasn't as though Izzy didn't understand Jewel's desire to roam. Not that long ago, she too had that same uncontrollable urge. Oh, to be young and carefree again.

A toddler's happy giggles, bright and cheerful, drifted to her from outside. A mother could recognize the voice of her child anywhere. Her lips curved into a subtle smile as she rose from the warm comfort of her bed. She ran her fingers through her hair, the silky strands cool against her skin, before pulling it into a messy bun and sauntering outside.

"Mama!" shouted little Pax as he ran toward her with arms open wide, begging to be picked up.

His slightly older brother, Caleb, was halfway up a pine tree. Beside him, standing alert and ready to catch the toddler if he fell, Bass sipped a hot tea. The moment he saw Izzy, he winked and nodded in greeting.

She lifted Pax and rested him on her hip, inhaling deeply. The scent of his soft hair and warm skin filled her senses as she kissed the top of his head.

Their dark hair was their mother's legacy, but the boys' blue eyes sparkled with Riggs-like mischief, their mannerisms and behavior undeniably their father's. Young Caleb was adventurous and fearless and already quite cunning for his age. As for little Pax, he was the boy with the big heart. Loyal to his older brother, if Caleb was up to something, Pax was not far behind.

Breakfast was over, and the afternoon meal preparations were in full swing; the savory aroma of smoked meat made her mouth water. Still carrying Pax on her hip, Izzy made her way over to the outdoor kitchen where she grabbed herself a bowl of raw meat, then strolled over to the fire where Raye was sitting quietly.

"Did I hear a motorcycle?" she asked as she took a seat. Pax squirmed on her lap until he was comfortable, then he shoved his two fingers into his mouth and rested his head against her chest.

The older woman nodded. "According to the sentries, it appears as though young Jewel has returned. This time with some newcomers."

Bass strolled up, carrying Caleb on his shoulders. "I heard some chatter about that," He said. He smiled up at the boy. "I've been a little busy. We figured you needed the rest." He turned his focus to Raye. "Any idea who her friends are?"

"We're about to find out," said Raye. She gestured with her head and, wearing a loving smile, rose to her feet with her hands outstretched. "Jewel, my darling. We're glad you're home."

Still seated by the fire, Izzy studied the young woman. The change in Jewel was astounding. Gone was the terrified, confused little girl she met years ago in a tiny desert town. In her place was a beautiful and powerful young woman. Despite everything she had suffered, she had come into her own, and it was a lovely sight to behold.

Bass removed Caleb from his shoulders and placed the boy on the ground. While the toddler followed him like a tiny shadow, he headed over to welcome Jewel home.

Still holding Pax, Izzy got up and strolled over.

The instant he laid eyes on his aunt, Pax squirmed and reached out. "Doo!" he shouted happily. Caleb who had already made it over to her, was busy hugging her legs.

Seeing the love the boys had for Jewel made Izzy smile. "You're adoring fans missed you."

Jewel reached out to hug Bass, then leaned down and picked up Caleb, resting him on her hip. With hardly a pause, she leaned down and scooped up Pax, settling the boy on her other hip. She smiled at Izzy, then planted several kisses on the sides of each boy's head.

The gleeful laughter made Izzy's heart soar. She would never grow tired of hearing that sound. "How were your travels?" she asked as she stepped back to get a good look at the girl.

Bass emitted a low, menacing growl, setting Izzy's hair on end. She turned to her brother, then followed his gaze.

A tall, pale blond stranger stood behind Jewel. He wasn't a Trickster; yet he wasn't entirely human.

Izzy stepped forward to stand beside Bass and studied the young man closer. There was obviously a supernatural component to him. Rather than cower or show any sort of shyness, he stood firm, his piercing eyes studying Bass through untamed locks of wavy, yellow hair, wearing a sly grin. He slid his eyes over to Izzy.

The grin melted into a wide smile, more cunning than friendly. "I've heard a lot about you," said the young man. He made no move to get closer.

"And I've heard nothing of you," she snapped in reply.

With folded arms, Bass grunted in agreement.

The young man had an odd accent that Izzy couldn't quite identify. With an almost arrogant swagger, he carried himself with a confidence rarely seen in others. His smile came easily, yet his eyes held a cunning glint. There was just one man she could think of who had that same swagger. Caleb.

Just thinking about him sent a sharp pain to her heart, followed by red-hot fury and protectiveness for the twins. Suddenly aware that the boys were too close to the stranger for her comfort, she quickly took them from Jewel, placing them on the ground behind her.

"Ahem," said Jewel, as she stepped over to stand beside the young man. "Everyone, this is Luca."

The way the stranger eyed the girl could only be likened to that of a hungry predator. His lips curled into a mischievous grin as he leaned close and whispered something in Jewel's ear.

She blushed and giggled like a schoolgirl while tucking a lock of hair behind her ear.

Before Izzy could do it, Bass stepped between the couple, breaking the younger man's gaze.

Luca sneered, his eyes blazing with anger as he glared at the big man, then, as swift as a viper's strike, he flashed an impish grin.

At that moment, Izzy decided she didn't like him. Based on her brother's reaction to the young man, neither did he. She locked eyes with Bass. As if that was his cue, he grabbed hold of Luca and shoved him against a tree.

The audible oof sound that escaped the lanky kid's lips made Izzy smile. She stormed over to stand beside her brother.

"Who the hell are you?" she demanded.

The kid grinned. "I believe she already told you, but somethin' tells me you either weren't listenin' or you don't care."

Bass punched him in the stomach, causing him to double over, holding his belly.

"Let's try this again," said Izzy. "Who the hell are you and what are you doing with a young girl?"

Luca stood tall. "Who is this young girl you're talking about? I only see a woman." He flashed that cocky smile of his and winked at Jewel.

Bass punched him again.

The sight of him in agony brought a cruel, triumphant smirk to Izzy's face. She wanted to do so much more to this creep. Behind her, she could hear Jewel muttering something, but she was no longer interested in what the girl had to say. She focused on Luca. "Need I remind you that you are the intruder here."

Luca broke into laughter only to be silenced by another blow to the belly. He doubled over and stayed that way for a moment, gasping for air.

Izzy stared at the newcomer. "What are you?" Jewel placed a hand on Izzy's shoulder, but she shrugged the girl off. She leaned close to Luca and inhaled, taking in his scent. "You're a half-breed," she hissed through sharp teeth.

The look in his eyes told her that he had been expecting this question. He stood tall and menacing, towering over Izzy. "I'm what you would call a Rougarou."

Izzy let the name roll around in her head. She had heard about this type of supernatural being, but she had never met one before. While both Tricksters and Rougarou were shapeshifters, the similarities ended there. For one thing, her kind were born—they were natural. His kind were made—they were unnatural. Both were fierce predators. However, due to their previous humanity, Rougarou tended to be far more brazen, vicious, and cunning when it came to prey. At least, this was what she was told growing up. Never having met one in person before, she honestly couldn't say if that was true or not. Based on the way Luca glared at her, she had an intense feeling that all the things she had heard about his kind were indeed true.

"You know," said Luca, leering over her. "You're kinda racist."

With a single grunt, Bass landed another blow, only this one was a direct hit to the kid's jaw.

Luca spat blood on the ground and wiped his mouth. He glared at Bass as tiny hairs sprung out around his neck, face and hands. His teeth were sharp blades in his mouth. "That's it," he growled. "I tried to be nice and polite; time to level the playin' field."

His arms grew long, with bulging muscles. Before their eyes, he grew a clear two feet or more, so much so that he was actually taller than Bass.

With a single growl, he shoved Bass away, sending the big man hurtling backward. Without pause, Luca stormed over to him. "If you want to fight, let's do this the right way!"

"Stop them!" shouted Jewel in a panicked voice.

Izzy had no intention of doing anything of the sort. She stepped back, wrapping her arms around Jewel to keep her in place, and watched.

Bass shoved Luca away, then shifted and launched after the kid.

It was hard not to be impressed. The Rougarou was enormous. So huge, in fact, that he made Bass seem average. Izzy had never seen anyone out-size her brother, who was by all measures, extremely large for their kind. She wondered how Bass would fare in this matchup.

"Izzy please!" begged Jewel, with tears streaming down her cheeks. "Please don't let him hurt him!"

The look on the girl's face cut through Izzy's ire, but she couldn't let go of her animosity toward the lanky kid.

Suddenly, Raye stepped forward, her form partially shifted. She placed her body between the two fighting men, then inhaled and released a menacing growl. "Enough!" she bellowed.

In unison, Luca and Bass froze in their tracks, their attention completely captured. The entire area fell silent. Even the twins stood still, listening intently.

Raye wheeled around on Bass. "What the hell do you think you're doing?"

"We're taking care of an intruder," said Izzy defiantly.

Raye glared at Bass, then Luca, and finally at Izzy. "This is not how we greet visitors. Whatever issues you two have with him, it's over now!" She stared directly into Izzy's eyes, daring her to defy her.

With no other choice than to accept her defeat, Izzy let her shoulders slump and sighed.

TWENTY-SIX

THEIR HEADS BOWED, the others submitted to the old woman's iron will, a sight both impressive and slightly unsettling. Wyatt stood back, hidden among the gaggle that had gathered to witness the drama.

Confusion roiled in his mind as he tried to figure out why the big man and his sister would have such a reaction to Luca. Weren't they all the same on some level? Or was it just hatred for outsiders? If so, it was probably best for him to remain out of the way for a bit. After all, he could be next.

A withering glare, sharp as shattered glass, shot from the old woman's eyes at Izzy, then melted into a warm, honeyed smile for Jewel. She held out her hands to Luca and said, "Your friend is welcome here."

The mood shifted as welcoming smiles appeared on everyone's faces. Wyatt glanced around surprised that none of the others even noticed him standing there among them. The older ones greeted Jewel, while the children seemed intrigued by Luca. Of course, both Izzy and the big man were not a part of any of that, choosing instead to stand off to the side, scowling with their arms crossed.

"We missed you," said the old woman. "It's always a good day when one of our own returns home." She turned her focus to Luca. "Now, let me get a proper view of this handsome young man you have brought to us."

Jewel wiped her cheeks. "Luca, this is Raye," she said, gesturing with her hands.

Raye nodded her head. "Any friend of Jewel's is a friend of ours. Welcome to our humble compound."

The look of utter astonishment and awkwardness on Luca's face, his mouth slightly agape, as the old woman wrapped her arms around him and pulled him close, nearly caused Wyatt to burst into laughter.

Raye stepped back and turned to Jewel. "I see you have a lot to tell us about your recent travels."

"There's one more," blurted Jewel. She gestured into the crowd.

An icy wave of fear washed over Wyatt, followed by an overwhelming urge to flee. Suddenly aware of his presence, a hush fell over the crowd as they parted. Their faces showed a kaleidoscope of emotions—wonder, apprehension, and even hostility.

"His name is Wyatt," continued Jewel, oblivious to his inner turmoil. She stepped closer and held out a hand for him.

Unable to move, he stood in place, his mouth had gone dry, his heart racing in his chest.

"Oh, dear!" gasped Raye as she placed a hand over her heart. Less than a second later, the old woman moved with terrifying speed. In a blur of motion, her arms wrapped tightly around him before he could react.

She pulled back, still holding tight, and gazed up at him with tearful eyes.

If he wasn't confused before, he was now.

"I know who you are," she choked. "Welcome home my dear."

A low murmur, like a hive of bees, spread through the crowd as they muttered to one another about the bizarre event. Wyatt's mind was a chaotic whirlwind, refusing to settle on a single thought. He was overwhelmed.

Welcome home. The words banged around in his skull like a metal ball in an old pinball machine. She said she knew who he was. He didn't even know the answer to that question. He licked his lips and tried to speak, but was unable.

"Izzy, my dear, and Bass, please come closer," said Raye. Her tear-filled eyes still locked on Wyatt. She turned her head to the duo and said, "Your brother, Micah, has returned to us."

The gasp that exploded among the crowd matched perfectly the gasp in Wyatt's own mind. He glanced around nervously, positive that he was imagining this whole thing.

The woman named Izzy stepped closer, her eyes piercing his soul as she studied him. Meanwhile, Bass crept uncomfortably close. A deep grumble emitted from his chest as he inhaled, taking in Wyatt's scent.

In a flash, the beast of a man's eyes widened and grew soft. He reached out for Wyatt and shook him, then wrapped his powerful arms around him and whispered, "Micah." His body trembled as he sobbed.

Unable to do anything more than stand there in shock, Wyatt reached his arms up and awkwardly patted the big man.

Wiping his eyes, Bass stepped aside, leaving Izzy to stare hard at Wyatt. She moved closer. Her face was much softer this time as she took him in.

"This can't be true," she muttered softly, shaking her head.

"My dear," said Raye. "Use your inner beast and see for yourself."

Izzy's amber eyes glowed vividly. The slightest shimmer of tears appeared in her eyes, pooling until her lids could hold no more, exploding and rolling down her cheeks. She hugged Wyatt. "It's true," she whispered. "You're home, my little brother."

No matter how confused Jewel and Luca appeared, theirs was nothing compared to Wyatt's. Was this some kind of elaborate hoax to get him to let down his guard? Was he dreaming?

Raye clapped her hands. "Come along," she announced. "I will ask that you all give us the space to process this. We must talk and get to know one another." She turned to a woman with brown hair, speckled with gray. "Mira, please organize a feast. We have much to celebrate this evening."

The other woman nodded in understanding, then shuffled off with an entourage of women, followed by a gaggle of small children.

"Come now," said Raye as she took Wyatt by the hand. "I can see you have questions. We have many answers."

TWENTY-SEVEN

OVERWHELMED with a mixture of disbelief and pure joy, Izzy followed Raye and the others to the fire. She had all but forgotten about Luca for the moment. As she struggled to listen to the older woman recount the story of Micah's disappearance, Izzy's mind flooded with her own memories of that fateful evening and the aftermath that would alter all their lives forever.

"Wake up my dear," whispered her mother, Rose.

Seven-year-old Izzy sat up in her bed, rubbing the sleep from her eyes. "What's going on Mama?"

In the bed next to hers, Bass sat up and glanced around the dark bedroom confused.

Rose sat baby Micah on Izzy's lap. "I need you to watch your baby brother."

Outside, one of the male members of the pack barked orders, his voice raspy and loud, echoing through the crisp night air. It sounded as though a hunt was taking place. Familiar with the way these things went, Izzy hugged her baby brother. The toddler responded by cooing, "Zee-zee," as he reached playfully for his older sister's hair.

"Is it a hunt?" asked Bass.

Their mother nodded. "A vehicle has broken down along the highway close to here," she explained. "I haven't been on a hunt since Micah was born, and I figure that since this one is so close to home, I'm gonna join." She reached back and pulled her long, dark hair out of a ponytail, allowing it to cascade down around her shoulders. "You and your brother watch Micah." She leaned over and kissed the toddler atop his head, then did the same to Izzy. With the grace of a dancer, she swirled around, tousled Bass's hair, and planted a kiss atop his head.

Snuggling her little brother, Izzy watched as her mother left the room, pulling the door closed behind her. As she sat there in the dark, she listened to the sound of Rose's footsteps pattering down the stairs.

Bass climbed out of his bed and peered out the window. "What do you think it's like?" he asked.

"What's what like?"

In her arms, baby Micah yawned and shoved his fingers into his mouth. She laid him down gently on the pillow.

"Going on a hunt," said Bass.

She climbed out of the bed and stood beside him. "I've heard the same stuff you have." She grinned. "It's exciting."

He sighed and stared dreamily up at the stars.

Bass was stoic from birth. Never one to share his thoughts freely, he tended to stand back and observe before acting. Izzy, on the other hand, managed to get all the emotions. First to jump into the fray, and last to listen to excuses, she took after her father more than anything.

Her father. Izzy hadn't allowed herself to think about him in a long while, the anger she felt over his decision to leave them was still too palpable. She remembered that day vividly. The pleading look in his eyes as he silently begged Izzy and Bass to understand why he was leaving them behind. Why he could not quell his desire to roam, even after fathering three young children, the youngest of which had only just been born.

As her own heart was breaking, she turned her gaze over to her mother, Rose, and shattered inside. The pain and heartache visible in her mother's eyes tore Izzy apart. From that moment on, she vowed she would never be any man's victim, let alone his incubator, while he wandered off in pursuit of excitement and adventure. She decided she hated her father.

A volley of coyote calls filled the night. Wrapped in soft blankets, little Micah stretched and continued sleeping.

Izzy crawled into the bed beside him, rested her head against her pillow and listened to the slow, rhythmic sound of his breathing.

The window slid open.

"What are you doing?" she asked.

"I just wanna see."

"See what? There's nothing out there." Izzy propped herself up on her elbows. "You heard mama, they're way out by the highway."

Bass sighed and bowed his head in defeat, then left the window open and crawled back into his own bed.

Silence descended, and before long, Izzy had fallen back to sleep, listening to the sound of both her brother's deep in sleep.

Her eyes flew open at the sound of gunshot. Startled, Izzy sat upright. Bass was already by the window.

"What's going on?" she whispered.

"I don't know," said Bass. "I think something's gone wrong with the hunt or something."

Izzy climbed out of bed, moving as cautiously as possible so as not to awaken baby Micah. She joined Bass by the window.

Shadows moved swiftly about the compound. Something was afoot. Tension lingered in the air, she didn't know what was happening, but her instinct told her it wasn't good. Where was Rose?

More gunshot—this time it was several in rapid fire. A woman's scream was followed by a man's cry of pain, all mixed with the sounds of growling and yipping from the pack.

Izzy and Bass remained in the window, staring out into the darkness, paralyzed by what they heard.

The sudden crash of glass downstairs made the siblings jump, their hearts pounding in their chests. They moved to the door and placed their ears against the wood. Someone was shuffling around in their house.

Fear clenched its icy fingers around Izzy's heart. She met her brother's gaze, and it melted away, replaced by confidence and anger. How dare someone think they could enter their home?

Bass reached for the doorknob and quietly pulled the door open.

Before leaving the room, Izzy glanced over at her still sleeping baby brother, feeling a slight twinge of guilt over leaving him alone. She convinced herself he would be fine, then followed Bass out into the hallway, taking care to close the bedroom door behind her.

The muffled sounds of hushed, panicked voices, laced with fear, drifted from downstairs.

With Bass in the lead, Izzy tiptoed down the creaky hallway and paused in the shadows. Holding her breath, she slowly crept down the stairs, peering into the dimly lit living room.

"What are we going to do?" asked a hysterical woman cowering under the window.

A man stood above her, peeping out through the curtain, his bloody hands staining the fabric.

"They killed them!" cried the woman.

"Stop it!" hissed the man.

The woman rocked back and forth. "What the hell are those things? They're not human."

The man crouched down facing the woman. "Maggie, I need you to calm down or we're not gonna get out of this."

Before anything more could be said, Izzy accidentally stepped on the one creaky floorboard at the bottom of the stairs.

Eerie silence descended, hanging heavily in the air as Izzy strained her ears, listening intently for any sound of movement. But all she could hear was the beating of her own heart in her chest.

An explosion of chaos erupted. The sound of skittering feet resounded as Bass scuffled with the man. The woman screamed and charged at Izzy, sending her tumbling to the floor, knocking the wind out of her lungs. By the time she climbed to her feet, the woman was halfway up the stairs.

In the living room, glass shattered, followed by the sound of Bass crying out in pain.

Instinct took hold. Izzy charged into the room and jumped onto the intruder's back.

Thrashing and crying out in pain, he tried his best to dislodge the young girl, but she hung on tightly, slashing and tearing at his face with her nails.

Her fingers sank into his eye sockets. As thick liquid gushed past her fingers, covering her hands, the man screamed and fell backward on top of Izzy.

Covered in bloody cuts and scrapes, Bass leaped atop the man and levelled one blow after another until the stranger was finally still.

Once again, silence descended upon the house.

"Are you okay?" asked Bass, pulling her to her feet.

Izzy did a quiet check of herself, and aside from a few scrapes and bruises, she was okay. The front door to the house burst open as the adults had finally arrived. Rose and Raye were the first to enter. As soon as she saw the state of her children, Rose ran over. "Are you okay?" she asked, spinning them around so she could get a good look at them. She glanced around the room. "Where's Micah?"

The silence spoke volumes.

Rose cried out, "Micah!" then she and Raye ran up the stairs.

Heart pounding in her chest, Izzy followed. Her bedroom door was barricaded shut. The woman must have closed herself in—with Micah!

Standing hand in hand, with their backs pressed against the wall, she and Bass watched as Raye and Rose slammed their bodies against the solid door, forcing it open one painful sliver at a time. The door finally swung open, and the two women burst into the room.

Silence. The curtains billowed in the breeze—the room was empty. No woman and no Micah.

A shriek, raw with pain and unlike anything Izzy had ever heard before, ripped from Rose's throat as she scrambled through the window.

"Stay here!" shouted Raye, then she took off behind her sister.

Standing in the dark bedroom, peering out at the surrounding forest, Izzy and Bass watched as their mother and her older sister disappeared into the woods, followed by several members of the pack.

Over three hours passed, filled with tears, worried whispers and anxious glances, before they returned. Their faces etched with sorrow as they told the story of what happened.

With Micah in her arms, the woman ran. Fearful of accidentally harming the toddler, the pack held back much of their strength. Before their eyes, the woman managed to flag down a truck on the highway. Rose attacked and tried as best as she could to rescue her baby boy. When the vehicle sped away, several members of the pack, including Raye and Rose, tried to keep up with the giant machine, but were unable. The woman got away.

Micah was gone.

Unfortunately for their mother, this was the final straw that broke her. Over the next few weeks, her vibrant spirit seemed to dim, replaced by a listless weariness that made her a shadow of her former self. Each time she looked at Izzy and Bass, her eyes, filled with unspoken grief and accusation, seemed to fixate on them as if they were responsible for their baby brother's disappearance.

Day after day, night after night, their mother went out alone, desperately searching for Micah, but there was no trail to follow. She stopped eating and hardly ever slept anymore.

Rose spent more and more time in her Trickster form. She wandered in and out of the woods looking more like a starving, feral coyote than the vibrant woman they used to know.

The elders spoke in hushed whispers about something called Feral. It seemed as though the clan had already given up on Rose as she took to disappearing for days on end, hardly bothering anymore to even acknowledge her two older children.

Then one day, she appeared along the edges of the trees just outside of the farmhouse. Something was different about her. For three days, the coyote lingered near her family's home, her presence a silent request for their approval. Then finally, she wandered into the forest and never returned.

As for Micah, at first, the clan did their best to help search for him, but any meaningful search was beyond them. Technology did not exist in their domain, and they had no knowledge of the ways of the outside world that could help them navigate. Both the woman and the toddler had vanished.

That night became Izzy's personal hell, its sights and sounds replaying in her mind for years, leaving her perpetually sad and bitter. She never discussed her feelings, and she never overcame her deep sense of guilt.

TWENTY-EIGHT

THIS WAS ALL TOO much for Wyatt to take in. He'd longed for this moment his whole life, but as he stood before his long, lost family, a wave of uncertainty crashed over him. He wanted to be happy, but all he could feel was numbness and confusion. Shouldn't he feel something else? Some sort of connection? A sense of relief?

As the story of how he became a ward of the state was recounted, a burning anger flared within him. Why did they stop looking? He was kidnapped and forced to live a shitty life surrounded by bullies and uncaring adults. All the while, these people went on with their lives as though nothing had happened at all. As though he ceased to exist.

Across the fire, he listened to Raye tell the tale of that night. Her voice was thick with sadness as she struggled to hold back tears. He glanced over at Izzy, staring down into the fire as though she were lost somewhere in the past. He felt sorry for her, after all, she was just a child herself.

Bass sat beside his sister, his gaze unwavering but kind, as he watched Wyatt.

The altercation between Luca and Bass played out in Wyatt's

mind. Try as he might, he couldn't understand why they had such a visceral reaction to him. In his mind, Luca was a friend. A little odd and annoying at times—but still a friend. Unlike Izzy or Bass, he had come into Wyatt's life when he needed someone the most. They also shared one key similarity—both of them came into this whole shapeshifter thing blind.

The subject of his mother, Rose came up.

Wyatt perked up his ears. Where was she? He scanned the crowd but saw no face that might be familiar. If she was here, why didn't she come forward?

"Where is she?" he blurted.

Tears welled up in Raye's eyes. "My dear boy, she is no longer among us."

"What does that mean? Is she dead?"

She leaned back against her chair and pulled out an ornate pipe, carved from bone, and a small leather pouch. As she packed the bowl with tobacco, everyone sat silently watching. When she finished, she pulled a twig from the fire and lit the bowl, then exhaled a plume of smoke. "After your disappearance, the heartache was too much for her. She pulled away from us all. There was no consoling her. In the end, the heartbreak of your disappearance was too much for her to bear, so she chose to go Feral."

Feral. Wyatt had no idea what that was. Fed up with these people talking to him as though he knew their lingo, he said, "What the hell does that mean?"

Jewel's hand rested on his arm softly.

He jerked his arm away. Instantly regretting his reaction, he glanced over at her, in silent apology.

She nodded in understanding. "It's when one of our kind decides to turn their back on the human half of the world we live in," she explained. "Your mother decided to embrace the wild beast in her."

Once again, Wyatt found himself struggling to understand what these people were telling him. Why did it seem as though they were talking in circles?

"It means she chose to live her days in full Trickster form. She wanted nothing to do with this world any longer, so she ran away," said Bass.

Startled, Wyatt stared at the big man. That had to be the longest sentence he had heard from him since they arrived. Thankful that someone had finally spit it out in plain English, he nodded at Bass.

"Micah, my dear," said Raye.

"Wyatt! My name's Wyatt," he replied with such force, even he was startled.

The old woman didn't even flinch. She nodded in acceptance. "Wyatt. You have a lot to process. I understand this is a lot to take in, but believe me when I say you are among family now. You're home where you belong." She tapped the ashes that remained in her pipe into the fire, then rose to her feet. "Jewel, my dear, please show both Wyatt and Luca around the compound." She nodded to Luca. "You, my young friend, are welcome to stay among us as long as you desire. Consider yourself a welcome guest. Another member of our family." She returned her gaze to Wyatt. "My dear, you take all the time you need. This is your home. We will all be here when you are ready."

The old woman rose to her feet and stretched, then sauntered away. As though that was some sort of signal, the crowd also dispersed, leaving Wyatt, Jewel and Luca on one side of the fire, with Izzy and Bass on the other.

TWENTY-NINE

AS MUCH AS he could appreciate the importance of the situation for Wyatt, Luca had all he could do to not walk away. His whole life he felt like an outsider—this situation did nothing to alter that. On a very deep level, he was envious of the kid, and he hated himself for feeling this way.

That said, he couldn't help but be enthralled by the whole story. Just when he thought he had the most messed up childhood, here comes someone who lived a nightmare that made his pale in comparison. At least he knew who his kin were—even if he didn't particularly appreciate many of them. For the first time since meeting Wyatt, Luca felt sad for him. He had a newfound respect for the sheer strength of will it took for the kid to function every day.

As the others talked, Luca studied each member of Wyatt's family.

Raye seemed genuine. In a way, she reminded him of his Mawmaw. She passed when he was still a young child. To this day he could recall the way the family changed after that. It seemed that the old woman took the glue that held the Boudreaux family together with her to the grave. As he watched the way Raye carried herself, he could understand the respect the others seemed to have for her. There was a strength and vitality to her that he had never seen before in someone her age. It was impressive. The term wise old elder came to mind.

For the most part, the other folks in the compound seemed okay. Truth be told, they weren't that much different from his kin. A little grubbier, but overall; quite similar.

He studied Bass and his sister Izzy.

His initial impression of the duo was less than stellar. After all, they sort of got off on the wrong foot—most of that could be laid at their feet for overreacting. On some level, he could understand their distrust of outsiders. Still, their dislike for him based on a now immutable characteristic didn't sit well with him. He wondered if the other members of the clan felt the same way. He'd had a lifetime of people hating him for his circumstances of birth, he was over it.

Jewel's soft hand rested on his. He laced his fingers through hers as he leaned back in his chair, allowing her calm to wash over him.

A middle-aged woman, her brown hair plastered to her scalp with sweat and grime, carried a chipped, wooden bowl to Jewel, who eagerly extended it toward Luca.

His hunger was strong. However, upon seeing the contents of the bowl, his mouth watered for a very different reason. Pink, fleshy chunks of meat floating in a soup of crimson. His stomach lurched, then growled in protest. The beast in him wanted to feed, but the human in him could not.

Another bowl was unceremoniously shoved in his face. This one was packed with smoked meat; the rich aroma filled his nostrils. Once again, his mouth watered, followed by his stomach crying out for food. He glanced up at the woman, gave a grateful nod, then took the bowl and dug in.

The conversation passed with little interest from Luca. Upon finishing one bowl, the motherly woman would materialize with another to replace it. It went on this way until his hunger was finally sated, and he waved her off with a hearty thank you.

He did his best to listen, but the urge to move around was far too strong. When the conversation ended and the crowd dispersed, Raye suggested Jewel show Luca and Wyatt around the compound, he was already on his feet before she even finished her sentence.

Wyatt seemed to welcome the suggestion.

The compound itself made Luca think of Gypsies. Trailers, cabins and ramshackle huts stood out against the thick forest backdrop. The sound of children laughing carried on the breeze. For a moment, he thought he heard a scream. He swayed his head around, hoping to figure out which direction it came from, but the sound never repeated itself. With a shrug, he continued on the tour.

Hidden deep within the woods, beneath the long shadows of the tall pine trees, the place remained hidden to all but those in the know. The compound had a distinctly feudal, almost medieval atmosphere. It seemed as though the inhabitants liked it that way.

There were no signs of modern conveniences. The rhythmic thud of axes chopping wood echoed as men worked, while women and children carrying buckets of water and other supplies moved around them, their footsteps muffled by the damp earth.

A giant still, its copper lid gleaming in the sparse sunlight, toiled away in a far corner under a rickety metal shelter. Beneath it, a bright, hot fire blazed, its flames licking the blackened bottom of the metal pot, the smell of wood smoke thick in the air. Luca was no expert, but he knew a moonshine still when he saw one.

Chatting happily, Jewel led them past the bustling outdoor kitchen, where a symphony of clanking pots filled the air, introducing them to each person with a warm smile and friendly conversation.

The names became a sea of words Luca could hardly recall.

"So, did you grow up here?" asked Wyatt.

Jewel sighed and shook her head. "No. I grew up in West Texas. I came here a few years ago. This clan welcomed me without hesitation. They made me feel like I had a new home. They're good folks."

A modest farmhouse loomed up ahead.

Upon seeing it, Jewel's face lit up. "Come on," she said, taking Luca and Wyatt in both hands as she led them to the steps.

The building's weathered exterior and dilapidated front porch made it clear that it was the oldest structure on the property. At least the oldest residential structure. The massive red barn at the far end of the compound seemed to be just as old. As they stood on the front porch of the farmhouse, Luca stared at the ominous building. Something about it set his nerves on end.

Inside the house felt exactly how he imagined. The old wooden floors groaned softly underfoot, partially concealed by worn, threadbare area rugs. Fine plaster dust, like a chalky snowfall from the ceiling, had settled between the aged floorboards.

Not a single photograph adorned the cracked and chipped walls.

The furniture was sparse and old.

"So, this was the house she stole me from," said Wyatt.

"Yes," said Jewel.

As though he knew where he was going, Wyatt made his way up the stairs, down the narrow hallway and into a bedroom. Two beds, each with dusty, faded linens and worn mattresses sagging in the middle, sat on either side of the window.

Luca followed Wyatt and Jewel, but not wanting to intrude, he stayed behind in the doorway as they entered the room.

"It looks like nobody lives here anymore," said Wyatt.

"As far as I know, nobody does," replied Jewel. "They never told me why, but after everything we just found out, I think we know."

Wyatt nodded. He strolled over to the window and gazed out through the grime covered glass. The boy's expression was a mask, concealing any hint of the thoughts churning inside.

"So strange," he whispered. "I don't remember any of this." He sat upon the bed, sending a plume of dust into the air around him like a billowy cloud. "So, where do Izzy and Bass stay now if they don't live in this house anymore?"

"Izzy and the twins stay in a trailer across the compound, behind the barn. Bass stays there occasionally, but spends most of his time moving from one bed to the other," said Jewel. A subtle grin spread across her lips. "Apparently, there's no shortage of women who would take him as their man."

Luca scoffed, folding his arms and leaning against the door frame.

He was beginning to feel overwhelmed by the depressing vibe that permeated the house. It was as if the ghosts of this place sucked the life out of you. He bit his tongue and kept his thoughts to himself, due to the fact that this was important to Wyatt. Still, he could hardly wait to get outside. When the boy finally signaled that he was ready to leave the building, Luca wasted no time dashing to the door.

Something about the barn was calling him. He needed to see what was inside, although deep down he knew he wouldn't like what he found. Thankfully, that was where Jewel was taking them.

The building's unimpressive facade featured faded, cracked siding and a rusty metal roof that groaned under the weight of years. As they neared, the door of the building opened with a rusty groan, revealing a man exiting with a hefty slab of meat in his arms. Even in its current state, Luca could clearly see that is was a human torso. As he watched the man stroll past, his mind went back to the memories of hunting when he was young. The torso was prepped the same way they would prep the deer they caught.

His stomach heaved, the sour taste of bile rising in his throat. His heart lurched in his chest. The acts performed in the barn became perfectly clear. Realization hit him like a punch to the gut; these Tricksters really aren't human. They're an entirely different species, and humans are their prey. Cattle. A source of food. Did they see him that way also?

He glanced at Jewel, who appeared unaffected, and then made eye contact with Wyatt, who simply stared back at him with his typical expressionless face, although his skin looked paler than usual. Luca took that as a good sign.

All at once, he felt a strong reluctance to enter the barn. He knew what was inside. He also knew what that meant as pertaining to the food in the smokers that permeated the air. The meat in the bowls—the meat he devoured.

Jewel linked her arm in his and pulled him away toward the trees. "Come on," she said to both him and Wyatt. "I'll show y'all one of my favorite places."

Thankful for the distraction and more than happy to get away from the barn, Luca followed her into the woods.

THIRTY

"WHAT DO YOU MEAN, you can't identify him?" asked Weston, his patience wearing thin.

The skinny man fiddled with the bottom of his tie. Clearly intimidated, he mumbled, "We found no one in the Oklahoma database that matches his identity."

"So, look in other databases!" shouted Weston.

The slight man flinched and stepped back. He licked his lips and swallowed nervously. "I-I have no jurisdiction to search databases from other states."

Weston glared at him, fighting the urge to rip the man apart. Sometimes—no, most times—he hated humans. Bureaucrats were on the top of the list with that spineless way of theirs, hiding behind rules that they seemed to make up as they went along. Rules that seemed to have only one purpose—to make everyone else as miserable as they were.

"Sir," said his man Sean, standing in the doorway. "This is Sarah Knowles, the caseworker to whom this office belongs."

As much as he wanted to continue to make the skinny little man uncomfortable, Weston wanted to know where Jewel and her companion might have gone more. He turned around with a fake, friendly smile and extended his hand to greet the woman.

"Good morning."

Annoyed, the woman, in all her dowdy, middle-aged glory, looked around at the crowd of strangers gathered in her cramped office.

"What can I do for you gentlemen?" she asked.

"Sarah," said the slender man. "These gentlemen are from the Texas Governor's office. They have some questions about the break-in." Without further explanation, he squeezed his way past everyone, leaving the woman to fend for herself.

She looked at Weston, showing no fear. "What exactly does the state of Texas have to do with my cases?"

The woman's lack of fear or deference toward Weston impressed him. It also irritated him greatly. He flashed a genuine smile. "I'm more interested in the young woman involved in the break-in. I was hoping you could offer some information."

Sarah shook her head. "I don't know either of them. Never seen them before, so I can't be of any help to you there." She walked over to her desk, took a seat and folded her hands, all the while glaring at him with annoyance. "Now, is there anything else I can do for you?"

Images of her screaming and begging for mercy while he tore out her insides, played in Weston's mind. It took every bit of resolve in his body to hold back. There would be plenty of time to do whatever he felt the urge to do later. For the time being, it was imperative that he maintain his politician facade. He could always revisit this woman another time.

"One more thing," said Weston. "Whose file did they take that night?"

"As far as I could tell, there was only one. It belonged to my charge, Wyatt Conroe."

"He's one of the members of the foster family that died in the fire. Correct?"

She nodded.

"Such a tragic thing," said Weston, doing his best to sound as though he cared. "Has there been any more word on that?"

Sarah shook her head.

It was clear the woman would not offer information without prodding. Weston put on his best face and said, "It appears as though we both want answers that revolve around the same set of circumstances. Perhaps we can work together on this. Is there anything about the boy that ties him to the girl and her tall friend?"

She continued to stare at him, only this time, something in her eyes told him she was considering his question. Once again, the woman shook her head. "Like I already said, I've never seen or heard of anyone who matched their descriptions before that video. As far as I've always known, Wyatt was an orphan—a loner. He never got along with anyone. He was just a strange kid. He had no friends."

"Strange. Don't you think? How could he have no friends? What about his extended family? Have you heard anything from them?"

"Again. He has no family," she replied dismissively.

"Everyone has a family."

"Not this kid. He's been in the system since before he could really talk. Never in all my years of handling him has a single family member surfaced."

Weston's curiosity was piqued. "How did he come to be in the system?"

The woman sighed. Her steely eyes fixed on him. "I suppose it can't hurt to fill you in. After all, I told all of this to the police, and you see what they've done with it." She shifted her gaze to her computer monitor and began tapping at the keys. "Okay, so Wyatt Conroe was handed over to the authorities. His age at the time was speculated to be around eighteen months. The woman who brought him to the hospital was named Maggie."

"You're sure that wasn't his mother?"

"Absolutely sure. She said so herself. The state even ran a DNA test to be positive. No match. Though there were some abnormalities on his end." The dire woman paused as though she were considering that last sentence, then she continued, "The only thing we've ever known about Maggie was that she showed up at the hospital, covered in filth and blood, carrying the baby, all the while screaming about shapeshifting beasts in the woods."

Weston perked up his ears. Shapeshifting beasts? The pieces were beginning to come together. Even though he had never met them, he knew there was a clan that hunted in eastern Oklahoma. The problem was, by every account, they were fiercely private. He had no way of knowing where to begin looking for them.

"Is this woman, Maggie—?" He paused, purposely waiting for her to offer the last name.

"Lawler," said Sarah.

He repeated the name. "Lawler. Is she still alive?"

"Yes. She's been in Griffin Memorial in Oklahoma City ever since she was released from the hospital."

"Have you checked in on her?"

The look that spread across the woman's face told him she hadn't, but he waited for her to answer.

"No," she said flatly. "Look, I have a full plate with all the kids I'm watching over. I simply don't have time to take a deep dive into the early life of a child who was simply another ward of the state."

Weston realized the woman had little regard for the boy. In fact, her feelings toward him seemed to border on contempt.

She cleared her throat. "As you can see," said Sarah. "I can't offer you any answers. There's nothing to share. Now, if you don't mind, I'd like to get back to work. I have a full day ahead of me and a lot of other kids to keep track of."

With a quick bow, Weston wished the woman a good day, then exited the office. He had all the actionable information he was going to get from her.

As the elevator doors closed, Weston turned to Sean. "Do me a favor—"

"Already on it, Boss," said Sean. "I'll call the hospital and let them know we'll be there in a little over an hour on official business."

THIRTY-ONE

AS SHE SAT ALONE, processing all that had happened, Izzy struggled with her emotions. Barely able to wrap her brain around Jewel's Rougarou boyfriend, she now had this whole new event that she could scarcely reconcile.

Her baby brother, Micah—Wyatt was home.

She recalled her childhood after his initial disappearance and how she'd lie in bed hoping for this very day. She took all the blame. Her childish heart overwhelmed by the possibility of terrible things happening to her innocent baby brother. Night by night, she sat up, staring out her window, longing for his safe return. Each day her mother would pull further away. Young Izzy's world was shattered— her heart broken to pieces. Only Bass understood how she felt. With his characteristic stoicism, he always seemed to know when she needed him most, appearing just when her spirits were at their lowest. He too felt responsible for what occurred. As the days turned into months that turned into years, Izzy had given up hope. In fact, she had literally forgotten about Micah, much to her shame.

But here he was. Home at last.

She ought to be thrilled, but she couldn't shake the feeling of immense guilt for having moved on. For removing him from her mind.

As for Luca; Izzy was left feeling uncertain about her feelings toward him. She couldn't help but question everything about him. A deep-rooted skepticism made trusting outsiders a constant challenge for her. She could see the wariness etched on Bass' face, showing his struggle to trust the strange young man. She mulled over every word he uttered, every nuance, looking for a tiny flaw in the retelling that she could pounce upon.

One thing was perfectly clear, she had to proceed with caution. Even a fool could see that Jewel had fallen hard for him. Nothing short of a catastrophic event would put a wedge between the pair. Even then, there was no predicting Jewel's response if something were to happen. A woman's first love was something precious— sacred. Her thoughts instantly shifted to Caleb, bringing with them the all too familiar stab of pain in the center of her soul.

Luca was either a skilled conman or the real deal. A not so small part of Izzy wanted him to be a lying con, as the alternative would mean he was going to be a part of her life for years to come. She wasn't entirely sure how she felt about that; her initial reflex was pure loathing over the idea.

As for Jewel, the girl was a hopeless, lost cause. Her eyes were filled with pure adoration as she stared at the half-breed. Come to think of it, the way he stared back at her was quite similar.

In the end, Izzy's intense anger boiled down to one desire: to hurl something at him with enough force to end his life. But this was a desire she could not act upon.

Little Pax squirmed and sighed on her lap, snuggling close. She kissed the top of his head and breathed in his scent.

Her thoughts went back to Micah. To the pain her mother must have felt when her baby disappeared. As she sat there holding one of the two most precious people in her life, Izzy finally understood how devastating that could be. In fact, she knew with every fiber of her being that she would never recover if one of her boys was suddenly ripped out of her life.

The anger she had harbored for her mother when she abandoned them melted away upon the realization. Izzy finally understood. She would watch the world burn to keep her boys safe from harm.

Her mind drifted to the single thing in this world that was a threat to her boys—Weston.

One thing was apparent most of all; every day that man breathed was a day that her sons were in danger. There was no question in her mind that he would do whatever it took to preserve his power and wealth. What would it matter if he had to murder another set of nephews? Even if they were small children. It was just another dark deed in a long list of atrocities.

Though she hid it well, the night they fled Sierra Diablo left a deep scar on Izzy's soul. Her heart ached with a stabbing pain every time she let her mind revisit the events of that night. Could she have altered the outcome? Perhaps if she didn't remain hidden, she could have intervened. The weight of the loss of the man she loved was so heavy, it felt as though it could swallow her whole.

Yet another instance where she finally understood her own mother.

Was she doomed to relive Rose's cursed life?

No, the situation with Weston was nothing like the trauma her mother endured. He was a monster in every sense of the word.

From a young age, she was taught to be wary of anyone who didn't belong to her clan, and that wariness extended to those who tried to hide among the humans. When the helicopter landed and the deafening roar of the rotors filled the air, Izzy quickly grabbed Jewel and discreetly retreated into the shadows of the barn. At first, the girl tried to shrug her off, but when Izzy insisted with a slight flash of the Trickster, the young girl allowed her to guide her out of sight.

Observing Caleb's reaction to the visitors, Izzy briefly felt a twinge of embarrassment for hiding. He knew them and was unafraid.

She, on the other hand, knew nothing of the men who had gathered outside the barn. It was obvious they were powerful and wealthy, but there was something in their demeanor that told her that these men were dangerous and to keep a safe distance.

Izzy's body trembled with rage as she witnessed Weston murder Caleb in cold blood. It took all her restraint to resist the temptation to charge forward and exact revenge. Despite everything, her priority remained her unborn child and, of course, Jewel. With her hand clamped tightly over the girl's mouth, she pulled her close and whispered, "Shh."

Izzy felt the young girl's tears, warm and wet, streaming down her hand as she whimpered helplessly.

Tears welled up in her own eyes as she fought against the overwhelming urge to cry. She wanted to collapse in a heap and sob uncontrollably. However, such a luxury was not granted to her. She had the baby in her womb to consider, as well as the girl.

As Caleb took his final breaths, Izzy seized the momentary diversion to grab Jewel by the hand, leading her out of the barn, toward the cave entrance. The tunnel was a dark, narrow passage that cut through the heart of the mountains. It was their quickest path to freedom. Despite knowing that Weston would be privy to the existence of the escape route, she couldn't afford to gamble by traveling across the open land. She could already hear the orders that the leaders barked.

Anxiety gripped her heart as she glanced around in search of Bass. He was nowhere to be found. A piercing cry echoed through the night, Izzy didn't have to see who made it, she knew her brother's voice. The sister in her wanted to charge toward the sound and fight —the new mother in her told her to flee.

Izzy leaned close to Jewel and whispered, "Change. Now!"

The young girl gave a quick nod, signaling that she understood.

A moment later, in their full Trickster forms, both Izzy and Jewel were nearly halfway to the chamber at the center of the tunnel when the sound of snarling rage bounced off the walls behind them. The men were after them. She knew, with no doubt that, given the opportunity, they would do to them exactly what they did to Caleb, Ezra and Bass.

Her brother's cry echoed in her ears. She couldn't see what happened, but she heard the pain in his voice loud and clear. She was sure he was now dead, like all the others.

Survive. She must survive.

Pushing and prodding Jewel along, they ran into the main chamber, pausing briefly by the cell. The cool breeze flowing gently through the tunnel tickled her fur.

As menacing growls bounced off the walls, she realized that the other Tricksters had finally caught up with them. Faced with no alternative but to fight, Izzy turned and, emitting a fierce growl, bravely stepped in front of Jewel, hoping to shield her from harm. In a perfect scenario, the young girl would continue to run. However, Jewel was very much Caleb's sister. Running wasn't instinctive to her. She stood firm and readied herself for a fight to the death.

Izzy lunged first, charging toward the larger opponent, hoping that Jewel could handle the other beast on her own. Her mother's instinct had taken over, what mattered most of all was that she survived so that her son could live.

When Bass appeared out of nowhere, no one was more relieved to see his giant form than Izzy. Her brother had survived. This was welcome news.

He made quick work of the two Tricksters, then after a moment of consolation, they turned their attention to escape. They needed to get as far away from West Texas as possible. Away from the reach of these monsters. There was only one place to go—back home.

Determined to stay strong, Izzy gritted her teeth and fought to keep her emotions in check. She needed to be strong, not only for Jewel but also for the tiny life that was growing inside her. They ran through the night, hardly pausing for breath. When dawn broke, they rested under cover of a copse of trees to rest—a struggle for Izzy. As soon as the sun set, they were off running once again. It was only after they came to the Red River that she finally let herself exhale, feeling the tension leave her body. The cool water rushing by tickled her feet. At the shoreline, she took a moment to relish the feeling of the soft, fine, rust-colored silt squishing between her toes.

When they arrived at the compound and Izzy rested her eyes on Raye, a sense of calm washed over her. She was home. Safely out of reach of the traitorous Weston and his men.

In Raye's comforting embrace, Izzy found solace and felt the weight of her anxiety lift, knowing she and her precious little one was safe. For the first time since fleeing Sierra Diablo, she allowed herself the luxury of emotions and broke down into uncontrollable sobs.

As luck would have it, Izzy wasn't carrying one child, she was carrying two. Several months after arriving at the compound, she gave birth to the twins. Two precious boys with dark brown hair and pale blue eyes. Without a second thought, she named them Caleb and Pax.

⋅-⋅⃜-⋅⋖-⋅⃤-⋗

She pinched a tear from her eyes and pulled little Pax close, relishing the warmth of his body and the sweet fragrance that filled the air.

Caleb was dead. Ezra was dead. Bass, Jewel, herself, and her precious twins were still alive through sheer grit. That man was supposed to be family, but he turned on everyone. How could he be so vile?

Weston Riggs was a monster in the worst form—a traitor of his own kind. No loyalty, no integrity, and no regard for others. If anything, he was far more human than Trickster.

THIRTY-TWO

WESTON WATCHED the pathetic woman rocking back and forth in the padded cell through the observation window, feeling nothing but disgust for her. Why were humans so fragile? Their minds broke so easily.

"Like I told your man over the phone, and as you can see for yourself, she is in no shape for an interview," said the burly RN.

Weston eyed the woman. It appeared as though this stop was a waste of time. "How long has she been this way?" he asked.

"Ever since the boy and his friend came to visit."

"Boy and his friend?" Maybe there was hope after all. "I thought she had no family."

The big man raked his fingers through his beard. "That was what we believed, but a few days ago this kid came in claiming to be her long, lost nephew."

"You don't sound as though you believe him."

"Not long into the visit, Maggie snapped. We still don't know why. She was hysterical, rambling on about shapeshifters again. We don't listen to private family conversations, so we have no idea what was said during the visit." He looked at the woman in the room.

"After they left, we did a little more digging and couldn't find anything that said she had a nephew. Or even a sister, for that matter."

"Clever ruse," said Weston. "What about his companion. You said the boy came here with a friend."

"Yes," replied the man. "A young woman, not much older than he was. Had I known any of this might happen, I never would've let them in to see her. That visit set her back years."

Weston glanced around the sterile halls, locking his eyes on the video camera hanging from the ceiling. "I'd like to see the security footage."

Nodding curtly, the large man spun around and guided them down the hall to a heavy metal door. He swiped his badge in the reader, and the door opened with a whoosh. "Pull up the footage of Maggie's visitors," he said to the two men inside.

The security room was exactly as expected. Weston had seen many of these cramped offices over the years. After a cursory greeting with the guards on duty, the older of the two set to typing on the computer keys.

Weston crept up behind the man, his eyes glued to the monitor as the guard sped up the video to the moment in question. The video paused. The face, hair, and eyes were painfully familiar. Jewel. A sinister grin played across his lips. Well, hello there dear niece.

"Is there any recording of the conversations they had in the waiting room or halls?" he asked.

The guard shook his head. "That would violate privacy."

"Mhm." Weston nodded and stared at the screen, committing the girl's face to memory, then turned back to the RN. "Tell me about how the woman, Maggie, came to be here."

"She was brought here from a local hospital years ago. Hysterical and suicidal, she kept screaming about shapeshifters in the woods."

"Yes, yes, I know all of that," said Weston, his patience wearing thin. "Where was she picked up exactly?"

"That would be in her file," said the RN.

"Can I see this file?"

The big man was taking far too long to consider Weston's request. Irritation swelled in his belly, threatening to explode to the surface.

"That would violate privacy."

Another attempt by the bureaucracy to get in his way. His irritation grew. Weston weighed his options. Should he end this man's life right now or wait until later in the evening?

As though he were reading Weston's mind, Sean piped up, "Surely you can make an exception. We're looking for the kid and have good reason to think he and the girl have something to do with the murder of a family a few counties over. We really need closure for this one."

Weston had forgotten about his most faithful man. He looked at Sean and nodded approvingly, thankful for his quick wit. He slid his gaze to the burly RN who was busy rubbing his jaw.

"If there's reason to believe they're somehow tied to a murder, I suppose it can't hurt," said the man. "Come with me."

With that, they returned to the hallway, the burly man leading them to a large room. Floor-to-ceiling shelves, overflowing with files, lined the walls. The smell of old paper and printer ink permeated the air, a stark contrast to the other parts of the building.

The RN vanished behind a tall shelf, reappearing moments later with a single file in hand. He gave it to Weston. "Here it is. This is all we have on Maggie."

Weston ran his hand across the smooth surface, then flipped open the folder.

Maggie Lawler. With wild hair and terrified eyes, she stared at the camera. The woman was a mirror image of the wretched creature in the other room. It was hard to imagine her in any other condition. He flipped the pages, taking his time to scan each one for the particular information he was searching for. Pages and pages of drivel. The woman had been in the state's care for so long, her file was filled with ridiculous amounts of unnecessary information.

Ten pages in, he finally found what he was looking for. Antlers,

Oklahoma. Covered in blood and dirt, she stumbled into a rural hospital emergency room with a small child in her arms, babbling about shapeshifting coyotes she'd encountered in the woods.

The next page; the police report, provided more information.

According to the truck driver who found her, he stumbled upon the woman and child just outside of a small town called Kosoma. Seeing her initial state, he drove immediately to the nearest hospital in Antlers.

A wicked grin played across Weston's lips. Alas, he had a location. Kosoma.

After a cursory glance at the remainder of the file, he handed the folder back to the RN, then thanked the man for his time and quickly made his way out of the hospital.

"Looks like Kosoma is a ghost town," said Sean, gazing down at the phone in his hand.

"Ghost town, huh?" said Weston. He locked eyes with his man. "Sounds like it would be a perfect area for a clan of Tricksters to live. Don't you think?"

"I was thinking the same thing, sir," said Sean.

After he entered his vehicle, Weston took the handheld radio from the glove compartment and told his team to assemble in Kosoma, Oklahoma, within two hours.

THIRTY-THREE

DARKNESS SURROUNDED Luca as he tossed and turned, his thoughts churning. No matter how hard he tried to wipe it from his memory, he couldn't shake the gruesome picture of the butchered body being carried out of the barn. The word cattle kept playing through his mind.

Snuggled close beside him, Jewel slept soundly. As he watched her, he wondered if she ever felt that way about humans. About someone like him. What if the Rougarou hadn't bitten him? Would she still be with him, or would she have already torn his heart from his chest and eaten it for breakfast?

What about the other members of the compound? Sure, they all seemed to like him—Izzy and Bass excluded. If he was a regular man, would he be dangling from a meat hook in the barn right now?

The barn. He couldn't stop visualizing all the gruesome things that could happen in there. His mind simply would not let it go. Sleepless and uneasy, he quietly slipped out of bed, careful not to wake Jewel.

In the far corner of the room, Wyatt was asleep, his eyelids fluttering as if he were caught in a turbulent dream. Now and then, his arm or leg would jolt, reminding Luca of a sleeping dog.

Boots in hand, he quietly slipped out of the tiny shed they chose as their temporary bedroom, closing the door gently behind him.

A wave of calmness washed over him with the first touch of the cool night air. He sat down on the front step and pulled on his boots. He wasn't entirely sure what he intended to do. Was he really gonna go peek inside the barn? He already had a good idea what he would find. Did he really want to know for sure? Deep inside he knew that if he was going to put the thoughts behind him, he needed to go see it with his own eyes. In many ways, not knowing for sure was only fueling his imagination.

The compound was eerily quiet. Unlike the daytime, there were no men and women busily going about chores. No children playing. In fact, from what he could see, the only building with lights on was the barn.

Since he was a child, Luca learned to confront his fears instead of running away. As he stared at the massive building, he couldn't decide if he felt fear or loathing for it. "Mais la couillion," he muttered under his breath. "Quit bein' such a pussy."

With a resolve to put the matter to rest once and for all, he exhaled and headed purposefully for the ominous building.

As he came within a few yards of the barn, a side door burst open, and out stepped Paul, one of the younger men in the compound. He was one of the more talkative and friendly members of the clan, who seemed to take to the strange newcomer immediately. Upon seeing Luca, his face broke into a cheerful smile.

"Luca!" he said. "What're you doin' up?"

"Couldn't sleep, so I figured I'd go for a walk. What're y'all doin'?"

"I was just steppin' out to go on patrol. Care to join?"

The door swung open a second time, offering Luca a clear view inside. And he was immediately sorry for it. Blood stained the straw that covered the floor, dripping from the flayed bodies swaying gently on meat hooks. It was exactly as he imagined. Somehow, seeing the reality did nothing to quell his anxiety. And he hadn't even seen all of it. He regretted getting out of bed.

Two more men stepped out, one man named Clay that Luca also met earlier, and, much to his dismay, Bass.

As soon as they locked eyes, Luca was sure he could hear the big man growl.

"Luca's gonna come on patrol," said Paul excitedly.

The two big men grunted in approval.

"Show him the ropes," said Clay. "And don't cut the route short. Make sure you cover your whole ground."

"And alert us if you see anything," said Bass. "You know how."

Each going their own way, the two large men left, but not before Bass made it a point to slam his shoulder into Luca as he passed by.

As soon as the two men were out of sight, Luca turned to Paul. "So, what are we doin'?"

"Come on. It's simple. Just follow me."

From the dark night sky, the icy light of the moon sliced through the trees, illuminating the surrounding woods. Small nocturnal animals scurried around in the shadows, doing their nightly business. Luca found this comforting. He liked the sound of the wilderness, whether it was swamp or piney forest, he felt at home among the creatures of the wild. Much more so than around people.

For the most part, Paul kept silent, which was fine with him. In fact, he preferred it that way as he was busy struggling with his own thoughts.

Nestled deep in the center of a vast swath of land that spanned the hills for miles, the compound was quite impressive. Just getting to the perimeter was a hike. More than once, Luca wondered why it was they hadn't shifted.

A cool breeze played on the leaves of the surrounding trees while they followed a well-worn footpath. How many others had walked this same trail over the years? How long had this clan lived here?

Somewhere in the shadows a twig snapped.

Simultaneously, Luca and Paul looked up to see a large stag and its female companions pass by. The majestic creature stared at them fearlessly, almost as though he was daring them to try something. The buck's confident swagger told Luca that even the creature understood that he and his does were not on the menu.

Farther down the trail, they came to a spot where the path they were following split off in two directions. Pausing, Paul turned to Luca. "You head that way and I'll go this way. It'll make it a lot faster."

"What exactly are we lookin' for?"

Paul shrugged. "Anyone who shouldn't be out here."

"So, people."

"Yep, People." He grinned. "If you see one, make sure it's incapacitated before you bring it back here. We don't want no escapees."

Luca nodded, then turned to the right and plodded along the trail.

Truth be told, he had no intention of capturing any poor soul who may be lost on this trail. But he also didn't want to be the one who allowed trespassers the ability to harm anyone in the compound. Hopefully, the choice wouldn't have to be made.

The sound of another twig snapping caught his attention. He spun around, expecting to see another deer, only to glimpse a large coyote. The animal leered at him through a cluster of short trees.

As he stood there mesmerized, another appeared a few feet away, then another and yet one more. With heads down and teeth bared, they crept closer, closing in on him.

Tricksters? What the hell are they doing? Was this some sort of an ambush?

He called his beast forward, feeling the surge of adrenaline course through his body. The familiar sensation of energy crawled under his skin. Something small and sharp pricked his neck. He reached up and pulled a tiny dart away. As he held it between his fingers, he whirled around to find a previously unseen, tall, sandy blond-haired man standing behind a tree holding what appeared to be a rifle. Something about the man was oddly familiar, but Luca's mind refused to cooperate. His thoughts were a jumbled mess.

Why?

The world was spinning—the darkness was closing in. He tried to call forth the beast, but his body was already shutting down. Luca collapsed, hands and knees hitting the ground, the air around him heavy with the smell of dirt and decomposing leaves. There was nothing he could do, whatever was in the dart was winning.

Intending to shout a warning to Paul, he took a deep breath, only to be struck on the side of his head with the butt of the rifle before he could utter a sound. Bright sparks erupted along the edges of his vision, then everything went pitch black.

THIRTY-FOUR

WITH THE MAN unconscious at his feet, Weston reflected. "One down." What were the odds that the first person they ran into was also Jewel's companion? This was a good omen for sure. He crouched down and sniffed the air, there was an unfamiliar scent to the young man. Not quite human, and definitely not a Trickster. A mystery for sure.

Weston hated mysteries.

His men surrounded him, awaiting their next order, which he gave using hand signals in order to maintain silence. A moment later, the team of Tricksters disappeared into the woods, quietly stalking their prey. At least now they had a scent to follow that would lead them right to their quarry.

Gazing down at the young man, Weston said, "Let's get him secured in the vehicle. I'm not sure what he is, and I don't want to take the chance that the drugs will wear off quickly."

"Are you sure you don't want to dispatch him right now while he's unconscious?" asked Sean.

The thought was tempting. But there was no telling what kind of opposition they would run into. The man could be helpful if for no other reason than to be a lure. "No. Let's just secure him. He might come in handy later."

"You're the boss," said Sean. He pulled a bundle of zip ties from his belt and went to work tying up their captive.

Hog-tied and still unconscious, Weston and Sean brought their prisoner back to their vehicle and locked him inside the trunk of their car. It was a tight fit, but that was for the best. Less wiggle room meant less of an opportunity for the man to escape.

Before heading into the woods, Weston turned to Sean. "I want you to stay here and stand guard."

A look of disbelief spread across Sean's face. "Sir, with all due respect—"

"I don't want to hear it. You're the only one I trust to make sure he doesn't escape."

Sean nodded in understanding. "If he wakes up and breaks free?"

"Then kill him."

Leaving his most trusted man on watch, Weston turned and stalked back into the forest.

There was no need for him to shift—at least, not yet. His men had already done so, and he knew without a doubt that they were capable of handling the task. He specifically chose each one of them for that reason.

Pulling the Trickster forward, he sniffed the air and perked up his ears to get a lock on their location. This was no simple task; his men were experts in stealth. It took a bit more concentration than he wanted, but before long, he was able to locate them.

All around him, the forest was calm. He could understand the draw of this place for the clan. It was rather nice with the soft breeze and the scent of pine wafting through the air. A twig snapped nearby, he turned his head and found himself staring into the eyes of a giant buck. The creature didn't move, nor did it show any fear. Brave stag, he thought. If he wasn't in the middle of a very different kind of hunt, Weston would have gone after him. Luckily for the buck and his entourage, he had another task to take care of.

A shout reached his ears, muffled and indistinct. Weston followed the sound until he reached a shadowy clearing. Three of his men stood around the mangled remains of a young man. He crouched down and sniffed. Trickster. What a fool to not have shifted while alone out here. But then again, this clan had lived here for so long with little to no intrusions; their guard would be down. A fatal assumption.

He poked the disembodied head to see the face. The young man's eyes stared up at him, cold and lifeless, seeing nothing. Such a skinny, undernourished thing. Unkempt too. This clan was feral. Based on what he could tell from what was left of the boy, they didn't care much for personal grooming.

Brushing his hands off, he rose to his feet and locked eyes with the largest Trickster in his group. With a quick nod of his head, the beast launched into the woods, the rest of his pack close behind. Following their trail, Weston kept pace, making sure to stay in the rear.

The scent of wood-smoke tickled his senses. They were close. The community couldn't be far. His mind danced with images of what sort of domiciles this clan lived in.

A piercing shriek broke the silence, bouncing off the trees. His men had found their quarry. An ancient bell tolled, its sound sharp and alarming, followed immediately by a pained cry and the sounds of fierce growling. The clan was officially alerted.

Weston pulled the Trickster forward and shifted. Now, to find his niece.

THIRTY-FIVE

JEWEL WOKE WITH A START. With wide eyes, she sat up in the bed she and Luca shared. His side was cold to the touch, he must have been gone for a while. Across the room, Wyatt was sitting up in his bed. How odd that they both awakened at the same time. Something was off. She could feel it in the air. The sound of alarm bells echoed outside.

"What's going on?" whispered Wyatt.

She strained her ears, trying to hear beyond the bells, but could not. "Whatever it is, it ain't good."

"I could swear I heard a muffled cry or something," said Wyatt. He stared at Jewel, his eyes shimmering in the darkness. "Something isn't right."

Feeling the same way, she rose out of bed and pulled on her jeans and boots, all the while listening intently for any sound out of the ordinary in their immediate vicinity. By the time she was finished, Wyatt was already waiting on her. She glanced around the room, wondering where the hell Luca had gone. It wasn't like him to wander off like that.

As she and Wyatt stepped outside, she scanned the area. She was just about ready to head over to the barn when she heard the sound of a woman crying out in pain.

"Help!" shouted the woman, her voice cut short by a thick gurgling sound.

The sound of coyote laughter bounced off the trees that surrounded them. Tricksters! But why? None of this was making any sense.

Chaos erupted. Everything around them was in an uproar, leaving Jewel completely disoriented. A sudden shove broke through her thoughts. She spun around and found herself face to face with Izzy, holding the twins. Without a second thought, she took Caleb in her arms.

"What's going on?" she asked.

Izzy leaned close. "I'm not sure. The alarms startled me awake, so I grabbed the boys and came to find you."

"Where's Bass?" asked Jewel. She glanced around and realized that Wyatt was nowhere to be found. Where the hell did he go? She wondered as she struggled to contain full blown panic.

"Come with me!" urged Izzy. She grabbed hold of Jewel's hand and tugged her along.

Wyatt suddenly appeared with Bass right on his heels.

Relief washed over Jewel as she rushed over to him. Before she could say anything, Izzy had already asked what was happening.

"Invaders," said Bass. "Tricksters." He Locked eyes with Izzy, then Jewel, his face saying what they all feared most.

There was only one member of their kind that she knew of who would be so brash and violent as to attack an entire clan in their home. Weston. He found them.

"Have you seen Luca?" asked Jewel.

"He came on patrol with us. I took my route, and he stayed with Paul."

Relief washed over her. "So, they should be back any moment."

Bass' silence weighed heavy on her heart. Once again, fear reared its ugly head.

"What are you not telling me?"

"We need to get the twins inside the barn," said Bass. "The others are already gathering the elderly and children there." Without another word, he pushed Izzy and Jewel ahead of him.

Little Caleb trembled in her arms. Too young to fully comprehend what was happening, he understood enough to know he was in danger. Bass was right, first get the twins to safety, then focus on Luca, and whatever the hell was going on.

Fire broke out at the old farmhouse. Bright red flames exploded into the night, casting a crimson glow on everything. All around them coyotes fought one another. Pandemonium reigned. Where the hell was Luca? Unable to contain her anxiety any longer, Jewel spun around and asked, "Where is he?"

Bass stared at her for a long, uncomfortable period. His shoulders slumped. "I don't know."

"What do you mean you don't know?"

"He was with Paul, but Paul's dead. We found his body spread all over the eastern perimeter."

"And Luca?"

"He was nowhere to be seen."

"Did you even bother to look?"

The big man glared at her. "Yes. I did, though only briefly, because we had to get back here to help the clan." His eyes glowed amber brown as he was already shifting. "Now get inside the barn and keep the young and elderly safe."

Jewel's mind was a million miles away as she imagined all the ways Luca could have met the same fate as Paul. Something deep inside her told her that wasn't possible. She had seen Luca transformed. He was far too large to succumb to a group of Tricksters. Surely, he escaped. But why wasn't he at the compound? The potential reason hung heavy on her heart. She knew he would never run away and leave her to fight alone.

Moving quickly, she carried Caleb through the main room of the barn, past the aging carcasses, and down to the basement beneath. In the holding cages, the bodies of two women, recently dispatched, slumped over in pools of their own coagulating blood. She needed no explanation. They simply couldn't risk them crying out for help.

Jewel turned and handed Caleb off to Raye, then spun around to make her way back up the wooden stairs to join the fight. Izzy and Bass stood in her way, blocking the exit.

From the compound above, she could hear the agonizing cries of combat.

"I'm coming with you," she said.

Izzy shook her head. "Not this time. Outside of myself and Bass, you are the only one I trust to protect the twins. I need you and Wyatt to stay here and keep the younglings and the elderly safe and quiet. Protect my boys with your life. Lock the hatch when I leave."

"No!" shouted Jewel, but it was too late. Bass was already up and out of sight. The telltale sound of him shifting in the barn came to her ears. Izzy climbed the stairs, then turned around to face Jewel. With a resounding thud, she slammed the door closed. Tiny bits of straw fell through the gaps, into her hair and eyes.

Angry, she stepped back and brushed herself off, then glanced around the room at all the faces, young and old, staring back at her. Resentment swelled in her heart. She turned to Wyatt, noting the look of fear on his face—the same look that was on everyone's faces. That is, except for Raye, who stood silent holding both of the twins.

There was no other choice but to accept things as they were. She was tasked with keeping the young safe—including the last remnants of her own family. Izzy was right, this was the most important task for her right now.

She slid the metal bar into place to secure the door above her head, then turned to Wyatt. "Keep an eye on the hatch. And help me calm the young so that they make no noise."

THIRTY-SIX

AS HE WANDERED around the compound, Weston couldn't help but feel repulsed. Everything about this place was vile. From the shanties they lived in to the way they stored and prepared food. Disgusting. Had they never heard of modern conveniences? Hell, a simple thing like an old icebox would be an improvement.

His disdain for his niece grew ever so much more after seeing how she had been living.

The clan's fighters were no match for his seasoned men, who outmaneuvered them with ease. Truth be told, he felt more than a little underwhelmed. This was all too easy. He expected more of a fight—he craved it. It was clear these Tricksters had little experience with outsiders and the threats they could bring.

While his men dealt with the pack, Weston weaved his way through the tiny makeshift village in search of one specific prey. She was here. He just needed to figure out where.

A sharp cry erupted in the night. One of his men had met his end. More fierce growling filled the air. For a second, Weston questioned his lack of emotion or curiosity over which of his men had perished. He shrugged it off with the mindset that they understood what they were getting into when they signed on with him.

To his left, the trees trembled. The sound of soft footsteps thumping on the forest floor met his ears. Something big was coming.

In battle, surprise was always the best weapon. Keeping to the shadows, he slinked around a corner of the barn and watched.

From the trees emerged a single enormous beast. Absolutely massive, its maw was covered in blood and gore as it snarled with rage.

Weston sniffed the air, filling his nostrils with the monster's scent. Familiar. This was the giant beast who had massacred his men back in Sierra Diablo. There was no mistaking it. He stood back and took in the magnificent creature. He had never seen a Trickster so large.

The giant creature sniffed the air, sending a jolt of fear through Weston momentarily as he feared being discovered. He pondered strategies for fighting such an enormous beast. Each one ended with his own death. The very notion of being afraid of anything or anyone, let alone a Trickster, enraged him. His respect for the creature quickly gave way to hatred.

As luck would have it, the massive beast took no notice of him. Its fierce eyes settled on the battle being waged in the heart of the compound. It gave out a lone howl, then launched off toward the fight.

Relief flooded over Weston. Alone with his thoughts, he contemplated how much further along he would be with his ambitions if he had such a magnificent Trickster by his side. Such a waste.

A brief, muffled sound, like that of a toddler calling for its mama, floated to his ears. Weston perked up and listened. Somewhere close by a small child was being silenced by what seemed to be a female. A young female.

Could he be so lucky?

He sniffed around the barn until he picked up a familiar smell. It was the same scent that lingered in the bureaucrat's office. Jewel. She was somewhere inside. He took a step back and studied the barn. The old building was desperately in need of repair. It was a miracle it hadn't been taken out by a tornado or heavy wind by now.

But the doors. The doors were made of solid, thick wood, held together by forged iron ties. Impressive. The clan must store something precious behind these walls.

He took the iron ring into his mouth and pulled. The doors hardly jiggled. They were locked from the inside. How curious.

Once again, the sound of a child crying wafted on the air. This time though, he successfully tracked the sound. His suspicions were validated. It was coming from inside the barn.

His mouth curled into a wicked smile. How quaint they hid the children in the barn. As if that would save them. He knew enough to expect that there would be a contingent of adult Tricksters with them, ready to fight to the death for their safety. No doubt, his niece was among them. He sniffed the ground once more, picking up a scent that led him to a single door on the side of the building. The trail ended there.

The door was fashioned of the same solid wood as the larger ones. He pulled at the handle. Nothing. There had to be another way inside. With his head down, he crept around the building, searching for any weakness—a false door, a loose board. Anything to allow entry.

His nose to the ground, he came upon a spot where the earth was recently disturbed. The telltale coyote prints heading away from the barn told him everything he needed to know.

A gentle push with his snout revealed the false door. A surge of excitement coursed through his body as he pushed forward. With a subtle creak, it gave way, creating an opening just large enough for him to pass through.

Inside, the barn was black as pitch, but he could see clearly. Scanning the vast space, he could see that he was surrounded by limbs and torsos hanging from hooks. The scent of human blood, both old and new permeated the air. A slaughterhouse. Clever little beasts, he thought.

He weaved his way through the dangling flesh, expecting at any moment to lay eyes on his niece. On anyone. But he was alone. No, Jewel—and no children. Could they have fled through another secret door?

If they had already run away, why go to such lengths to secure the building? He stalked over to the main doors, noting the massive metal arm that secured them closed. The only way this bar could have been set into place was from the inside.

Weston sniffed the metal rod, unable to identify the hands that put it into place. He turned and scanned the barn once again. He was missing a crucial piece of the puzzle. Someone was in here to secure the doors, and then whoever it was, snuck out through the secret exit. That much he already knew. But why go to such lengths? Surely meat couldn't be that scarce out here.

Perhaps the children hadn't escaped after all.

Where was the precious cargo they took such pains to hide?

There had to be a basement or false floor somewhere. He inspected the floor, noting the subtlest displacement of straw. With his nose down, he followed the scent from the hidden door, across the barn, where it stopped abruptly inside a stall.

The faint outline of a square on the floor was plainly visible.

Bingo!

Unable to contain his glee, he cackled in celebration, then lunged forward, gnawing away with his powerful jaws at the wooden floorboards.

THIRTY-SEVEN

WITH HER TRICKSTER ears perked up, Jewel listened intently to the shuffling sound of footsteps overhead. Someone was inside the barn.

Right beside her, Wyatt stood quiet and alert. The poor boy reeked of fear. She felt bad for him. The past week had been such a whirlwind for him, only to have it come to something like this.

A few steps away stood Raye, holding both of the twins. To their credit neither of the boys made a sound, merely tracing the footsteps overhead with their eyes. Their father would be proud.

In a far corner, the elder women managed to keep the other children quiet. It was as though everyone was holding their breath.

Why would Tricksters attack a compound of their own like this? But she knew why. Weston. Of all the cunning and vile members of their kind, he was the only one she had ever known to be so willing to attack his own. How could they have been so stupid to believe he would leave them alone? Thier foolishness brought destruction upon this entire compound.

She wanted to charge up the steps and face him. But Izzy was right, the boys were the most important thing right now, and she was the only one who had a chance at fighting for them. Raye would be no match for Weston. And Wyatt—he was still a child himself.

The sound of soft footsteps on the straw covered floor overhead met her ears. She locked eyes with Raye who nodded in understanding.

Silence hung heavy in the air.

Jewel perked up her ears and listened to the soft shuffle of feet slowly stalking across the floor. She could hear him as he sniffed, searching for a scent to follow. Was this her uncle? Did he know she was down here?

The air vibrated with the sound of gleeful cackling, followed immediately by furious digging. The beast had discovered the entry to their hiding place. Snarling and growling, the invader pulled and scratched at the hatch. It wouldn't be long before he gained entry.

The time for hiding was over. Raye handed the twins over to one of the other women, then stepped up to the base of the steps to stand alongside Wyatt.

Jewel glanced at Wyatt and Raye. She was going into the fight of her life with an old woman and a gangly teenage boy. Their odds weren't great. In fact, they were stacked heavily against them. Regardless, she was ready to fight until her last breath to protect her nephews and finally get revenge for the murder of her brother. She pulled the Trickster forward, making the shift effortlessly.

At the base of the steps, the brave trio stood firm.

Tiny shards of splintered wood mixed with straw and dust floated down atop their heads. She could see the beast's teeth poking through the holes as tiny droplets of saliva leaked through. The door was making him work for it.

In a flash of fury and rage, the beast dug and gnawed, but the hatch remained steady, never giving an inch. The clan had built this one to last.

A slight smile played across Jewel's lips as she imagined the anger the intruder above must be feeling over potential failure.

Silence.

Time froze.

The sound of her own heartbeat echoed in her ears. Had the beast given up? Could they be so lucky? No. Something was wrong. A shared glance with Raye confirmed that the older woman was feeling the same way. Jewel leaned closer to the stairs. Nothing. No sign that anyone was even inside the barn.

The sound of rapid footsteps scraping on the straw floor erupted followed by a whoosh, then a blast of bright orange and yellow light poked through the gaps in the wood. Fire!

Thin wisps of smoke crept in through the cracks while tiny flames licked and lapped their way around the edges of the hatch. Orange light glowed brightly, illuminating the cracks between the floorboards overhead. The barn was on fire.

Thick black smoke churned and billowed as it crept down the ladder, filling the basement with a thick haze, making it difficult to breathe. The children coughed and gagged. There was no other option, they had to escape. But that meant running right into the maw of whoever was waiting upstairs.

Overhead, the giant barn groaned as parts of the roof splintered and toppled down to the wooden floor.

A loud crash echoed from above, followed by fierce growls. The clan was coming to the rescue. It was time. The children needed to evacuate before the entire barn fell in a fiery heap upon their heads. She climbed the steps, slid the metal bar free, and flung to door open.

All around her red-hot flames devoured the walls, culminating in an undulating ocean of red and orange that spanned the entire building. In a far corner, two Tricksters fought one another in a fierce battle. The smoke was far too thick for her to identify them.

With little time left, she turned to the others and signaled for them to come. The group below needed no further prodding. She stood guard while Raye and Wyatt ushered the children and elders out of the basement and through the trapdoor.

Fresh air assaulted her senses. All around her the children and elders coughed.

They were surrounded by pandemonium. Fire burned brightly, illuminating the compound. The ground was littered with bodies, tossed about like discarded toys. Jewel identified a significant number of them as belonging to the clan. Bass. She could see him over by the cooking area, a lone figure fighting four intruders at once.

With a loud crash, a single Trickster burst through the flaming wall of the barn. It was Izzy. Another, larger beast was on her tail. He launched atop her, tackling her to the ground. In a flurry of snapping jaws and tearing claws, the two fought.

Another intruder rushed over, joining the battle. While Izzy fought against the newcomer, the original beast she was fighting turned and stared directly into Jewel's eyes with pure malice. She knew who this was. Weston.

He launched toward her only to be sideswiped by Raye who slammed headfirst into him, knocking him into a pile of stacked wood.

Two more Tricksters rounded the corner.

Jewel and Wyatt jumped to action, both attacking the beasts. Much to her surprise, the intruders weren't doing much to fight back. In fact, all they were doing was corralling her away from Wyatt, the elders, and the children.

Raye fought against Weston valiantly. She gave no ground, lunging and biting with such ferocity, Jewel could almost imagine it wasn't the old woman who was fighting.

Suddenly, Weston reared up and seized Raye by her throat and tore. A crimson torrent erupted, showering the ground. Jewel stared in shock at the spectacle while the children cried out in a mixture of sorrow and fear. The gaggle of remaining elders placed their charges on the ground, shooing them into the woods, then shifted, all ready to die protecting the young.

Standing triumphantly over Raye's body, Weston turned and glared at Jewel as he slowly stalked closer.

Her uncle had finally come for her. The sight of him ignited a rage she had never known before as images of the night he murdered Caleb played out in her mind.

In a flurry of teeth and claws, she launched at him, managing to get a good hold on the side of his face. She tore. The metallic taste of blood rushed into her mouth as he cried out in shock and pain.

Wyatt lunged for Weston's throat. His powerful jaws missed the mark by less than an inch, slamming closed with a resounding hollow thud.

Weston reeled and turned his attention to Wyatt. Without a moment's hesitation, he attacked. The poor boy was no match for the larger, more cunning beast. Pinning the younger Trickster beneath him, he slashed and tore.

Using every bit of strength she had, Jewel jumped onto Weston's back, biting and tearing with the only intent to get him off of Wyatt.

It worked.

Howling in pain, he reared up and shook, trying to dislodge her. But she refused to let go. He moved away from the boy, bucking around like an enraged bull being ridden by a cowboy.

Still, she held on.

She was so focused on holding on; she was surprised when Weston slammed his body against a tree, pinning her between him and the unyielding trunk.

The air was knocked from her lungs as she toppled to the ground.

With bared teeth, he leaned close, gazing down at her in a way that let her know he knew exactly who she was. And there would be no mercy.

Jewel tried to rear up, but her uncle was having none of that. Using the full weight of his body, he pinned her down against the soft dirt of the forest floor. Slowly, he dragged a single claw across her throat. The taste of her own blood gushed up from her wound, into her mouth as she closed her eyes and tried to focus on healing.

Several feet away, Wyatt struggled to move, the sound of gurgling blood filling the air. He was alive—for now. But there was no telling how long it would take his young body to heal enough to help her.

A volley of fierce, low growls erupted; the three elders had joined the battle. Waiting for nothing, they launched at once, knocking Weston off of Jewel.

He tumbled away.

As she lay there on the ground, she could do nothing more than listen as one by one, the elders were murdered by her uncle. Then suddenly it was silent. Too silent.

The children!

She glanced over, seeing their terrified faces peering out from the brush. She had to protect them. If anything happened to the boys, she had no reason to go on living.

With every ounce of strength she had left, Jewel willed the jagged tear in her throat closed. Still healing, she rolled over and stared in horror as Weston stood before her. He leered down at her and snarled, then lifted his head and released a triumphant howl that shook her to her core.

THIRTY-EIGHT

LUCA'S EYES SNAPPED OPEN. His head hurt, and his mind was cloudy. He blinked, hoping his vision would return, only to realize the problem wasn't his eyesight. Darkness enveloped him. Where the hell was he? The one thing he knew for certain was that he was in a small, cramped space, and his arms and legs were tied behind his back with plastic zip ties. Making things worse, whoever applied them, tied them so tight, he couldn't feel his hands or his legs.

That said, tight or no, zip ties weren't a big problem. Even without his Rougarou strength, he knew how to get out of them. Never had he appreciated his upbringing as he did now. No restraints could hold a Boudreaux for long. However, this time, there was no need to rely on tricks or hacks, he had all the strength he needed. He brought forth his inner beast and pulled. The thin plastic strips shattered like ribbons of Christmas candy.

Next step was figuring out where the hell he was.

Movement was close to impossible. Using his Rougarou senses, he managed to discern that he was locked inside the trunk of a vehicle. This should be easy, he thought.

This time he unleashed the beast completely. Pushing and

207

punching with all his might, he sent the metal hood of the trunk careening through the air. The sound of it crashing to the ground somewhere nearby met his ears, followed by a threatening growl close by. He turned and found himself eye to eye with a large Trickster.

The beast launched at him.

Luca snatched the coyote from the air as if it were a toy. With a single tug, he tore the animal in two. Thick crimson blood showered down upon him. He tossed the halves to the side and scanned the area, ready for another attempt. But there was no one around. That must have been his only sentinel.

He glanced down at the pieces at his feet. Whoever that was, they weren't very smart.

A lone howl echoed through the trees, accompanied by the sound of an alarm bell ringing. He turned his gaze in the direction it came from and saw the ominous glow of fire. Thick black smoke billowed above the trees. The compound was burning.

Moving as fast as his supernatural legs would carry him, Luca charged through the forest with one thought on his mind. Jewel!

He arrived at the compound only to find it in a state of chaos. It was a war zone. Pieces of clan members lay strewn about. Pools of their coagulated blood seeped into the ground. Every building was engulfed in flames. Thick smoke wafted around like noxious fog, making it difficult to see.

Following the sound of battle, he ran toward the barn where he found Bass fighting four Tricksters.

Luca ran over, grabbed two at once, hurling one into the trees and holding on to the other. As soon as Bass dispatched their companions, Luca tossed the coyote he was holding over to him like a dog treat. While Bass made quick work of that one, the first beast recovered and launched for Luca. The coyote sank its deadly teeth deep into his arm. The pain was sharp and instant.

But a Trickster is no match for an enraged Rougarou.

He took hold of the beast's muzzle with his free hand and pulled. When his arm was released, he took hold of the bottom jaw and tore until the top of the Trickster's head was no longer attached to its body. It fell to the ground at his feet.

While Bass charged after Izzy and the duo she was fighting, Luca raced around the barn in search of Jewel.

When he came upon the body of Raye, he halted. Panic washed over him.

A lone howl echoed, vibrating all around them.

Luca turned his head to follow the sound. A single Trickster hovered over Jewel. Covered in her own blood, she was struggling to climb to her feet. Several yards away, Wyatt lay bleeding on the ground. There was no time to worry about the boy's condition, his focus was entirely on saving Jewel.

The beast stood with its back to Luca, staring directly at her, snarling and waiting for her to rise. He wanted her to fight to the death.

All at once, Luca knew exactly who this Trickster was. The fabled backstabbing uncle had finally found his niece.

Rage erupted inside him. He lunged forward, grabbing hold of the beast by the scruff of its neck, dangling it in the air like an errant pup. Confused and angry, Weston flailed and snapped with his sharp teeth in a desperate attempt to get free from the Rougarou's grip. But could not do anything more than look pathetic.

Fueled by hatred and disgust, Luca lifted Weston to stare directly into his eyes and growled. He wanted to end it all right then and there, but he turned his head and made eye contact with Jewel who had finally managed enough strength to stand on her feet. This was her kill. She should be the one to end this once and for all.

She stepped forward.

Weston snapped and clawed in an attempt to get to her, only to have Luca shake him around like a rag doll. When he finished, he stared directly into Weston's eyes and growled, making sure he knew exactly where he stood on the food chain.

The survivors of the battle surrounded them—all eyes were on Jewel and her uncle.

Luca held Weston out in front of her.

The beast growled, but made no move to attack. Perhaps he was still reeling from the good shaking he just received—or perhaps it was the extra pressure Luca applied to the back of his neck with his claws.

Jewel changed into a more humanoid form, then stepped close enough to reach out and touch Weston. He growled and seethed in defiance, but could do nothing more.

Fighting back the urge to rip him to pieces himself, Luca waited for Jewel to decide the Trickster's fate. This was, after all, her family matter.

She flashed a menacing grin, then stepped back and gazed at her uncle with disgust.

To his credit, Weston no longer made any attempt to escape Luca's hold. He seemed to know this was his end, and he accepted it rather than give Jewel the satisfaction of seeing him afraid.

She locked eyes with Weston and said, "You lose, Uncle. This blood feud of yours ends tonight." She stepped closer.

Weston's body tensed, preparing himself for the final blow.

But she stopped and took a single step back slowly shaking her head. "I won't be like you; I won't have the blood of a family member on my hands." Her lips curled into a malevolent sneer. She slid her eyes over to Luca. "My love, would you do me the favor of sending this vile creature to hell?"

If this was how she wanted it done, Luca was more than willing to do it. He pulled Weston back and stared directly into his eyes, relishing the fearful look in them, then he wrapped his arms around the beast, and took hold of its muzzle with one hand, pulling slowly. The wet sound of tearing flesh filled the air.

The Trickster cried out in pain as it struggled against the pressure.

Taking his time, in order to inflict as much pain as possible, Luka pulled Weston's head free, spinal cord and all. He dropped the body to the ground like an empty bag of flesh and bones, then he lifted the bloody prize into the air and released a triumphant howl.

All around him, the survivors joined in the celebration.

Izzy stepped forward, holding the twins in her arms. She didn't need to say a word, the look on her face said it all. Luca was now a welcomed member of her pack. He glanced over at Bass, who gave a curt nod of his head, then helped Wyatt to his feet. The boy survived.

Calm descended. The battle was over, and the clan won. Jewel won.

THIRTY-NINE

AS THE RISING sun cast its warm glow over the forest, Izzy surveyed the damage. The compound was destroyed; the pack decimated. Decades of living and thriving was erased in a single night. Far beyond the material devastation, losing lives was the most painful aspect. Raye was gone. As were nearly all the strong, agile members of the clan. Who would take up the mantle of leader?

Bass and Izzy were the most obvious choices, but she had her heart set elsewhere—Sierra Diablo. It was highly unlikely her brother would stay behind without her.

After much discussion, the clan divided. Those who chose to remain would rebuild on their own. Those who chose to leave would either follow Izzy and Bass or go their own way.

As she loaded up what remained of the things she cared about most, Izzy couldn't help but feel a sense of melancholy over the end of an era. This was home. When she was scared and had no place else to go in this world, this was where she ran without hesitation. She would miss this place—she already missed Raye.

But every ending is a new beginning. Her story was far from over, and the twins' lives had only just begun. With Weston gone, there was no longer any reason to hide. The time had come to bring the twins to their rightful home.

As she glanced through the rearview mirror watching the compound disappear from view, her mood shifted from somber to hopeful.

The drive back to Sierra Diablo was a mix of pleasant scenery and nervous anticipation, as she wondered what they would find upon their arrival. Was the ranch still be there? Had Weston burned it all down, or let it rot in place? With a calm resolve, she decided that no matter the state it was in, they would rebuild. Caleb's sons deserved to grow up surrounded by their ancestors. In the very home their father and uncle—their namesakes, grew up in. The home they were destined to inherit.

As the forest gave way to wide open fields, gradually trans-forming into towering mountains, Izzy was filled with a nostalgic sense of homecoming. She couldn't help but find it strange that she felt like she was returning home.

"You look happier than you have for weeks," said Bass.

"I am. Is it strange that it feels like we're going home?"

He smiled, gazing out at the road ahead, and nodded in agreement.

It dawned on Izzy that Bass had remained silent about their return to Sierra Diablo. She had no idea if he intended to stay with her or if he would head out on his own. She couldn't shake the feeling of dread that washed over her when she contemplated a life without her brother by her side.

"What about you?" she asked apprehensively, not entirely sure if she wanted to hear the answer. "Will you stay with us, or do you have other plans in that head of yours?"

"My home is wherever you and the boys are." He turned his head to her and gestured at the twins sleeping soundly in the back seat, snuggled up against Wyatt. "Those two are gonna need a man in their lives to help them grow." He smiled warmly. "I can't have you spoiling them rotten."

With a smile on her face, she sighed. "You make it sound as though I'm one of those over-coddling mothers."

He chuckled. "That's exactly what I'm saying."

"Thank you," she said. "For staying with me—with us."

"Like I said, my home is wherever you are."

"Mine too," said Wyatt from the backseat.

Izzy turned to smile at him. "You would have to fight me before I would let you go, little brother. Your home is with us."

A happy glint settled in his eyes, then he turned his gaze out at the scrolling landscape.

Images of the ranch in Sierra Diablo played out in her mind. "How do you suppose the West Texas clan is going to react after hearing what we did?"

"You mean, how will they feel about us getting rid of Weston and his group?" He quickly glanced in her direction. "My guess is that they'll be happy. I imagine there's no love lost for the ones who turned against their own."

He had a good point.

At ease with the thought of returning for now, she stared out the windshield at the motorcycle rumbling ahead of them, carrying Luca and Jewel. "How do you think they'll take to Luca?"

Bass exhaled slowly. "I don't know. But that boy has a strange way of growing on you. He'll grow on them too. And if anyone has a problem with him, they'll have to go through me first."

Izzy couldn't help but laugh, realizing that Bass meant every word. Luca's unique personality had a knack for winning people over. As for Jewel, Sierra Diablo was her home—her birthright. The clan would welcome her back with open arms. A tiny ember of apprehension sparked in her belly. Even though she had lived in that tiny desert town for some time, Izzy never forged a bond with any members the clan outside of Caleb, Pax and Ezra. When they learn about the boys, would they show kindness toward her?

"Woo-hoo!" yelled Jewel. She stretched out her arm, pointing to a green and white road sign ahead, showing that Sierra Diablo was only five miles away.

Izzy stuck her head out the window and breathed in the familiar scent of the West Texas desert.

The exit for the town loomed up ahead. Before heading to the ranch, there was one last task that needed to be taken care of. They turned down Main Street, past the old bar, and parked in front of the sheriff's office.

Izzy scanned the empty street. "I see it's as vibrant and alive as usual."

"Wouldn't have it any other way," said Bass.

She stepped out of the truck and strolled up to the motorcycle. "You ready?"

Jewel climbed off the bike. "I am."

Leaving Wyatt to watch over the boys in the truck, Izzy, Bass, Jewel and Luca entered the building.

The tiny bell atop the door jingled, announcing their presence, as they entered the dusty little office. When he realized who had stepped into his domain, the old man's expression turned grim. He glanced around nervously; the air filled with the stench of his fear. Ramirez pushed his chair back, its legs scraping against the floor, as he stood up.

"H-hello," he said with a trembling voice. His eyes darted anxiously around the room, making brief stops at Bass, Luca, Izzy, and finally Jewel. Tiny beads of sweat seeped from his pores, glistening against his skin.

With a mischievous grin, Luca settled into the chair at the opposite side of the room and began spinning it around playfully.

Bass strolled over beside him. Casually leaning against the desk, he folded his arms.

"Hey," said Luca. He pointed to another chair. "Grab that one. I'll race ya." When he received no response, he shrugged and went back to spinning around until Bass stopped him by placing one hand on the backside of the chair, freezing him in place.

Izzy allowed herself a brief smile at the antics, then set her focus on what they had come here to do.

"You seem surprised to see us," said Jewel.

Ramirez swallowed nervously and licked his lips. "I-I just wasn't expecting—"

"Now, why would that be?" asked Izzy, moving closer.

The old man stepped back. Unable to speak, he simply shook his head. "I-I thought—"

"You thought what?" said Izzy. "Did you think we were dead too?"

"He must have," said Jewel, as she moved closer.

Slowly and deliberately, Izzy closed the distance between herself and the sheriff. "Maybe he thought we were run off. Pushed away, never to be seen again." She glared at Ramirez. "Is that it, old man? Did you think that you and Weston had made us go away forever?" She paused and glared into his eyes. "Or perhaps that he had somehow managed to make us suffer the same fate as Caleb?"

Terror washed over the sheriff's sun-dried face as his eyes darted around the room, unsure as to who would be the biggest threat.

Suppressing a laugh, Izzy closed what little space remained between herself and the old man, wrinkling her nose at the stench of whiskey, stale cigarettes and B.O. that emanated from him.

His efforts to back away from her only resulted in him bumping into Jewel. He stepped to the side and found himself backed up against the wall.

With a rumble deep in her chest, Jewel leaned in closer, her teeth jutting out from her snarling lips.

"Don't worry," Izzy said softly. "This won't take very long." She grinned, sporting her sharp teeth. "But it's gonna hurt like hell."

Ramirez raised his hands in a feeble attempt to protect himself as both Izzy and Jewel descended upon him. The room filled with the sounds of tearing flesh and the old man's screams. By the time they were finished, there wasn't much left of him, but blood and gore mixed with shreds of torn fabric from his uniform.

"Whoo lawd!" chirped Luca. "You girls fucked old boy up!" He glanced up at Bass. "Remind me to never piss these ladies off."

Izzy poked the tattered remains of the sheriff's shirt, exposing the shiny, bronze shield. After freeing it, she carefully wiped it clean on her jeans, then casually strolled over to Bass and pinned it on him.

"Looks like there's a new sheriff in town," she said, grinning widely.

"Hell yeah!" shouted Luca. "Hey man," he said as he tapped Bass on the arm. "Can I be your deputy? I always wanted to be a dick with a badge."

"Now why does that not surprise me?" said Bass.

Laughter filled the air, bringing a much-needed moment of joy and relief.

Izzy turned to Jewel. "You ready to go home little sister?"

Jewel nodded. "I am."

FORTY
ONE YEAR LATER

"YOU SURE YOU WANT TO GO?" asked Izzy.

Jewel carefully divided the bouquet of desert wildflowers she had collected on the walk to the family gravesite into four equal parts. She laid one bundle on her father's grave, then turned to her mother's and placed a bouquet on the ground, then softly kissed her fingertips before pressing them against the rough surface of the stone. After a moment of pause, she gently laid the remaining bundles atop the graves of her brothers.

Since her return a little over a year ago, she made it a habit to visit the cemetery frequently. Everything she had known since birth was buried beneath the hard, rocky soil. The bittersweet feeling of being in such proximity to the ones she loved dearly, but still feeling a great distance between them, was unbearable, yet strangely comforting.

She lifted her eyes to the vivid blue sky, a mixture of hope and sadness in her heart, as she silently sent her thoughts and wishes to her family.

Turning her attention to the future, Jewel dusted her hands off on her thighs and then turned to Izzy, flashing a bright smile. Motherhood had created a profound change in her. She was more calm, yet far more lethal should anyone ever cross her or her family. Izzy was always quite capable of taking care of herself, but something about the way she had grown since the boys were born made her far more-so.

Recalling Izzy's question, Jewel replied, "Yeah." She smiled. "Weren't you my age when you left home to explore the world?"

Izzy sighed. "I could use the help around here."

"Bass is here. So is Micah, not to mention the whole West Texas clan."

Much to their surprise, the clan welcomed their return with open arms. The fact that they also took care of Weston and the rest of his pack of traitors was a bonus. As it turned out, Ezra's family wasn't buying Weston's explanation at all. In fact, they pushed for a tribunal to bring him and his men to justice, but the Elders were too fearful of Weston and his proclivity toward violence against anyone who crossed him.

The news that the Riggs family line would continue had the West Texas clan buzzing with excitement. They immediately embraced the twins and even Izzy, treating her as if she had always been part of their group. As for Bass taking over the role of town sheriff, they couldn't be happier. In fact, they were so happy about the change, Jewel couldn't help but ask herself why the thought of putting one of their kind in the position never occurred to any of them before.

As for Wyatt, the past year had brought about a sea of change for him, both in his circumstances and his physique. With the help and guidance of his family, he learned to embrace his true self, even going so far as to adopt his birth name—Micah. Gone was the scared and confused loner. In his place was a young man with the stature of Bass, the insight of someone who understood things about the world of humans that many of them could not, and of course, a hefty dose of Luca's bizarre sense of humor.

Ah, Luca. The clan's acceptance of him was a different story altogether. To say they had a strong aversion to him would be an understatement. After all, he was a Rougarou. None of them knew what to think. Perhaps they would have embraced him warmly if he were a simple human, but his status as a half-breed made their initial reception less welcoming.

At first, the behavior of the elders toward him enraged Jewel, but Luca didn't take any mind to it. After all, he had an entire lifetime of being ignored, mistreated and hated long before he was even bit. That didn't make her feel any better. In fact, his nonchalant acceptance of it being just the way things were only made her angrier.

Gradually, he won them over in that way that only he could do, but only after he proved his value to them.

Izzy wrapped her arm around Jewel's shoulder. "It's hard not to look at you and see the lost little girl I met when I first arrived." She pulled away and smiled. "I guess I better get used to letting go."

"You have your hands too full to worry about me," said Jewel. "Those boys will be a handful the older they get."

"Hush," said Izzy, playfully. "Don't say that."

"Oh, come on, they take after my brothers in so many ways beyond their names."

Izzy laughed. As she peered down at Caleb's grave, a solemn look swept across her face. With tears welling up in her eyes, she looked at Jewel. "I'm gonna miss you."

"I'll come back," replied Jewel. "Until that night, I never even thought I would ever be able to leave. I mean, I even tried to, but couldn't." A pang of regret washed over her as she recalled the night she tried to run away. Just thinking about it was difficult. What would have happened if she had been successful? Where did she think she was going? The thought that she once considered Weston a wise uncle made her cringe.

"Well, don't forget your people," said Izzy.

With arms intertwined, they turned and headed back to the house.

"I can't possibly forget y'all," said Jewel. She paused and wiped the tears from her cheeks. "Besides, I have two nephews now, so I gotta come back for them."

Izzy pulled her in for a long hug.

When they separated from one another, both women had fresh tears streaming down their cheeks.

"Girl," said Izzy. "Look what you do to me."

They walked the remaining stretch in silence.

Back at the house, Jewel wandered off alone, taking in every detail as she meandered through her childhood home. There was a time in her life when these walls encompassed her entire world, filled with memories and emotions. With each step down the hall, she trailed her fingertips along the smooth surface of the walls. As she closed her eyes, images of her childhood played like a movie in her mind. She could still hear the laughter, each joyful sound echoing and resonating within her.

In the living room, she strolled around, taking in the faces of her family one by one, recalling all the times as a child she would saunter around this room and do this very thing.

She paused before the picture of her mother and father on their wedding day. As she traced her finger over their smiling faces, she wondered what they would think of her decision to leave. After deciding that they would support her, she moved on to the image of Pax. The photo taken a month prior to his death was the most recent one she could find. He stared out at her, forever frozen in time with that wistful smile of his. Oh, how she missed him.

Caleb. A bittersweet feeling consumed her as she stared at his picture on the wall. Born with that cunning glint in his eyes, the elders called him an old soul. With a nod of her head, she agreed, that was exactly what he was.

Pushing aside the new onslaught of emotions, she swiftly turned on her heels and exited the room. When she stepped outside, Jewel found Luca waiting beside the two motorcycles, while the twins gleefully ran circles around him.

As soon as he laid eyes on her, a bright smile appeared on his face. "There she is. We were wondering how you were doin'."

Jewel walked over to Izzy and gave her a hug. "You take care of my nephews."

Wiping away tears, she hugged Bass. "You keep this place safe. You hear?"

The big man responded with a simple nod; his face blotchy with emotion.

She turned to Micah and brushed a speck of sand off of his shiny new deputy badge. Knowing that he and Bass were officially in charge of keeping the town safe set her mind at ease. "Keep these two out of trouble, okay?"

He smiled. "I can only do my best."

Crouching down, she extended her arms, beckoning the boys to come closer. "Come here," she said aloud. "Give me a hug." As they wrapped their tiny arms around her neck, she hugged them tightly then pulled back and gazed into their eyes. "Y'all listen to your mama. You hear?" Then she let the boys go back to running around in circles.

Sorrow threatened to derail her plans. She stood up and nodded to Luca. Without another word, he climbed upon his motorcycle.

The roar of their engines reverberated through the hillside.

After a final wave goodbye, Jewel and Luca drove off. As she rolled down the driveway, she watched as Bass, Izzy, Wyatt, and the boys disappeared behind a cloud of dust and gravel.

FORTY-ONE
A NEW BEGINNING

THE HEAVY AFTERNOON sun dominated the bright blue sky, sending down its warm rays that bathed the blacktop in a gentle glow. As they cruised down the picturesque Louisana road, Jewel's mind was full of visions of all the places they would go—all the things they would see.

The canopy of trees spread out in front of them, creating a lush green tunnel dotted here and there with the occasional shard of sunlight.

Her belly grumbled, reminding her that it was time to find some food. Or was it simply the vibrations of the motorcycle? How long had they been riding? She glanced up at the clear blue sky, noting the sun hovering high among the puffy white clouds. It must be well past noon. In front of her, Luca's bike slowed and coasted off to the shoulder where he rolled to a stop.

Once again, her belly groaned. The moment she stopped her bike, she said, "Please tell me you want to eat something. I'm starving!"

"I was just about to ask you the same thing." He grinned. "Lunch it is."

Jewel giggled. "What are we having? Something rare or made?"

He smiled at her. "I was thinkin' something more along the lines of a greasy cheeseburger."

"Okay." She scanned the road ahead. "Seems like our only option is to ride along until we find a diner or something."

He nodded his head in agreement.

"How long's that gonna be?"

He responded with a shrug.

"You are no help at all. I'm gonna die of hunger," she whined playfully.

"You and me both," said Luca. He glanced down the road. "We're bound to come up on a diner or town or something real soon. Think you can hold off dyin' till then?"

Jewel chuckled. "I think I can, but the first human or deer we come across before we find a diner very well might not."

A large white SUV materialized on the horizon. As it approached, the vehicle's wheels ground to a gentle stop. The driver's window rolled down, exposing a friendly looking man sporting a well-groomed beard. A pretty woman peered out at them from the passenger seat while a young boy about ten years old, popped his head out between the seats. Somewhere in the back, a younger child called out, "I wanna see!" The man flashed a cheerful smile. "Y'all need any help?"

Jewel locked eyes with Luca. He gave her a slight shake of his head, then turned his focus to the man in the vehicle.

"Thanks a lot brother," he said. "But we're good."

"Suit yourself. Y'all have a nice day," said the man as he moved to roll up his window.

"Hold up!" shouted Luca. "You wouldn't, by any chance, know of any place nearby where we can get a bite to eat, would you?"

The man nodded. "I most certainly do. We just left a small diner about a mile back." He pointed behind him. "It doesn't look like much on the outside, but the burgers are top tier."

Just hearing the word burger made Jewel's mouth water. At this point, any food would be more than welcome. Her stomach screamed in agreement.

After a quick thank you and a wave goodbye, the man and his family were back on their way, and the two motorcycles were rolling down the road toward a hearty meal.

At first glance, the diner seemed kind of derelict, had it not been for the man telling them it was open, they would have assumed it had closed long ago.

The savory scent of meat cooking on the grill wafted on the afternoon air. Jewel waited for Luca to dismount and then climbed off her bike. She was so hungry; she could have eaten an entire cow on her own in a matter of minutes.

Stepping inside, the warm aroma of coffee and day-old bacon excited her senses, confirming the diner was exactly as she'd envisioned when they rolled into the parking lot. A cloud of smoke floated around the cramped space like a savory fog. A single long counter spanned the length of the building, the polished wood top gleaming under the fluorescent lights. It was the cleanest thing in the whole place. The rhythmic sizzle of the grill filled the space like background music as a large man skillfully tended to the food on the grill.

"Take a seat anywhere," said the woman behind the counter as she poured a cup of coffee for a gnarly haired old man.

Jewel's mouth watered. Luca casually slid up to the counter and waited for her to take a seat before claiming one of his own beside her.

As she approached, the woman pulled out a pen and pad. "What can I get for ya?"

"I'll take the biggest burger you can make. Medium rare," said Luca.

"I'll have double that," said Jewel. "Though I want mine rare. Oh! And no vegetables!"

The woman regarded her with a skeptical eye. "You sure?"

Grinning from ear to ear, Jewel bobbed her head up and down and winked at Luca.

"Okay then," said the woman. "Nice and simple, I like it that way. Make yourselves comfortable, Frank'll get right on it for ya." She shoved her pen and notepad back in her pocket and strolled over to the other end of the counter where the grizzly looking old man was sitting and struck up a conversation.

Time ticked slowly. Each second felt like hours as Jewel's body cannibalized itself. As her hunger grew, so did her irritation. Every little thing was grating on her nerves.

She cast a glance at Luca and found him gazing attentively out the grimy window at a young woman who had just climbed out of a fancy sports car.

The woman's hair was long and dark as coal. Her makeup was flawless. She glanced at the building, then brought an elegant hand up to her hair, the jewels on her fingers reflecting the sun's rays. Every aspect of her, from her clothes to her mannerisms, spoke of wealth and privilege. In an ironic twist, she was wearing a black T-shirt with the words—Eat the Rich—emblazoned in blood-red lettering on it.

Instant jealousy, fiery and hot ignited in Jewel's belly. Seething, she watched as the woman entered the diner.

Clearly disgusted, she gazed around the cramped space, scrunching her nose and fanning her hand, as if the air itself was revolting.

"What can I do for you miss?" asked the waitress.

The newcomer glanced around.

Her eyes settled on Luca and then Jewel. A subtle sneer played on her lips, then she turned her attention back to the waitress. "I just need to use your restroom."

The older woman was having none of the girl's attitude. She glared and said flatly, "Restroom's for patrons only."

"But it's the only one for miles."

"That it is," said the woman with a smirk and a curt nod. "We ain't no gas station. If you wanna use the toilet, you'll have to order some food."

The girl rolled her eyes and huffed, then spun on her heels.

"Whatever!" she said over her shoulder. "Keep your nasty little diner. The bathroom's probably just as disgusting as the rest of this place. I wouldn't eat here if you paid me."

As she opened the door, the older woman called out, "There's a nice thick patch of trees about a mile up the road. Perfect for squattin'. Just make sure you keep an eye out for snakes and poison ivy."

The leathery faced old man at the counter chuckled loudly.

Luca erupted into a boisterous fit of laughter, joining both the old man and waitress.

Jewel, however, still seethed. When she saw that Luca's focus on the girl was not attraction but a manifestation of his dislike for their kind, her jealousy lessened. But her hatred toward the girl remained strong. That said, she had good taste in clothes. She leaned close to Luca and whispered in his ear, "I like her shirt." Her eyes flickered with mischief.

"You do?" He glanced out the window as the car sped away, then turned back to Jewel. "You want it?"

With the wildest grin on her face, she nodded.

He winked at her, then made a show of searching his pockets. "I must've dropped my wallet back on the road when we stopped." He shared his most innocent smile with the waitress. "Imma go run back and see if I can find it. We'll be right back."

Focused on filling the sugar containers, the woman acknowledged him with a brief nod. "Don't be too long. Food's about done."

Jewel sprang from her seat and went toward the door. Luca held it open and with a flourish, guided her outside.

Leaving her motorcycle in the parking lot of the diner, she quickly mounted Luca's and, with the sound of the revving engine and crunching gravel filling the air, they rolled out onto the blacktop. As they sped down the narrow road, Jewel's heart pounded with anticipation, her eyes locked on the horizon for the slightest glimpse of the tiny sports car. A little over a mile up the road, they came upon the car sitting idle on the shoulder.

Trying not to attract attention, Luca cut the engine, then he turned off into the woods. Before he was even off the bike, Jewel was already several feet away, her eyes fixed on her target.

"I got the girl," she said over her shoulder. "I wanna make sure the shirt isn't damaged."

"Then I suppose that means I got the guy," said Luca with a nod.

As she snuck past the vehicle, Jewel glimpsed the man sitting in the driver's seat with his eyes closed, singing aloud to a catchy pop song. His taste in music only deepened her dislike for him. Everyone knew metal was the only music worth listening to.

Behind her, Luca was creeping closer. It was surprising how easy it was. These types of people lived in their own isolated bubble, completely oblivious to the world around them. They feared nothing—not because they could protect themselves, but because they lived behind gates in guarded neighborhoods so that none of the violence of the world could ever touch them. Far from fearless, they were ignorant. In their eyes, bad things only happened to other people.

Staying hidden behind a cluster of trees, Jewel concentrated on the girl, whose trail was easy to follow through the thick under-growth. Her expensive perfume acted as a beacon.

With an angry mutter, the woman relieved herself, all the while trying to fend off the hoard of buzzing flies and mosquitoes that were circling around her.

Jewel stifled a giggle as she watched the girl's every move with a sense of quiet amusement. It was only fair to wait for her to finish her business. When she stood up, Jewel stepped out from her hiding place and gave a playful wave. "Hey there," she said in her most inno-cent tone.

The woman stumbled backward, nearly tripping over a fallen tree limb. Her hand instinctively reached for her throat. "Oh!" she exclaimed. "You startled me." She glanced around. "I thought I was alone."

"You were," replied Jewel. "Sorta." She flashed a wide grin, showing off her sharp teeth.

Her face became a mask of confusion and fear as she recoiled and stepped back.

"Where are you going? I just want to talk."

"What do you want from me?" Her eyes darted from left to right as though she might find someone who could intervene.

"Well, for starters, you can give me your shirt."

The woman seemed stunned at the request. She gaped at Jewel with a look of disbelief.

"Come on." Jewel held out her hand. "Hand it over." She wiggled her fingers for emphasis. "Don't make me ask again." A soft growl emanated from her chest.

Trembling with fear, the girl removed her shirt, then tossed it to the ground where it landed at Jewel's feet.

"Now, was that so hard to do?"

Frozen in place, the woman shook her head. She licked her lips and swallowed nervously, then took a step to the side.

"Where do you think you're going?" asked Jewel.

"I-I was just," stammered the woman.

Jewel wasn't quite ready to kill her just yet, she wanted to play with her for a little while first. "I-I was just, what?" she taunted, stepping closer.

Quick as a deer in the forest, the girl turned and made a run for it, but Jewel was ready—she expected this. She allowed her prey a five-foot head start, then launched after her. It didn't take much effort to catch up, knocking her to the ground. She grabbed a fistful of shiny black hair and yanked the girl's head back.

A single piercing scream erupted from her lips as Jewel, with a sharp claw, slashed the soft pink flesh of her neck wide open. A cascade of deep crimson blood spewed out, soaking into the soil.

Jewel leaned close enough for her lips to brush the woman's ear. "Thanks for the shirt," she whispered. She ran her tongue along the woman's neck, savoring the metallic flavor of the warm blood, then released her grip, letting her head fall to the ground with a soft thud.

She pulled the rings from her fingers and earrings from her ears then stepped back and watched the woman gasp, with eyes wide, like a fish out of water as she bled out. It was all over so quickly, Jewel was a little disappointed. Her lips curled into a gleeful grin as she recalled she had a new T-shirt.

Leaving the corpse on the ground, she quickly pulled her top off, replacing it with the new one.

Twigs snapped nearby. She spun around in time to glimpse Luca making his way through the trees.

She stuck her arms out and twirled around, happily showing off the new addition to her wardrobe. "What do you think?"

"Eat the rich," said Luca, with a nod of approval. "Fitting."

"I thought so too," she replied with a playful giggle. She peered down at the woman's lifeless body, poking it with the toe of her boot. "It'd be a shame to let this go to waste. Care for a quick bite?"

Luca shook his head. "I kinda got my heart set on that greasy burger back at the diner."

Jewel shrugged. "Okay," she sighed. "So, what should we do with her?"

"Is she dead?"

She nodded and flashed a sharp toothed grin. "She most certainly is."

Luca lifted the body over his shoulder. "Follow me. We can put her where her man is."

"What did you do with her man?" asked Jewel, trailing along behind him.

"I used a little too much force on him." He grinned sheepishly. "I tried to grab him by the head and pull him out. In the process, his neck snapped." He chuckled. "I guess I don't know my own strength."

"Anyway, I carried his body away from the roadside, lookin' for someplace to get rid of it. That's when I found this pond here." He dropped the woman's body on the ground. "I filled his clothes and pockets with rocks, then tossed him in."

"We doin' the same with her?"

"What else would we do with her?"

Jewel batted her eyes and smiled.

He gave her a playful side-eye. "I thought we agreed on burgers this time."

She poked out her bottom lip in a pout, then quickly sighed. "Okay, it's your call. This time."

The pond was surprisingly deep. Taking care not to dirty her new T-shirt, Jewel helped Luca get the woman properly weighted, then he nonchalantly threw her into the pond. The body slammed into the water with a loud splash, then quickly vanished beneath the murky depths.

"Well," said Jewel, wiping her hands together. "That's that."

"It most certainly is," he replied.

"Did you get their cash?"

"Mon Sha, what kind of fool do you take me for?" He flashed a mischievous grin. "I even got the money from her purse and dug the change out of the console." He held up his arm. "Like my new watch?"

"Oh! That looks very expensive!" She ran her fingers through his hair. "It was made for you."

He wrapped his arms around her waist and kissed her, then pulled away with a loving smile. "Now let's get back to the diner. I want my burger."

Jewel chuckled playfully, then gave him a quick peck on the cheek before turning and walking back to the motorcycle.

As they entered the diner, Luca wiggled his wallet in the air. "Found it!" he announced.

"Perfect timing," replied the waitress. "Grab a seat, your food's comin' out right now."

She didn't even notice Jewel's change of clothes.

THE END

AFTERWORD

Well, here we are. I wouldn't call this the end of the road, more like a pause before a twisted turn. If you know me, you know.

It's been a blast hanging out with the Tricksters. But I have other supernatural beings to spend time with, who have been patiently waiting their turn.

Will I revisit the Tricksters at a later date? I mean, I can't just leave Jewel and Luca out there alone, can I? Of course not. We shall see what the future brings.

Thank you to everyone who has joined me on this wild ride. Stick around, there's much more chaos to come.

While you're here, please be sure to leave a rating or review. These are so important for us Indie Authors.

Feel free to drop me a message through my website, if you like, and let me know your thoughts. I'm always up for a good chat about characters and chaos.

For now, I hope you enjoyed my little nightmare. And always remember the three rules of a roadtrip...

- Never stop for hitchhikers
- Always stay on the main road
- And don't play with the wildlife

I'll meet you at the Crossroads.

www.nancylmclaughlin.com

ABOUT THE AUTHOR

Nancy was born and raised in Massachusetts. After serving in the USMC, she returned home and went to college. Not long after, she moved to California and married. Six kids and multiple moves around the US later, she and her family call Texas home.

ALSO BY N.L. MCLAUGHLIN

Crossroads, Volume 1

Crossroads, Volume 2

Tricksters

American Nomads

Lost Boys

Imaginary Dragons

True North

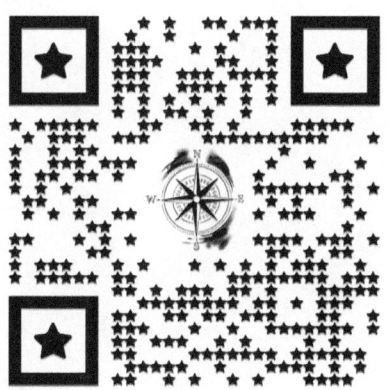